THE
NAZI'S ENGINEER

A James Acton Thriller

By J. Robert Kennedy

James Acton Thrillers

The Protocol
Brass Monkey
Broken Dove
The Templar's Relic
Flags of Sin
The Arab Fall
The Circle of Eight
The Venice Code
Pompeii's Ghosts
Amazon Burning

The Riddle
Blood Relics
Sins of the Titanic
Saint Peter's Soldiers
The Thirteenth Legion
Raging Sun
Wages of Sin
Wrath of the Gods
The Templar's Revenge
The Nazi's Engineer

Special Agent Dylan Kane Thrillers

Rogue Operator
Containment Failure
Cold Warriors

Death to America
Black Widow
The Agenda

Retribution

Delta Force Unleashed Thrillers

Payback
Infidels

The Lazarus Moment
Kill Chain

Forgotten

Templar Detective Thrillers

The Templar Detective

Detective Shakespeare Mysteries

Depraved Difference
Tick Tock
The Redeemer

Zander Varga, Vampire Detective

The Turned

THE
NAZI'S ENGINEER

A James Acton Thriller

J. ROBERT KENNEDY

ISBN: 9781998005475

First Edition

10 9 8 7 6 5 4 3 2 1

For the Monuments Men, who risked their lives in an attempt to save
the over 5 million pieces of art looted by the Nazis.

THE
NAZI'S ENGINEER

A James Acton Thriller

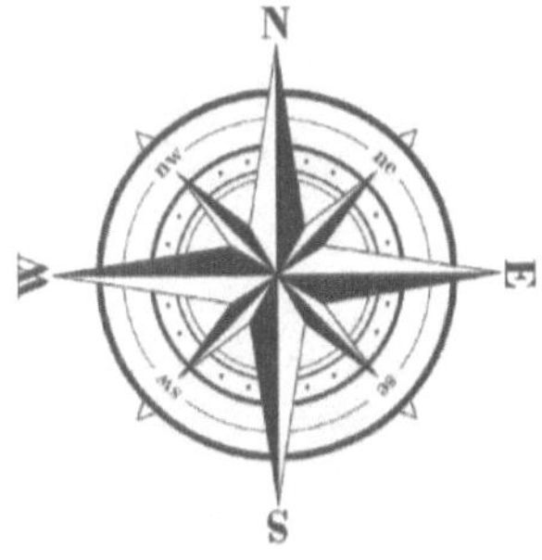

AUTHOR'S NOTE

This is to confirm that "The Nazi's Engineer" is grammatically correct, as it refers to a single Nazi, and the engineer he provides.

"I vow to you, Adolf Hitler, as Führer and chancellor of the German Reich, loyalty and bravery. I vow to you and to the leaders that you set for me, absolute allegiance until death. So help me God."

SS Oath of Loyalty

"Art belongs to humanity. Without this we are animals. We just fight, we live, we die. Art is what makes us human."

Mikhail Piotrovsky, Director, Hermitage Museum

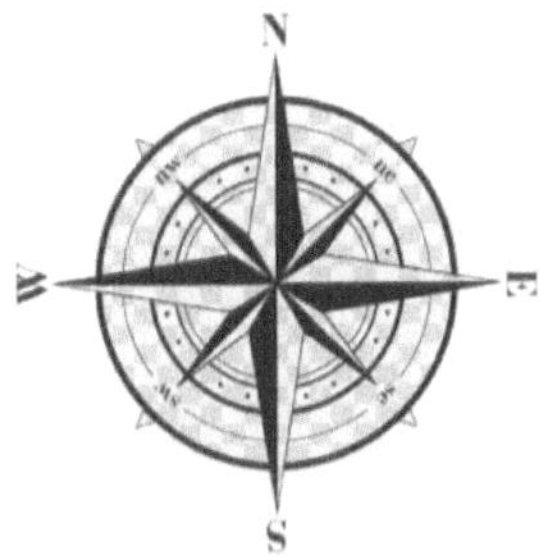

PREFACE

In January 1945, Adolf Hitler issued orders to begin evacuation of artwork kept in Königsberg, Prussia, in anticipation of the eventual arrival of the Red Army. During the reign of the Nazis, millions of pieces of art were stolen from across Europe. Many were destroyed intentionally when the defeat of Nazi Germany was imminent, others fell victim to Allied bombing, and still others disappeared without a trace, never to be seen again.

Including the subject of this book, an artistic wonder so valuable, it is heartbreaking to contemplate what might have happened to it. Some say it was destroyed, though the sheer scale of this masterpiece suggests that were it destroyed where it was last known to have been kept, surely some evidence of it would have remained.

Leaving only one possibility.

It was moved before it was too late.

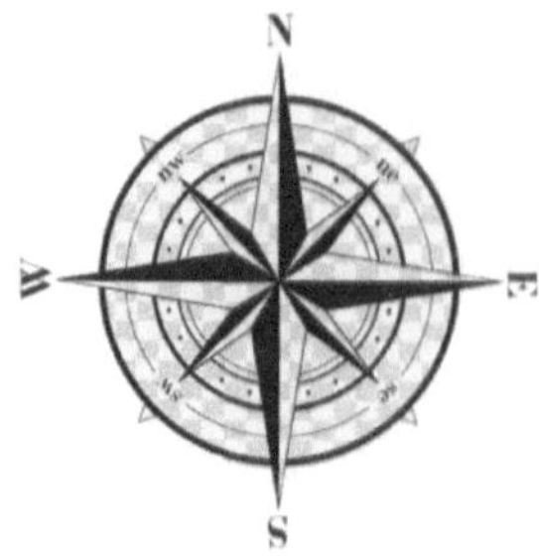

South of Marienwerder, West Prussia

Nazi Germany

January 28, 1945

Something had changed. Hermann Lang was sure of it. As he slowed his locomotive to a crawl, he peered into the darkness, his dimmed lights barely giving him a track's length of visibility, having one's train well-lit never wise in case Allied aircraft made it a target of opportunity.

Yet something had definitely changed. He knew these tracks like the back of his hand. He had been here scores of times, usually to pick up ore from the mine somewhere in the darkness ahead, sometimes to deliver supplies or workers. When the war was going well, which it hadn't been for some time, these runs were made in broad daylight, or at night with lights ablaze.

But no longer.

His hometown of Berlin was under near-constant bombardment by the Allies, and whispered reports were that the Russians could be on their doorstep within months.

The Thousand-Year Reich would soon be defeated.

He wasn't sure how he felt about that. He had grown up during the Great Depression, far worse in Germany than anywhere else in the world thanks to the punitive Treaty of Versailles. The war reparations Germany had been forced to pay as punishment for its actions, were crippling.

And Adolf Hitler had offered a way out to the impoverished, desperate citizens of a defeated Germany.

To fight back.

To take back what had been stolen, and rebuild.

He had embraced the idea, almost from the beginning. He had even joined the Party, thinking it was his patriotic duty, though mostly because it meant you went to the head of the line for jobs. He was fortunate he hadn't been required to fight. As a trained engineer, a skill in desperate need, he had been spared that horror, though most of his friends hadn't.

It racked him with guilt every time he saw the dead and wounded, or heard another widow or mother cry out in agony when the telegram arrived.

He just prayed his wife never received such a message.

Though with what he had been told yesterday, he was terrified *he* would be the one receiving a telegram.

What had his wife been thinking? Speaking out against the Reich? The very idea seemed nonsensical to him, completely unbelievable, though not because she was fiercely loyal to the Führer. It was because she wasn't an idiot. She knew what could happen.

And that was why he had refused to believe the accusations.

Until the names of three other women were provided, all friends of hers, all women that regularly gathered to gossip.

And it was apparently one of these sessions that was reported to the Gestapo, probably by one of the women whose husband needed to prove his loyalty for a promotion.

They had threatened to take her in for interrogation if he didn't cooperate, and he knew what that meant. He would never see her again. Too many disappeared these days, convincing him it had little to do with people fleeing the city, and everything to do with the Gestapo rounding up anyone they suspected of not being 100% loyal to the cause.

The lights caught a glint of metal, and he recognized the gates of the mine outside Marienwerder. In the shadows, he saw the silhouettes of several guards and a couple of canine units, but the entire area was under a complete blackout.

This was the strangest run on which he had ever been. They had called him in at the last minute, just before he was about to head home to Berlin to see his wife for the first time in months, and sent on what was a regular run except for the cargo.

What that cargo was, he had no idea, and the pickup location was unusual. Königsberg. He had never picked up anything destined for the mine from there before, though perhaps others had. Those who served this region worked most of the routes, rotating through them to relieve the boredom.

But this load he was transporting was like no other before. There were only two boxcars, already hooked up and sealed when he had arrived, and the train had been surrounded by SS soldiers. He had been ordered to leave his fireman at the last junction, left to travel the final leg by himself.

That was unheard of.

If he were going anywhere else, he'd think his cargo was some top-secret military equipment. But he wasn't going anywhere else, he was going to a regular old mine, one he had heard was due to be shut down as it was now almost barren.

The locomotive jerked to the left unexpectedly, and he leaned out the window, peering into the dark, his dim lights glimmering off brand new track.

Something had changed, but this wasn't it.

Then it dawned on him.

There were no sounds. Normally when he was here, over the engine he could hear equipment operating, men shouting—the sounds of everyday life at a mine. Even with minimal lighting at night, the mine still operated, its materials essential to the war effort.

But tonight, there was nothing beyond the sound of his engine.

And a dog barking in the darkness.

A flashlight shone in his face and he raised a hand to block the glare. Somebody hopped on the running board, the beam lowered.

"Just keep going, I'll tell you where to stop."

Hermann nodded, then sweat broke out over his entire body as he caught a glimpse of the SS emblem on the man's collar, a skull and crossbones on his hat. He kept them moving forward, slow and steady, his heart pounding hard as he tried to appear calm.

And why was that? He had done nothing wrong. He was doing his job and doing it well, as ordered. If he had arrived unexpectedly, or in some incorrect fashion, would this man have climbed on board and told him to keep going as he was? No, there would have been cursing and beratement as was typical of an SS officer.

Yet he was still terrified of this man.

And it was the second time in one night he had encountered the SS.

First at the beginning of his run, and now at the end of it.

He was certain that whatever cargo he carried was of the utmost importance to the SS, and if it was important to them, it was important to the Reich. The SS were the *Schutzstaffel,* or Protection Squadron, under the direct command of *Reichsführer* Heinrich Himmler himself, and fiercely loyal to the Führer, the Nazi Party, and the ideals of the Reich.

And with a notoriously low opinion of anyone who didn't have their insignia on their collar.

He spotted the entrance to the mine, but it wasn't the usual one. The tracks were still new, and he had never been this way. In fact, he had never known this entrance existed. Either a new shaft in the mine had been opened, or an old one had been reopened. Whatever the answer was, he was about to find out, as his dim lights that failed to pick up the emptiness that surrounded the tracks outside, suddenly lit the tight confines of the tunnel they were now in with little problem.

And it was all old construction.

Very old.

In fact, if he had to guess, this area of the mine had been shut down for years if not decades. As they slowly rounded a bend, he spotted a bright glow ahead, and moments later the train emerged into a large hollowed out area filled with several other boxcars, all with crates being offloaded. Dozens of men he recognized from the mine were moving the crates, and they appeared exhausted. He counted at least a dozen SS coordinating the effort, all fresh in their crisp uniforms, not a hair out of place as they did none of the manual labor.

"Stop here."

"Yes, sir."

He brought his train to a halt, the screeching of the brakes piercing in the confined space, only the SS wincing with pain, the workers used to the noise. He was quickly uncoupled and directed ahead, then switched onto a siding track and ordered to reverse out. He kept his eyes on the job, trying not to look at the goings on, and as they were about to leave the lighted chamber, the SS colonel swatted him on the shoulder.

"Back it out then wait for me, understood?"

"Yes, sir."

The colonel hopped to the ground and began barking orders for the two cars he had just delivered to be opened, but not unloaded. Hermann wondered what made his cargo so special to be left aboard, though decided asking such questions, even of himself, was unwise. As he reversed out of the mine and returned to the crisp January air, he again could see little in the overcast sky beyond the shiny new tracks and the snow covering the ground. He brought the locomotive to a halt and put it in idle, waiting for the return of the colonel.

I wonder what he wants.

It could be as simple as a lift back to the city. It wouldn't be the first time, though he couldn't recall transporting an SS officer unscheduled, and definitely never where he would have had to share his cab, as there were no passenger cars on this train.

As he waited, he could pick out the shadows moving around him. The mine might be closed, but the security detail seemed larger than normal.

"Turn off your lights!" shouted someone from the darkness.

"Yes, sir!" He immediately complied, cursing for being so foolish. When underway, there was a need for at least some minimal lighting ahead, though to be honest, at high speed, if the tracks were out ten feet beyond, you were screwed no matter what. At least, though, you'd have a few seconds to say a prayer before your fate was sealed.

But at idle, the lights should never be on in blackout conditions.

A flashlight bobbed ahead, and his now adjusted eyes spotted what appeared to be the SS colonel, followed by several armed soldiers.

"Get down!"

Hermann's eyes narrowed, wondering what possible reason this man could have for wanting him out of the locomotive. "Sir?"

"Now!"

The soldiers all aimed their weapons at him as the echoes of gunshots and the screams of men erupted from the tunnel.

Oh my God!

It was then that he realized what was happening. The miners were being executed, as they had seen what had happened here on this dark, cold night.

They were witnesses.

And so was he.

He hit the reversing lever, throwing the train into full reverse as he ducked. Gunfire pelted the locomotive as the three soldiers opened up on him. The glass shattered, showering him with shards, and he kept his head down as the train slowly gained speed.

But not fast enough.

Someone grunted on the other side of the door, one of the soldiers obviously having jumped on board. He rushed to the other side of the cab, though it was too late.

"Halt!"

He spun around to see the SS colonel half through the window, his flashlight in one hand, his Luger P08 pistol in the other.

"Please, don't! I swear I won't tell anyone what I saw!"

"You're right about that."

The trigger squeezed once, then twice more, Hermann shaking with each hit before he sank to the floor, his blood unseen in the dark, but the dampness of his shirt and overalls leaving little doubt what was happening.

That and the searing pain.

And as the life drained from him and the brakes squealed, bringing them to a halt, his heart hammered out its last few beats as he paid the ultimate price for a desperate Reich and a desperate leadership that he could only hope would die soon, before it took his daughter, as it had taken his daughter's father.

He closed his eyes and pictured his wife, her golden blond hair an ideal in the Reich, and wished he had made it home to see her one last time.

And ached at the thought of the telegram she was about to receive.

Goodbye, my love.

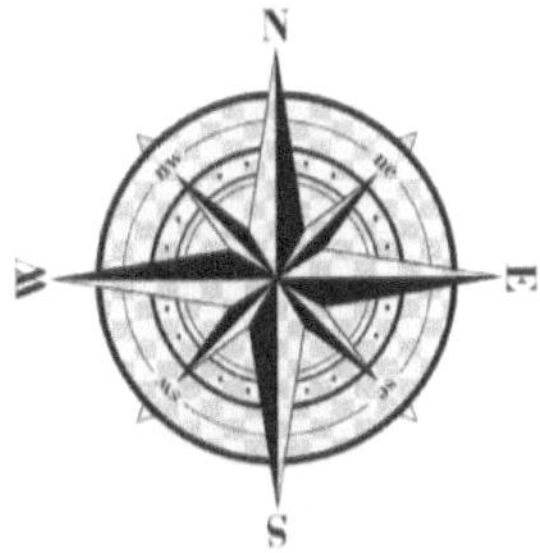

Granger Residence

St. Paul, Maryland

Present Day

Tommy Granger sat in the corner of his bedroom, the same one he had lived in his entire life. Mai Lien Trinh, the woman his heart ached for every time she wasn't with him, lay on her back beside him, her head propped up on a pillow as she chatted with friends back in Vietnam on Facebook.

It was a perfect day.

Except for the fact his parents were downstairs, and his bed creaked, so any fooling around had to happen on the hardwood floor, and his mother could walk in at any moment.

I have to move out.

It was beyond ridiculous that he still lived with his parents. He was in his twenties, already had his degree, and was ready.

"What's in that box?"

He glanced down at Mai.

God, she's beautiful.

"Huh?"

"That box in your closet. I don't remember seeing it before."

He glanced at the open closet, and his eyes widened slightly. "Oh, I forgot about that. It belonged to my great-grandfather. Some stuff my grandmother thought I might be interested in since I'm dating a history buff."

Mai rolled to her knees, her eyes wide. "You mean it has old stuff in it?"

He shrugged. "Mostly papers, I think. All in German. My family on my mother's side was German originally. I think they came here after the war. I'm not really sure."

"Can we look at it?"

He smiled at her eagerness.

How can I ever say no to you?

"Sure, I guess."

She jumped to her feet and rushed over to the closet, grunting as she bent over and pulled out the heavy box. Tommy forgot all about it though, the sight of her perfect posterior raising a flag. He pressed against her and she stood.

"Not again! Your mother will never let me visit you if she catches us."

"I'm an adult."

"Not as long as you live here, you're not."

The words stung, but she was right. "Maybe I'll get my own place."

"Sounds good. Something close to me would be nice."

He grinned, the hurt gone. "*Very* nice." He squeezed her butt, and she swatted his hand away.

"Give me a hand with this. It's heavy."

He made a show of flexing, then grabbed the box, heaving it onto his bed with a little more difficulty than his male ego could take. He sat on one side of the box, Mai the other, and removed the lid, revealing a bunch of boring old papers and photographs.

Mai was delighted, quickly reaching in and pulling out each piece of paper, one at a time, examining them carefully. "I wish I spoke German. I wonder what these say. Some of them look like official papers." She held up several. "These look like ID. Was your great-grandfather in the military?"

Tommy shrugged. "No idea. Mom might know."

He rose and grabbed his laptop off his desk, then his cellphone. He grabbed an envelope from the box, something scrawled on the front of it, and snapped a photo, uploading it into some optical character recognition software, then pushing the result to a translation program.

"Huh, I wonder what that means."

Mai glanced at him. "What does it say?"

"It says, 'My biggest regret.'"

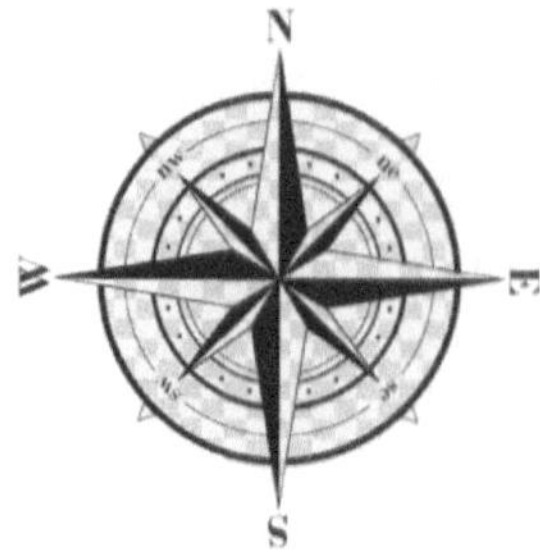

Königsberg Castle

Königsberg, Nazi Germany

January 26, 1945

Two days earlier

Klaus Becker adjusted his tie then made certain his Nazi Party pin was in place and unblemished as SS *Standartenführer* Steiner strode into his office after inspecting the proceedings in the museum. The colonel's arrival had been unannounced, though not unexpected. The war wasn't going well, the Russians were closing in, and his museum contained a large number of precious artifacts, including one prize display worth more than the rest combined.

And it had to be protected.

"I trust everything was to your satisfaction."

Colonel Steiner sat, crossing his legs and laying his black leather gloves on his knee. "Yes, a pleasant surprise, I must say. Too often German efficiency has been left to wane in these dark days."

"Not here, I assure you."

Steiner regarded him for a moment. "And you are certain you can have it dismantled within forty-eight hours and ready for transport?"

"Absolutely. We will work day and night. We cannot risk its capture, or worse, having it damaged in an air raid."

"I would rather see it destroyed than fall into Russian hands."

Becker was about to express his horror at the very idea of destroying a unique, priceless creation, but bit his tongue.

It was never wise to contradict a senior SS officer.

"Of course. I'm sure, however, that won't be necessary. We will have it ready for your return in two days. Where will you be transporting it?"

"None of your concern. Let's just say it is somewhere very safe, no matter the outcome of the war." Steiner leaned in. "Secrecy is of the utmost importance. As discussed, I want different men transporting the crated items to the rail yard, and yet another crew loading it onto my train. No man must know what they are handling, nor where it came from before they handled it."

"Understood. I will arrange for outside transport from a trusted source, and use the crews already at the rail yard to offload the trucks and load the railcars. They won't know what they're loading, nor will they know where it came from."

"Or where it's going. Only I and the engineer will know. Unfortunately, one of our trains was hit by the Allies yesterday, and my man was killed. I have yet to secure a trustworthy engineer, though I'm sure I'll find someone in time."

Becker cleared his throat. "I might be able to help you with that."

"You know someone?"

"Not exactly. Let's just say I know someone who probably does. He's my go-to man if I ever need anything done quickly."

"Who?"

"Oh, umm, you probably don't want to know, Colonel. Rest assured, he's a good Nazi. He's been a member of the Party since the beginning, and can absolutely be trusted."

"And he can get us an engineer we can trust?"

"I'm sure he can. He seems to have a man for every job. You need a baker, he's got a baker. You need a plumber, he's got a plumber."

Steiner slapped his knee with his gloves. "All I need is an engineer to take the damned train where I need it to go, and who can be relied upon to keep his mouth shut."

Becker gulped, perhaps having pushed the sales job a little too far. "I-I'm sure he can find us one."

"Find out."

"Y-yes, sir." He grabbed his phone and placed the call, the line ringing a few moments later, each second increasingly uncomfortable as Steiner stared at him.

I wonder how many men he's killed.

"Hello?"

"Konrad, it's Klaus Becker at the Königsberg Castle Museum. How are you, my friend?"

"Busy. What do you want?"

Becker was thankful the colonel couldn't hear the other side of the conversation, Konrad apparently not in a good mood, and never very friendly when he was. "I need a favor."

"Of course you do. Everybody needs a favor. Again, what do you want?"

Becker smiled at Steiner, adjusting the knot of his tie once again. "Well, actually, the favor isn't for me, it's for the SS."

"The SS?"

Becker sensed an immediate change in tone, a hint of fear in Konrad's voice, and for a brief moment, he felt the surge the colonel must feel every time someone cowered in front of him.

Right now, at this moment, *he* was representing the SS, and *he* had the power to put fear into the heart of a man far more powerful than him.

"Yes, the SS. I won't mention any names, but I need your help."

"Well, umm, of course I'd be very pleased to help the SS. What is it you need?"

"I need an engineer that can be trusted with an important mission."

"An engineer? No problem. Civil? Mechanical?"

"A train engineer. You know, someone that operates a locomotive."

"Ahh, I see. Give me a moment."

He heard the phone put down followed by footsteps. A filing cabinet drawer opened then closed, and the receiver was once again picked up. "You're in luck. I actually have someone on file. He'd be perfect for the job."

"Trustworthy?"

"Better. Compromised."

Becker smiled. "Compromised? How?

"His wife. She's apparently said some things that could be considered treasonous."

Becker tensed, not keen on the idea of using a man's wife against him. He wondered if his own wife might have said something she shouldn't have at some point, and if Konrad had his name on a list somewhere, should there be a need for a museum administrator in the future. "Does he know?"

"Not yet, but I'll see that he does. I assure you, he will be most cooperative after I'm finished with him. And discreet."

Becker forced a smile. "Perfect. Have him report to the rail yard here in forty-eight hours."

"Consider it done."

Becker hung up the phone and leaned back in his chair slightly. "Done. You'll have your engineer on schedule."

Steiner smiled. "Nothing beats a good Nazi when you're in a hurry."

Becker chuckled. "Too true, too true. And our good Nazi's engineer will fit the bill perfectly. Apparently, his wife's tongue has been wagging. He'll cooperate once he finds out, if he wants to see her alive again."

Steiner rose from his chair. "You've done well, Herr Becker. Your name would feature prominently in my report, if there were to be one."

He straightened his jacket. "But there won't be. You will keep no records of what is happening here, neither will your transport company, or the rail yard. There will be no record made of this shipment anywhere. Understood?"

Becker bowed slightly. "I understand completely."

Steiner snapped to attention, extending his arm. "Heil Hitler!"

Becker sucked in a breath and mimicked the colonel as best he could. "Heil Hitler!"

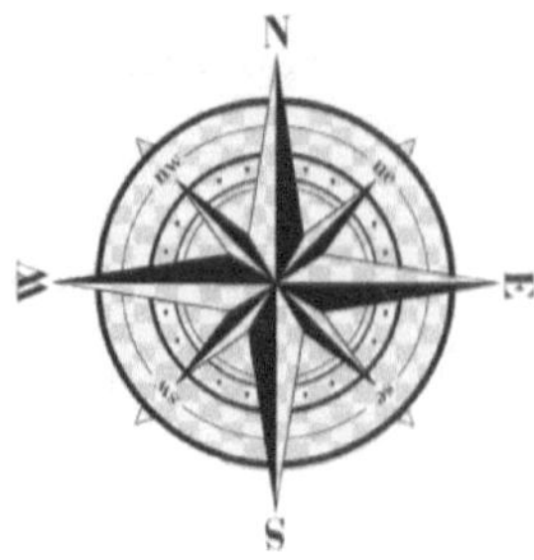

Acton Residence

St. Paul, Maryland

Present Day

Archaeology Professor James Acton lay in his two-person hammock, the other half occupied by his wife, Archaeology Professor Laura Palmer. An iPad lay in his lap as they shared a set of earbuds, listening to an audiobook they had been competing for, finally agreeing just to listen to it together.

The hammock had been his choice, the sunroom at the back of the house and a bright sun enough to let them enjoy the experience without suffering the chill on the other side of the glass.

And there was nothing like shared body heat.

He stared at her chest, a hint of cleavage visible as she was slightly squished against him.

He kissed the top of her head.

She snuggled a little closer.

He tilted her chin up and smiled.

She eyed him. "It's a book on the Templars. How is this making you horny?"

Acton grinned. "It's not, you are."

"You're like one of your students."

"Hey, enjoy it while you can. One of these days I'm going to need pharmacological assistance."

"Then maybe the girls will get a breather."

His busy hands froze. "I thought they were always enthusiastic participants."

She groaned. "Oh well, I suppose I could spare a few minutes." She leaned over to put the iPad on the floor when Acton felt them tip.

"Oh shit!"

He rolled over her and slammed onto the floor first, Laura landing on top of him with a thud. He groaned in pain, then forgot about it as a hand reached for his crotch.

"You don't waste any time."

She smiled. "Now you've got me feeling frisky."

He groaned. "Meet Frisky."

She squeezed. "Is that his new name?"

Acton tilted his head back, his ecstasy only beginning, when the doorbell rang. "Ignore it."

"Your wish is my command."

Oh yeah!

The doorbell rang again. "Oh, for Pete's sake, you're killing me!" He grabbed his phone and swiped his thumb, a live video of the front porch displayed. He held it up for Laura to see.

Tommy and Mai, two of their students.

"Yes?"

"Hi, Professor, I hope we're not disturbing you, but we found something we think you should see."

Acton sighed as Laura put Frisky away then gave the hidden bundle a pat before climbing off him. "What is it?"

"Some old papers of my great-grandfather. There's something here I think you should read."

Acton rolled to his feet. "Just a second." He extended a hand and pulled Laura up, copping a few extra feels under the guise of straightening her clothes.

She stared at him. "Don't think you're fooling anyone."

He grinned. "Am I that obvious?"

"Get the door."

"Yes'm." Acton opened the front door with a genuine smile. Mai Trinh had helped save their lives in Vietnam, and had paid the price by having to flee her country, the communist regime none too happy with her. He had invited her to his university, and over the past couple of years had come to think of her almost as a daughter, now very protective of the young woman.

Which was why he had been a little concerned when Tommy Granger, hacker extraordinaire, who as a teenager had broken too many laws to count, had taken an interest in her. Fortunately, his fears had been unfounded, the young man having turned his life around, now Acton's go-to guy if he needed something computer related.

"Come on in guys." He gave Mai a hug and would have shaken Tommy's hand if he weren't carrying what appeared to be a very heavy box. He stepped aside, letting Tommy rush past him to find relief through a flat surface somewhere. "What brings you two here?"

Tommy sighed around the corner after a heavy thump, as Acton took Mai's coat and hung it up.

"We found something in some old papers that Tommy got recently from his grandmother. They belonged to his great-grandfather, and, well…" She smiled. "Maybe he should tell you."

Tommy gasped from around the corner. "You're doing fine."

Acton followed Mai into the living area, Tommy standing with one hand on the wall, the other on his hip, the box sitting on the kitchen island. Mai retrieved an envelope from the top and handed it to Acton.

"We found this inside."

Acton examined the envelope, something written on the front in black ink. "What language is this? German?"

Tommy nodded. "Yeah, my mom said her family is part German. My great-grandfather, her grandfather, was German, then immigrated here."

"I assume you know what it says?"

"It says, 'My biggest regret.'"

Acton exchanged a glance with Laura, his eyebrows rising slightly. He carefully removed a sheaf of papers inside, opening the dry foolscap pages, praying they didn't crack. It appeared to be a handwritten letter of sorts, dated January 28, 1965. "We're going to have to get this translated."

Tommy emerged from the kitchen, a glass of ice water in his hand. He grabbed a blue file folder from the box and handed it to Mai, who passed it to Acton.

"Tommy already used his computer to translate everything. It's rough in some spots, but it's accurate enough to get the gist."

Acton scanned the pages, handing each one off to Laura as he finished. His eyes were wide when done, and he waited for Laura before saying anything.

She looked at him. "Is this saying what I think it's saying?"

Acton shrugged. "I don't know what *you* think it's saying, but to me, it's a retired cop telling about his last murder case, and how there might be a Nazi gold train sitting in the side of a mountain!"

Laura patted his shoulder. "Stay calm, dear, nowhere in here did it say there was a Nazi train loaded with gold sitting inside a mountain."

Acton grunted. "You're no fun."

"That wasn't the impression I got just a few minutes ago."

"All right, Docs!"

Acton laughed at Tommy who delivered a remote fist bump. "Keep it clean." He waved the sheaf of papers. "Okay, let's cover what we know. Your great-grandfather was a cop. I assume there are things in that box to confirm this?"

"Yes."

"And he's talking about his last case. His big regret is that he was never able to tell the wives of the victims what had actually happened.

As an archaeologist, there's not much we can do with any of this story concerning the murders and the case itself, but I return to the fact that we have a dead train engineer, who must have delivered something to this mine he refers to, something that was worth killing for." He pointed at Tommy, typing furiously on his laptop. "Have you looked up this mine?"

He nodded. "Yup. It was abandoned at the end of the war. Google is just showing green. Looks like there's nothing there at all."

"But it did exist."

"Yup."

Acton paused. "Wait. Where is it? Germany's no longer Germany."

"Poland."

Acton's eyes narrowed. "Poland? Why would they hide their gold in Poland?"

Laura shook her head. "You're fixated on gold."

"I like gold."

"Uh huh." She tilted her head toward Tommy. "Where in Poland?"

"South of Gdansk."

A smile spread on Acton's face, and Laura's. "Formerly known as Danzig, a major city in what was formerly known as Prussia."

Tommy's eyes narrowed. "What's Prussia? Some sort of Russian offshoot?"

"There were tight ties before the Russian Revolution, of course, but what's important here is that Prussia was traditionally German. That means that it is plausible the Nazis would hide something on Prussian territory, thinking that even if they lost the war, it would remain German."

"Boy were they wrong."

Acton agreed. "Who do we know in Poland?"

Laura thought for a moment. "What about Professor Lisowski? She's always asking us to visit. This would be a golden opportunity to meet her in person finally, and satisfy your curiosity."

Acton grinned. "Road trip!"

"I'll take a plane."

"Suit yourself." He stared once again at the translation. "It would be nice to get some answers, but also perhaps provide some closure to these families. I wonder if there's some way to track them down."

"Found them."

Acton's eyebrows shot up. "Excuse me?"

Tommy held up his notebook. "I already found them. Everything's computerized now, which means there's no way to keep anything secret from me." He flashed a toothy smile at Mai, who giggled.

Acton shook his head, the boy's skills never ceasing to amaze him. "If you broke any laws, then I don't want to know." He rose. "We should make plans to leave right away."

Laura pulled out her phone. "I'll call our agent and have her get the jet ready."

Tommy cleared his throat, raising a finger. "Umm, professors, ahh, can we come?"

Acton stared at him for a moment, then looked at Laura, who shrugged. "Why not?"

"You're right, why not." Acton thought for a second. "But how about this? There are two things we're trying to accomplish here, and we don't have a lot of time to do it, since classes resume in a week. Laura and I will go to Poland to see if there's anything in this mine, and you two go to Germany and see if you can track down the two families. Have copies made of the pertinent documents so you can give them to the descendants of the victims, and if we find something at the mine, we can share that information with them as well. It did say one of the engineers was missing and presumed dead. I have a sneaking suspicion we're going to find his body with his train."

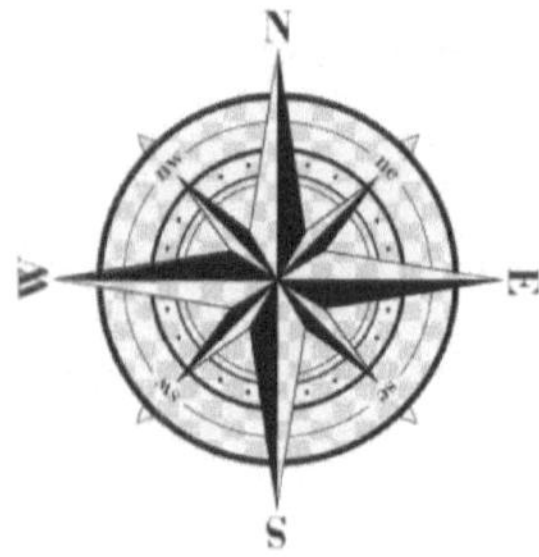

South of Marienwerder, West Prussia

Nazi Germany

January 28, 1945

SS Colonel Friedrich Steiner watched the locomotive back out of the chamber. He shouted at the men unloading the already arrived boxcars to hurry up, then waved off another crew heading for the newly delivered cargo.

"Leave those be!"

The men stared at him for a moment, then returned to help the others. He could tell they were curious why these two cars weren't to be touched, but he didn't care. It was none of their business, and he didn't owe them an explanation.

Though perhaps it didn't matter if they knew.

He turned to see the lamps of the locomotive now gone, its engine still echoing through the chamber. He beckoned his second-in-command to join him.

"Yes, sir?"

"As soon as they're finished, execute them."

His second-in-command's eyes widened for a moment, but he snapped back to attention. "Yes, sir!"

Steiner pointed at three of his men. "You three, come with me." He strode briskly after the locomotive, and shook his head as someone shouted for the idiot to turn off his lights, their beams a beacon for Allied air power in the pitch dark.

He emerged into the frigid cold of a Prussian winter, but suppressed the shiver, never one to let his men see any sign of weakness. He turned on his flashlight, the beam slicing through the night, though not carrying far, just enough to make sure he didn't twist an ankle on the uneven ground. He spotted the engineer leaning out his window.

"Get down!"

There was hesitation, as if the man sensed something not to his liking was about to happen.

And he was right.

The plan had never been to allow him to leave alive. He needed a trustworthy, reliable man—either through loyalty to the Führer and the Party, or, as in this case, through leverage—who could be counted on not to speak to anyone of his priority mission.

And now that his job was done, his life was forfeit.

As was everyone's here.

There could be no witnesses to what had just taken place. The priceless artifacts transported here over the past several days would be safe, but only as long as no one knew where they were.

And that meant no witnesses who had seen the crates, could be left alive.

Including this engineer.

"Sir?"

"Now!"

He motioned to his men, and they all raised their weapons, aiming them at the cab of the massive locomotive. Gunshots erupted from the tunnel entrance as his men executed his orders, the crew inside evidently finished their task.

Unfortunate timing.

The sound of the engine changed, and the wheels screeched as they spun, the train reversing as the engineer apparently realized he was about to die. Steiner pointed at the cab and his men opened fire, their MP35 submachine guns pumping lead as the train slowly pulled away. Windows shattered and bullets ricocheted, but there was no evidence they had found their mark, and the train continued to pick up speed.

He rushed ahead, drawing his weapon, and leaped onto the side of the train, hauling himself up. He slipped on the built-up ice, his feet dragging along the ground, and he regretted having drawn his weapon before securing his footing. Dangling by one hand, he shoved his Luger back in its holster, then dragged himself onto the running board. Stable, he drew his weapon and thrust his head through the shattered window, his pistol leading the way. He couldn't see the engineer. He pulled out his flashlight, shining it into the cab.

And spotted him on the other side.

"Halt!"

The engineer spun toward him, raising his hands. "Please, don't! I swear I won't tell anyone what I saw!"

Steiner chuckled. "You're right about that."

He fired three shots into the man, his victim collapsing in a heap in the corner. He opened the door and stepped inside, staring at the controls for a moment before taking a guess at what were the brakes.

He was right.

He shone his flashlight on the man's face, still alive, though not for long, and wondered what his final thoughts were.

Probably of his wife.

He jumped down to the ground as the train came to a halt, making a note that the wife should be picked up.

After all, we can't have anyone speaking ill of the Reich.

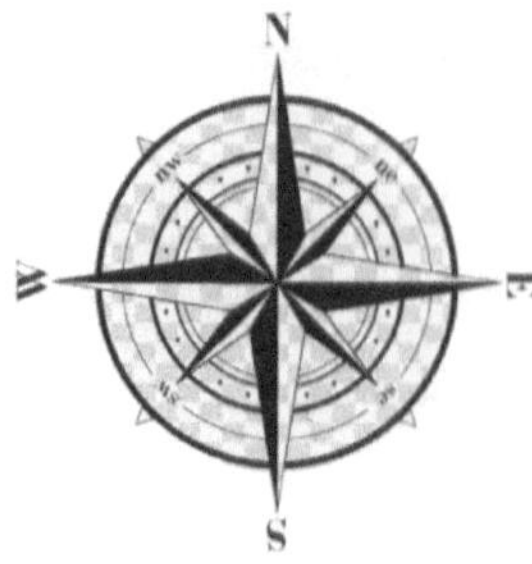

South of Kwidzyn (formerly Marienwerder), Poland

Present Day

Professor James Acton stared at the sight before them. Or lack thereof. It was an empty field with a good-sized hill, and no evidence whatsoever that anything had ever been here. He was beginning to think they were on a wild goose chase, though it wouldn't be the first time what appeared to be a blank canvas was merely time healing the earth of the scars man had inflicted upon it.

Professor Aleksandra Lisowski sighed. "And you're sure this is the place?"

Laura Palmer nodded. "Absolutely. Assuming the letter was telling the truth."

Acton pursed his lips. "I doubt he'd lie. But there *was* a mine here, right?"

Lisowski held up a printout of some official records from before the war, clearly showing there had been a mine at this location. "The records don't lie."

Acton smiled at her. "Oh, how much I have to teach you, my friend!"

Lisowski laughed. "Yeah, you're right. I just sounded as foolish as one of my students."

Laura stepped toward the hillside. "You know, if there was an old mine here, there should be some evidence of it. The old entrance, railroad tracks, maybe some old buildings. But there's *nothing.*"

Acton grunted. "I think that's the point, isn't it? We must be in the wrong place."

Laura shook her head. "No, *you're* missing the point."

Acton smiled. "Enlighten me."

"I shall." She winked at Lisowski. "If *I* were trying to hide the fact I hid something in an old mine, I would try to hide the fact that there was even a mine in the first place."

Acton's eyes widened. "You mean it's sitting right in front of us, purposefully hidden."

"Exactly."

Acton's disappointment at his initial assessment was shoved aside as renewed hope fueled him. He grabbed a metal detector from the back of their SUV, and headed for the side of the hill as he fit the headphones in place. He quickly scanned for any signs of metal, forcing himself to slow down, as Laura and Lisowski waited behind him, having a conversation he couldn't hear.

The indicator jumped, and the device wailed in his ears.

"I've got something! Bring me a shovel."

He continued scanning the area, the hits almost constant, the fact something was behind the dirt in front of him now indisputable. Lisowski approached with a shovel.

"Where?"

Acton pointed. "Right in front of me. The whole area seems to be giving indications of metal."

Lisowski began digging as Acton continued to scan the hillside, just in case his initial discovery proved to be nothing. He found several more minor hits, but nothing like his initial find.

The shovel scraped something, ending his search.

"Huh? What's this?"

Acton rushed back to where Lisowski had been digging, Laura already using a spade to clear more dirt away. "What is it?"

Laura stood back, a smile on her face. "It looks like a cinderblock wall, perhaps with rebar inside to reinforce it."

Acton grinned at the ladies. "Sounds to me like somebody might be trying to hide something!"

Lisowski tapped her shovel against the wall now facing them. "I think we're going to need a bigger shovel."

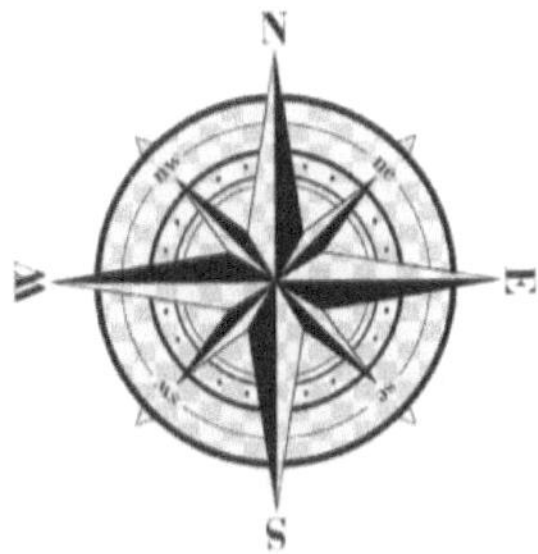

South of Marienwerder, West Prussia

Nazi Germany

January 29, 1945

"Wake up!"

Dieter Maier woke, still tired. He stretched and executed an exaggerated yawn before opening his eyes. As far as he was concerned, whoever wanted him here on such short notice, could wait. He had a four-day pass, and was supposed to be on a train for home right now. Instead, he'd been driven—yes, driven!—for almost two hours in the dead of night, dawn just cracking the horizon.

Hopefully the others got away.

Four of them had been given leave passes, though only after two trains had run into each other last week, the engineer asleep at the controls.

They were exhausted.

They all were. With the war going poorly, no matter what Goebbels and his radio broadcasts would suggest, there were fewer and fewer engineers as the Allies shot up more of the trains as they closed in on the Fatherland.

Defeat couldn't come soon enough. He was tired of the war, had already lost a son to the Russian Front, and had sent his only remaining son to stay with relatives outside of the city, with orders to keep him out of sight.

They were drafting boys now.

And his son, indoctrinated by the Hitler Youth, would eagerly volunteer.

I just pray that Renatta can keep him from doing anything stupid.

If he knew anyone in the west of the country, he'd have sent him farther, but he didn't. The idea of living under Russian control terrified him, and his repeated requests for transfer to the western routes, were always denied.

Once you were assigned to the east, you were fated to die in the east.

And every run he took was another chance to fulfill the belief.

Which was another reason four days off with his wife would have been a blessing. He had every intention of keeping the neighbors up all night as he worked off several months of pent-up frustrations, but he also just wanted to sleep in his bed with his wife in his arms, and the war something in the distance.

A fairytale, he knew—the Allied bombers were decimating Berlin.

"Are you waiting for the Führer himself to invite you?"

He opened his eyes, having drifted off again. "Is he here?"

The driver grunted. "Careful, friend. This place is swarming with SS, and they don't have a sense of humor."

Dieter tensed, finally taking in his surroundings, a chill sweeping over him that went beyond the frosty air filling the interior of the car, heaters a luxury during a gas shortage. His driver was right. At least a couple of dozen soldiers were spread out around the exterior of the old mine.

And not a single worker.

Something was going on here, and if it involved the SS, he wanted nothing to do with it. Unfortunately, the fact he was here, and the fact an SS colonel was marching toward them, meant he was already involved, whether he liked it or not.

Just keep your head down and your mouth shut.

He scrambled out of the car and stood at his best impression of attention as he could.

"Good luck, my friend," whispered the driver as he reversed the car quickly. The kind words were delivered with a finality that suggested he not only needed it, but it was offered uselessly.

No amount of luck would save him.

The colonel came to a halt directly in front of him, his eyes piercing, Dieter making a point to keep his chin high, his eyes directed upward, over the man's head and his jet-black uniform. "Engineer Dieter Maier reporting as ordered, sir!"

"It's about time! You're over an hour late."

"I apologize, sir. I was at the mercy of my driver, and he to the weather."

The colonel grunted, a growl threatening to erupt, before he spun on his heel, heading toward a locomotive that sat inside the fence surrounding the mine.

"Are you coming?"

"Yes, sir!" He scrambled after the man, his heart pounding.

The colonel pointed at the locomotive. "Take this back to the yard."

His eyes narrowed as they approached the over 80 tons of metal. "Where's the engineer who brought it here?"

The colonel's head snapped around, his glare emasculating. "There are no questions to be asked, understood?"

Maier dropped his gaze to the ground. "Y-yes, sir. I apologize, sir!"

He stopped in his tracks when he finally reached the front of the locomotive. Dozens of bullets scarred the exterior, and several of the windows were shattered. His jaw dropped as he was about to ask what happened.

He snapped it shut.

"Polish partisans."

"Huh?"

The colonel pointed at the locomotive. "Polish partisans attacked the mine last night. Killed the engineer and a few of the miners. They were stopped and executed." The colonel spit on the ground. "A fruitless effort. The mine was just closed, so they accomplished nothing."

They killed one of my colleagues, so they did something.

"What was his name?"

"Who?"

"The engineer who died."

"I have no idea, and you aren't to ask any questions. His death is not to be discussed with anyone, understood?"

"Y-yes, sir. I doubt anyone will ask, anyway. Engineers are dying and being reassigned every day. I'm sure no one will notice except those who need to know."

The colonel assessed him for a moment then grunted, pointing toward the locomotive. "Get it out of here, and make it quick."

"Yes, sir."

Dieter climbed up into the cab and gulped. Blood was everywhere, apparently little if any effort made at cleaning it up. He checked the controls, and nothing seemed damaged. It was still at idle, so he should be able to leave within minutes. He turned and nearly cried out when he saw the colonel's head sticking through the shattered window.

"Is everything in order?"

Dieter nodded. "Y-yes, sir. I should be leaving momentarily."

"Good. Discuss with no one what you saw here today, or even the fact you were here." He jabbed a gloved finger at him. "And should you ignore my warnings, remember this. Not only will your life be forfeit, but your family's as well."

The colonel disappeared from the window, leaving Dieter shaking from terror and the cold.

And consumed with the thought of his wife and son.

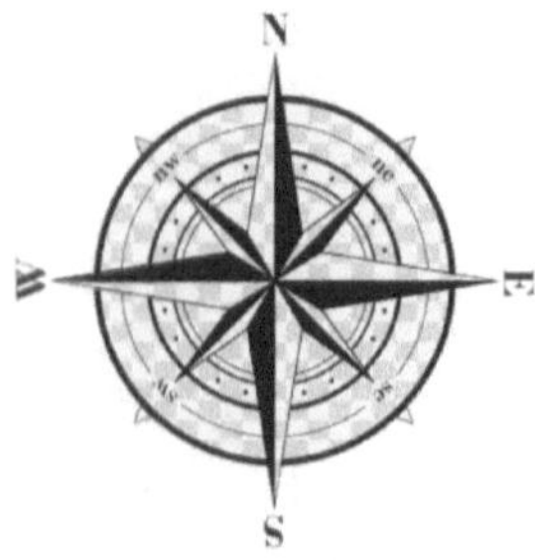

South of Kwidzyn (formerly Marienwerder), Poland
Present Day

James Acton could barely control his giddiness. It had taken several hours for the heavy equipment to arrive, a backhoe now making quick work of the hillside, the couple of hours of shovel work he had put into it now appearing a fool's errand.

The teeth on the bucket finally sank into the dirt behind the cinderblock wall, and the operator expertly pulled it down, the wall collapsing outward, revealing a dark cavern behind it. Acton desperately wanted to rush right in, but it was still too dangerous. The crew chief directed his operator to move the downed wall away from the entrance, and when he was done, two city engineers tentatively stepped inside, inspecting the remaining structure for stability.

Acton spun in a circle, hopping up and down.

Nazi gold train! Nazi gold train! Nazi gold train!

"You'd think it was Christmas and you were five."

Acton grinned at his wife. "It *is* Christmas, and I *feel* five!"

One of the inspectors stepped back into the light, giving a thumbs-up and shouting something in Polish.

Lisowski smiled at Acton's expectant stare. "We're good to go. It does indeed appear to be an old mineshaft."

Acton hopped in the air like a little schoolgirl, then rushed forward, stopping short of the entrance as he urged Laura and Lisowski to hurry up. He pulled his flashlight from his belt and tapped his hardhat. "Ready to make history?"

"Don't be surprised if disappointment is the only discovery."

Acton frowned mockingly at his wife. "Aren't we the pessimist today?"

Laura remained serious. "Have you considered the fact that they may not have been hiding gold in here, but something else."

Acton paused, then felt sick. "A mass grave."

Laura nodded, her face grim. "Exactly. Let's just not get too excited here. We may be about to find hundreds or even thousands of bodies, and they deserve respect."

Acton sighed, his head bobbing slowly as all the joy of the moment drained from him. "You're right, of course." He turned to the gathered crew, Lisowski translating. "Remember, we don't know what we're going to find, or if the shaft is completely stable. Don't touch anything, and if you see or hear something, don't hesitate to speak up." He motioned toward the engineers. "I assume you'll want to lead the way?"

"Yes," replied the lead man in English. He and his partner forged ahead with Acton, Laura, and Lisowski on their heels, as several others followed. He'd prefer a smaller crew, but there had been a heated argument between Lisowski and the foreman sent by the city, settled in the opposing side's favor.

Acton played his light out ahead, first scanning the ground for any hidden dangers, then the walls for signs of stability issues, just in case the experts missed something. Having been in tunnels and shafts far older than this on too many occasions to count, he was willing to pit his gut against their skills any day.

Laura paused, rubbing the toe of her shoe against the track they had been walking along. "Seems to be in good shape."

Acton kneeled, running a finger along it. "Yeah, a little too good. How long was this mine worked?"

Lisowski took a knee beside him. "Decades, but this track looks barely used."

Acton suppressed a smile. "It could have been laid just to move something inside."

Laura agreed, resuming their march ahead. "Possibly. That's a lot of work for something so temporary, though."

Acton held out a hand, pointing ahead of them. "Look!" He rushed forward and took a knee beside the body of a man sitting against the wall in overalls and a small hat. "This is an engineer's uniform. A train engineer!"

Laura gasped as she joined him, pointing at the dust-covered uniform. "Are those bullet holes?"

Acton nodded. "I think so." His eyes widened. "This must be the engineer that Tommy's great-grandfather spoke of in the letter. They must have shot him so he couldn't tell anyone what he had brought here."

Laura took several photos. "But what did he bring that was worth dying for?"

Acton rose, heading deeper into the shaft, several more bodies, these wearing military uniforms, lying about in their final resting places, some appearing to have been running away from their killer or killers.

He gasped as they entered a large chamber, the engineers ahead of them already playing their flashlights about the massive area, revealing hundreds of crates.

And two fully loaded boxcars.

Acton grabbed Laura by the hand, excitement returning. "This isn't a mass grave."

She squeezed his hand as they stepped deeper inside. "No, it's not." She smiled at him. "I think you were right all along!"

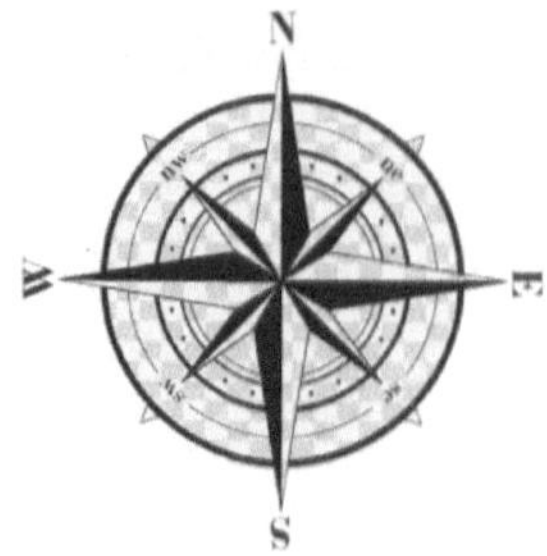

Lang Residence

Berlin, Nazi Germany

January 30, 1945

Erika Lang polished the kitchen counter for the umpteenth time today. She had to do something, anything, to occupy her time. Unfortunately, keeping house wasn't distracting enough, and she constantly found herself in mid-wipe, frozen in place, shaking.

Her husband was missing.

Though was he?

He was late. Two days late. He was supposed to have returned home on a four-day pass, yet hadn't. And there had been no word. She had phoned his supervisor, but had been given the runaround, then cut off. She would go in person tomorrow, though expected little more. Two years ago, German efficiency would have told her exactly where he was and why.

But now, in a nearly defeated Germany?

She was lucky to still have a roof over her head.

The bombing by the enemy was too frequent now, even residential areas sometimes targeted. Fortunately, her neighborhood hadn't been touched yet, though everyone was feeling the effects. When it had first started, she had run for the shelters like everyone else, and cowered in fear.

But no longer.

If she heard the sirens, she would prepare to flee while waiting for the sound of the bombs. If they sounded close, she'd head for the air raid shelter, though if they remained in the distance, as they usually did, she wouldn't bother.

And if a stray bomb killed her, then so be it.

If only Hermann knew!

He'd be furious if he knew she wasn't going to the shelter every time the siren sounded, but he didn't know what it was like. They had seen each other only twice in six months, and the last time he had been here, the bombings hadn't been as frequent. To head to the shelter every night would mean she'd never get any sleep, and she'd be useless.

But none of that mattered now. He wasn't home, and she didn't know what to do.

Every sound in the hallway had her running for the door, an ear pressed against the wood in hopes that it would be him, terrified it would be a telegram informing her of his glorious death in the service to the Reich.

Though she had loved the Führer and what he had accomplished for her great nation, that faith had wavered over the past couple of years, and she did not want to sacrifice her husband to the cause, nor their daughter. Hitler had failed. He had promised to restore Germany to greatness, then peace.

Instead, he had restored the Fatherland to its former prominence, then squandered it with over-ambitious plans of ruling the entire continent, including Russia.

If only we hadn't made an enemy of them.

If she had been in charge—a laughable notion—she would have left the Russians alone, and thrown everything they had at England. Eliminate that thorn, and the Allies would have nowhere to amass their troops. And once secured, the focus could turn to Africa and its untapped resources, then finally, when ready, the Soviet Union.

But it was all the musings of wives with too much time on their hands, coffee and the occasional schnapps leading to idle speculation of what they would have done differently should the men not be in charge.

In some circles, it might have even been considered treasonous.

The very thought sent a shiver up and down her spine, speaking out against the Führer or the Reich certain to get one shot, but not before a healthy bout of torture to force out the names of any others who might share similar views.

She paused as a thought occurred to her.

What about Michaella?

Michaella Maier was one of her best friends, and her husband was due back yesterday. He worked with Hermann, and might at least be able to tell her something. Even just knowing he was alive would be a relief.

She scribbled a note, just in case Hermann arrived while she was out, then grabbed her coat and hat, bundling up for the chill outside. She stepped out into the hallway and locked the door, then rushed toward the stairwell and down the stairs, emerging onto the street. She looked in both directions before crossing to the other side, the stop for the streetcar a block away.

She made a point to go behind an idling black car with a dented rear fender, just in case the driver got underway, the waste of gas unheard of these days. She noticed a pile of cigarettes by the driver's window, and her heart pounded at the sight of the man's shoulder—a shoulder clad in leather.

Gestapo?

She shuddered at the thought, resisting the urge to look back at the vehicle. One never wanted to draw the attention of the Gestapo. Her recent activities replayed themselves in her mind as she rushed for the streetcar, its screeching sounds bringing her comfort, reminding her of Hermann and the times he had brought her to the rail yard to see the massive equipment he operated.

An engineer.

She had been so proud of him when he got his first job after training. They had been holding off having a baby until he had steady work, and the day he was officially hired, they had made love repeatedly, and she swore their daughter had been conceived that night.

The thought made her warm all over.

She spotted the streetcar and picked up her pace, reaching it just in time. She found a seat near the back and caught her breath, smiling at her seatmate.

"Chilly one today."

The old woman grunted. "With nothing to heat the apartment, I sometimes wonder if there's a difference anymore between inside and out."

Erika was about to reply with something supportive, when she noticed the same black car that had been parked across from her building, pulling in behind them.

I wonder who they're following.

She stared at the others on the streetcar with her, watching for anyone who appeared nervous, instead finding too many blank, defeated expressions. Everyone knew that the end was near, and everyone knew it would be the Russians who conquered Berlin.

A terrifying prospect, best not thought about.

They had sent their daughter to stay with relatives outside of the city, but they were still in the path of the vengeful Russians. There was no hope now to get them to the west, where Americans or British might conquer them.

Should Germany be conquered, Berlin would be under Soviet control, and though she wasn't much of a fascist anymore, she had no desire to be a communist.

Life under Hitler would be far better than under Stalin.

She glanced behind her, the black car still visible, her search for a suspect among those on board a failure.

Herr Vogel would have spotted the criminal in a heartbeat.

Vogel was a good man, and she always felt safe when she heard him return home. He was a *Kriminalinspektor*, a Detective Inspector, and lived directly across from her. His wife was a terrific woman, plenty of fun, but Erika hadn't seen her or their children in months.

Vogel had sent them away when things began to look hopeless.

She had no idea where they had gone, though she knew they had family in the southwest.

I hope the Americans get there first.

She felt envious, sometimes a little angry, that they were so safe compared to her daughter, though they could hardly be blamed for where their relatives lived.

They were lucky, and she was happy for them.

Sort of.

She spotted her stop and hopped off a little early, saving her half a block's walk. She quickly made her way to the Maiers' building and stepped into the lobby, shaking the snow off her jacket, and removing her hat and gloves while giving her feet a few good stomps. She headed for the stairs, winding up several flights, then paused as she glanced out the window.

The black car, the same one with the dented rear fender, was now parked across the street.

She stopped and listened for someone else in the stairwell with her, but heard nothing. Whoever they were following wasn't here with her.

Then her heart slammed and she gripped the railing hard.

They're following you!

She forced herself to continue forward, up the final two flights of stairs, just in case she was wrong. Or right.

Looking suspicious either way could mean her doom.

Out of sight of any windows, she pressed her back against the wall and steadied her breathing. Why would the Gestapo follow her? She had done nothing wrong.

Your idle gossip!

So many people she knew had either fled the city or were dead, that she would have no idea if any had actually been arrested and forced to name names. And under torture, perhaps someone had named her as having said something against the Führer or the Reich.

She knew if she were tortured, she would tell them anything they wanted to hear, even if it weren't true, just to make it stop. Could one of her friends that she had presumed left the city, instead been arrested and forced into confessing to crimes they hadn't committed?

The thought terrified her.

Then her jaw dropped.

Maybe they've already arrested Hermann, and that's why he's late!

She collapsed in a heap.

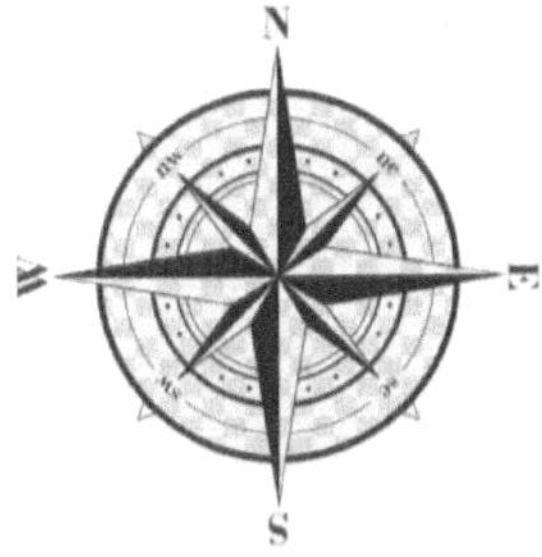

South of Kwidzyn (formerly Marienwerder), Poland

Present Day

Acton forced himself to take a seat as yet another priceless work of art was revealed. It was a treasure trove like no other. There was gold here, but that wasn't what was valuable.

Art, missing since the end of the war, looted from all across Europe from families and museums alike, filled the chamber. The trove they had discovered seemed to be much of what had been stolen from those on the eastern front, including Polish and Russian sources.

A find like this could answer so many questions, could restore dignity to families left impoverished, could once and for all let so many rest in peace.

It was overwhelming.

So overwhelming, he was battling tears.

"Are you okay?"

He looked up at Laura and shrugged. "I don't know. I'm just so overwhelmed with emotion right now, I-I don't know what to do."

"Professors! You have to see this!"

Acton turned to see Professor Lisowski standing inside one of the train cars, waving at them. Acton rose and strode toward the train, Laura holding his hand, as he refocused. "What is it?"

"I'll let you tell me," grinned a clearly ecstatic Lisowski. "I'm too scared to say it."

This had Acton's curiosity piqued, and as he approached, getting a better angle of the opened crate that had his colleague so excited, his jaw dropped and he gasped. "Oh my God! Is that what I think it is?"

Laura inhaled rapidly, her hand darting to her mouth. "It can't be!"

Acton climbed up into the boxcar, pulling Laura up after him, then dropped to his knees, carefully running his fingers over the find. "But what else could it be?"

Lisowski kneeled beside him. "If it's genuine, it can be nothing but."

Laura reached out to touch it, then hesitated. "I thought it had been destroyed during the bombings."

Lisowski grunted. "*Everyone* thought that."

Acton sighed. "Not everyone. Some thought it had been taken apart and moved, only to be lost at the bottom of the sea." He dropped back on his backside, staring at one of the most expensive missing pieces of artwork ever created. "I can't believe we found it," he whispered, finally noticing the entire crew was now standing at the door, shining their flashlights inside, revealing the stunningly preserved find in even more detail.

"What is it?" asked one of the workers in English as he snapped a selfie, the opened crate in the background.

"It's the Amber Room," replied Lisowski, who then began a data dump in Polish to those gathered as Acton climbed to his feet, opening several more crates, each containing a panel of the fabled room.

Built between 1701 and 1707 in Berlin by artisans on behalf of King Frederick of Prussia, it was gifted in 1716 to the Russian Tsar Peter the Great, who expanded it to be more than 590 square feet with 13,000 pounds of amber, with an estimated value of as much as 500 million dollars today. When the Nazis invaded, the curators responsible were too scared to dismantle the room, as they were concerned it could shatter due to the materials having dried out and becoming brittle. They instead wallpapered over it, but the Nazis, always on the hunt for art, knew of the room's existence and quickly found it. And they had no qualms of dismantling it, bringing it back to Königsberg, and reassembling it at the Königsberg Castle, where it had remained until January 1945, at which point it was lost to history.

Half a billion dollars.

He froze as another camera flashed. He spun on his heel, pointing at those gathered. "Aleksandra, tell them to stop taking photos, and to delete any they've already taken."

Lisowski stared at him. "Why?"

Acton leaned closer. "It's worth half a billion dollars. Do you really want word getting out before we can protect this properly?"

Lisowski's jaw dropped, and she quickly issued the orders in Polish, those gathered clearly not happy, though fingers were swiping rapidly as they complied.

Acton stared at the find once again. "We're going to need security here right away."

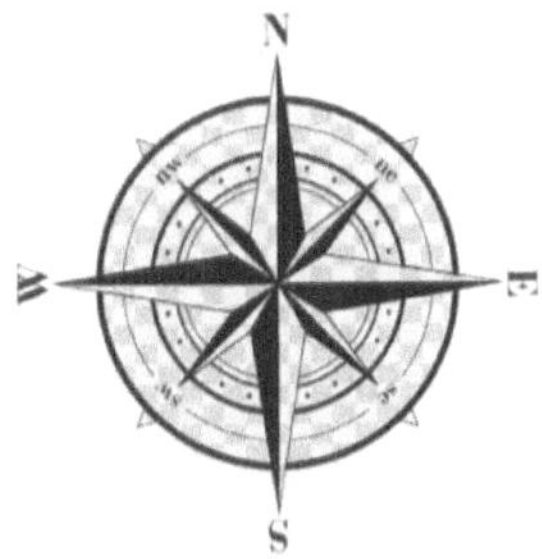

Maier Residence

Berlin, Nazi Germany

January 30, 1945

Erika Lang wasn't certain how long she lay in the hallway, but it couldn't have been too long as the sun was still bright, and as she picked herself up, she didn't feel overly stiff, though her hip did hurt from the fall.

Thank God for my winter jacket.

She straightened her thick coat then drew a long, slow breath, calming her still frayed nerves. She resisted the urge to look behind her, where a window lay just around the corner. The Gestapo would still be there if they were indeed following her.

She rushed to the Maiers' door and knocked as calmly as she could.

"Just a minute!" she heard Michaella's sweet voice call, dripping with contentment.

There's no way Dieter isn't home.

Which filled her with a sense of foreboding. If Dieter had made it home, then why hadn't Hermann? A wave of nausea washed over her, and her forehead felt cold and clammy as sweat trickled down her back.

The door opened and Michaella smiled at her. "Erika! What a wonderful surprise!" She leaned past her, checking the hallway. "Where's Hermann?"

"Umm, that's why I've come. He never made it home. Did-did Dieter?"

Michaella nodded, concern written across her face as she ushered Erika inside before closing the door and taking her jacket. "Yes, last night. He was a day late, but that's to be expected these days." She hung the accouterments of winter, then led a shaking Erika inside. "I'm sure it's nothing to worry about. I wouldn't be surprised if he's home by the time you get back."

She directed Erika into a chair, then stared at her for a moment. "You look cold. I'll make us some tea."

Erika gave a weak smile, then glanced around the apartment. "Wh-where's Dieter?"

"Asleep." Michaella blushed. "We, umm, were up pretty late last night, umm, celebrating."

Erika's smile widened as her own troubles were forgotten for a moment, then clouded again just as quickly. "Can-can you ask him if he saw my Hermann?"

Michaella pursed her lips, clearly not wanting to disturb her husband, though finally agreed. "I'll see if he's awake." She disappeared down the hall, and Erika heard a murmured conversation, then two sets of footfalls. She stood, her purse clasped in front of her, and forced a worried smile as a groggy Dieter appeared, scratching behind his ear.

He yawned. "You wanted to ask me something?"

"Have you seen my Hermann?"

His eyes narrowed as they focused on her for the first time. "What do you mean? When?"

"He was supposed to arrive two days ago, but never did."

Dieter shrugged. "Hardly unusual. I almost didn't make it."

"Yes, but it's been two days, and when I called, they gave me the runaround. It was as if they didn't want to tell me something."

Dieter motioned for Michaella to bring him a coffee. "I don't know what to tell you. We're at war. People are going to be late. Maybe his train was bombed."

"Dieter!"

Dieter batted his hand at his wife. "Calm down, woman, that's not what I meant. I meant the transport train to bring him here. He might be waiting for another transport because the one he was supposed to be on was bombed. I'm sure he's fine. If he weren't, they'd have notified you. If there's one thing they're efficient at, it's letting people know their husbands and sons are dead."

Erika dropped back into her chair, trembling at the thought of her beloved husband dying in some Allied attack. "But what about the car?"

Dieter paused in mid-sip. "What car?"

"I think someone has been following me."

Dieter slammed his coffee onto the counter, the dark brew sloshing over the sides, Michaella already springing into action to wipe up the mess. He rushed to the window and peered out from the side at the street below. "Black car, two men inside?"

"Y-yes."

Dieter carefully backed away from the window. "They're still there. Are you sure they're following you?"

"No, not really, but they were outside my building when I left to come here, and now here they are again."

"Are you sure it's the same men?"

She nodded. "Pretty sure, but it's the car. It has a dented rear fender."

Dieter peered out the window again then cursed. He strode quickly toward her, urging her to get up. "You have to leave, now!"

Erika's heart leaped into her throat. "Why?"

"I can't say. You just have to leave. It's too dangerous for you to be here."

Erika rose, shaking all over, as Michaella rushed to her side, putting an arm around her to try and steady her. "Why? I don't understand!"

Dieter furiously shook his head. "I'm sorry, but I can't explain. You just have to leave."

Tears erupted from Erika as she stared at Dieter, terror gripping her. "Something's happened to my Hermann, hasn't it? What do you know?"

"Nothing!" Dieter herded her toward the door, grabbing Erika's winter garb off the rack and shoving it into her hands. He opened the door and pushed her none too gently into the hallway. He jabbed a finger at her. "Don't come back. Ever!"

He slammed the door, leaving Erika alone in the hallway, sobbing and shaking.

And wondering what could have Dieter so scared that he would act in such a way.

But she knew the answer.

Something had happened to her husband.

And the Gestapo was following her because of it.

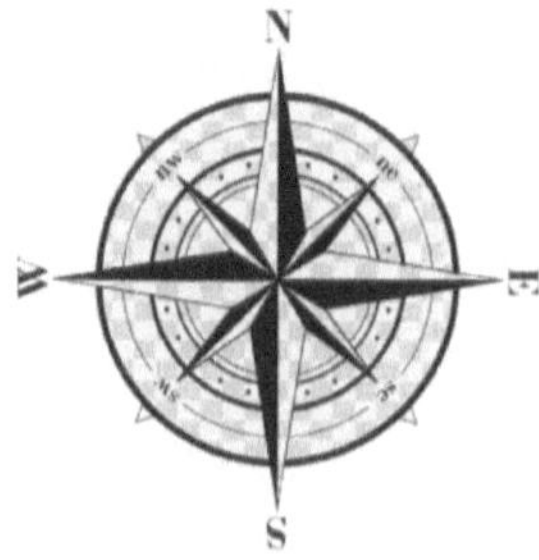

Bar Abazuram

Kwidzyn (formerly Marienwerder), Poland

Present Day

Stefan Bosko fired back another shot of vodka, this easily his twelfth of the night. It was Friday, it was payday, and he was out with his boys, everyone talking about what had happened earlier in the day, more details revealing themselves as the liquor flowed and more joined their table who hadn't been party to the discovery.

"I'm surprised they let you see it," said Milan, his best friend since high school, and far smarter than him.

Stefan pushed a shot toward him, his friend far too sober. "I don't think they were expecting to find what they did."

"But once they did, I would have thought they'd swear you to secrecy or something."

Stefan laughed, the others who had been working the equipment with him joining in. "They did, but I'm not going to listen to some Yankee in my own country!" He pulled out his phone, bringing up his selfie. "Look at it if you don't believe me. It's worth like half a billion dollars or something."

Milan's eyes widened. "What is it?"

"I think they called it the Amber Room."

Milan's eyes became almost saucers. "Are you kidding me? They found the missing Amber Room?"

"You've heard of it?"

"Of course I have!" He lowered his voice. "This is huge. No wonder they swore you to secrecy."

Stefan tapped at his phone, sending the photo to his Facebook page, quickly typing a clever caption.

Me with the Amber Room. Shhh. Don't tell anyone.

He posted it with a tap.

Milan gulped. "You shouldn't have done that."

Stefan shrugged. "Who cares? What's some American going to do about it?"

Milan shook his head, finally taking his shot. "It's not the American I'd be worried about."

"Then who?"

"Every thief in the world who now knows *you* know where one of the most valuable pieces of missing artwork is located."

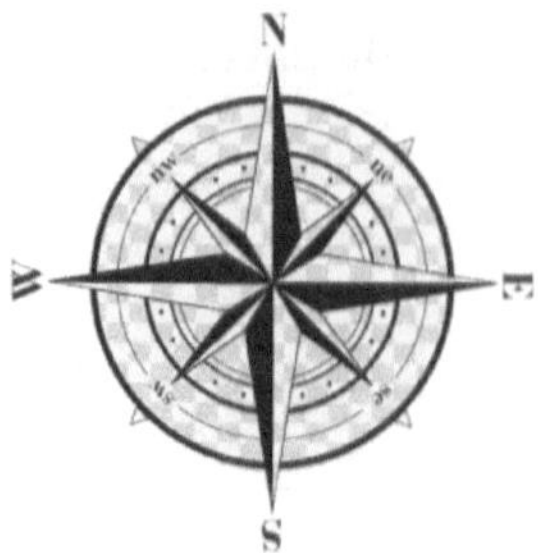

Marseilles, France

Alexie Tankov stared appreciatively at the half-dozen bronzed and fit women lounging around the pool. He could have any one of them he wanted, any time he wanted. And he had.

They were all bought and paid for.

He preferred professionals. His life left him with little time to meet women, and women were simply baggage not worth the effort. Why waste time with an emotional relationship, when a sexual one could be had for a few hundred Euros a night? He had the money, his entire team did, their new line of work since leaving the Russian Special Forces, Spetsnaz, very lucrative.

Lucrative enough for him to have half a dozen houses around the globe, cars that would be the envy of any adrenaline junkie, and all the women he could possibly want, in all shapes, sizes, and colors.

It was a good life.

Yet decadence without excitement wasn't the life for him. He had enough in the bank—or banks—to last him several lifetimes, but he wasn't in it for the money.

At least not entirely.

He was in it for the thrill of the chase.

His phone vibrated beside him, and he picked it up, checking the call display.

Dimitri.

He smiled. Dimitri would never call him unless he had found something worth his while. He swiped his thumb. "Da?"

"I've got something for you. Something big."

His smile grew. "What is it?"

"Are you sitting down?"

"Dimitri, you're killing me!"

His friend laughed. "Someone might have just found the Amber Room."

Tankov bolted upright. "Please tell me this isn't one of your jokes."

"No joke, my friend. From what I can tell, it was found just a few hours ago, which means it's probably not properly secured yet, considering the size of it."

Tankov rose. "Where?"

"Poland."

"Okay. Notify the team. Wheels up in two hours."

"We're going to need a special buyer for this one."

"What's the estimated value?"

"Anywhere from one hundred to five hundred."

Tankov stared at the bevy of beauties as he headed inside, already thinking of doubling his stable. "I've got someone in mind who this would be perfect for. And a hundred million would be nothing to him."

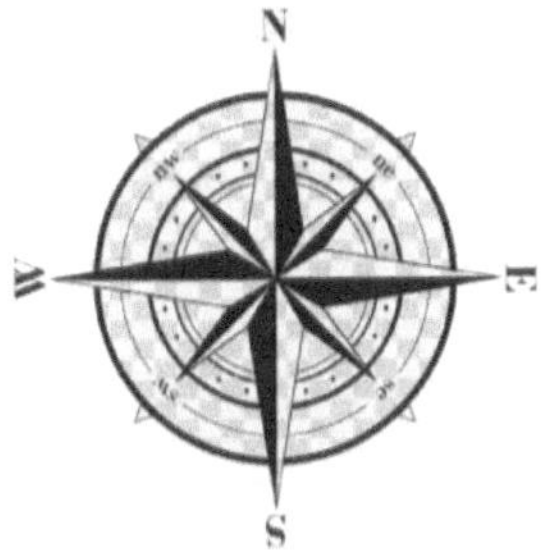

Outside Riyadh, Kingdom of Saudi Arabia

Sheikh Khalid bin Al Jabar lounged in a ridiculously comfortable chair, the overstuffed cushions enveloping him, something normally not enjoyed in the desert climate, though this room was climate controlled, both temperature and humidity strictly monitored lest the priceless artwork contained within be damaged in any way.

He might be a collector of stolen art, but he was also an aficionado.

He could never let anything happen to his prized possessions.

Part of an underground community of ultra-rich individuals with questionable scruples, he purchased pieces on a regular basis, and rid himself of items he had become bored with.

Like the Delamain Grande Champagne Extra Cognac he had been enjoying at $600 a bottle, and was now tired of.

Too much of a good thing...

He stared at Caravaggio's "Nativity with St. Francis and St. Lawrence," stolen in 1969 from Palermo. He was bored of it, too.

Sometimes having billions at one's disposal was tiresome. Once one had everything, there was little chance of experiencing the excitement of something new.

And that was where his art collection came into the picture. Something new was always on the market, something exciting, unseen for perhaps decades, even centuries, something he alone would get to enjoy until once again bored.

He'd have his people begin making inquiries immediately.

There was a knock at the door, two quick raps followed by a third, a combination uniquely favored by his trusted man.

"Enter."

Nadeem entered, a phone in his hand. "Sir, I have Mr. Tankov on the line for you."

Khalid smiled, the timing fortuitous, and he glanced up at the heavens, giving silent thanks for the answer to his prayer. He took the phone and dismissed Nadeem with the flick of his wrist. "Mr. Tankov, your timing couldn't be better. I'm in a buying mood today."

He could almost hear the smile over the phone. "I'm happy to hear that, sir. I'm on my way to pick up something I know you'll be interested in, but it's expensive."

Khalid liked what he was hearing. Expensive to him meant out of this world to the proletariat. That meant it had to be exceptional. "How expensive?"

"One hundred million Euros. Firm."

The smile spreading across Khalid's face, such a rare occurrence these days, threatened to become painful. "Then it must be an exciting acquisition."

"It is. Something thought lost for over seventy years."

Khalid's heart slammed as he leaned forward. "Yes?"

"The missing Amber Room."

Khalid felt faint, the room spinning as he fell back in his chair, almost losing grip of the phone. The Amber Room would be the ultimate possession, something that would make him the envy of everyone, something it would take a long time for him to tire of.

And something he absolutely must possess.

"Are there any other bidders?"

"I came to you first, since you're my best client."

"I bet you say that to all your best clients."

Tankov chuckled. "I do, but I called you first. Do we have a deal?"

"Absolutely. Contact me when you have it, and I'll wire fifty million to your account, the other fifty when it's in my possession."

"Always a pleasure, sir."

Khalid ended the call, leaning back in his chair, his smile still broad. He raised his cognac to the room and took a drink, now tasting so much more interesting than only moments before.

Life is good.

Vogel Residence

Berlin, Nazi Germany

January 30, 1945

Kriminalinspektor Wolfgang Vogel yawned and pressed his forehead against the cool wood of the door to his apartment. He closed his burning eyes for a moment before inserting his key in the lock and turning it, ending what had been a long, exhausting day.

They all were.

Being a detective inspector in the *Kriminalpolizei* was a tough job even in normal times. Before the war, he had investigated crimes, just as he did now, though without the added stresses of bombings, blackouts, rationing, and panic.

And he had always had his wife and children there to support him.

But tonight he was entering an empty apartment.

Yet again.

It had been a heart-wrenching decision sending his wife and children away, yet there had been little choice. Once Berlin began to be bombed in earnest, he knew it was time, though his wife had fought him every step of the way. Once it was clear that the Russians were winning on the Eastern Front, the argument had been settled.

There was no way he would let his family be taken by the Russians.

He had relatives in the southwest of Germany, an area where he was confident the Americans or British would arrive at first, and living under occupation with them would be far preferable to the Soviet Red Army.

It was the right decision, but it hadn't made it any easier.

He pushed open the door, and his neighbor's door behind him burst open.

"Herr Vogel! Thank God you're here!"

He closed his eyes for another brief respite and sighed before facing what was clearly a very agitated Erika Lang. "Yes, Frau Lang? What can I do for you?"

"My Hermann! He never came home!"

She was clearly in a state, and her cries were echoing down the empty hallway. He ushered her back into her apartment and closed the door. "Please calm down, Frau Lang. Why don't you start from the beginning? When was he supposed to be home?"

"Two days ago."

"From his assignment in Poland?"

She nodded. "Yes."

He directed her to a chair, then sat across from her. "We are at war, Frau Lang. To be late by a day or two is hardly unheard of."

She sighed, wringing a handkerchief gripped in her hands. "Yes, I know, and Herr Maier said the same thing."

Vogel's eyes narrowed. "Who?"

"Oh, my friend's husband. He's an engineer too. He works with my husband on occasion."

"He sounds like a wise man."

She agreed. "And a friendly one, or at least I thought so until today."

"Why, what happened?"

"I went over to visit Frau Maier and see if her husband had seen my Hermann, because I knew they worked together. He said he hadn't, but when I told him about the car, he became scared and kicked me out, telling me to never come back again!"

She wailed, and Vogel cringed, stepping closer and patting her on the shoulder. "That's all right, I'm sure there's just some sort of misunderstanding that can all be sorted out with time." His eyes narrowed as he picked up on something she said. "What car?"

She pointed at the window. "Just look, I'm sure it's still there."

Vogel stepped over to the window and moved the blackout curtain slightly, quickly spotting the idling car across the street. He closed the curtain back before the air raid warden noticed, and sat across from Frau Lang. "Tell me about this car."

She blew her nose then dabbed her eyes dry. "I-I first noticed it this morning when I left to see Michaella—Frau Maier. Two men inside a black car with a dented rear fender. I noticed them following the streetcar, then park across from the Maiers' apartment building. Then when I got home, I looked outside, and it was there again."

Vogel frowned. The woman was probably paranoid, as there was no reason he could think of for anyone to have any interest in her, though there was one way to find out. "Wait here."

He left the apartment and hurried down the stairs, stepping out into the chill, then crossed the street. He pressed his identification against the driver's window, and it rolled down.

"Go away."

He kneeled and quickly evaluated the two men. Young, committed, Nazi Party pins on their leather jackets, hair closely cropped.

Poster boys for the Reich.

And that meant they were dangerous, though unimportant within the organization—senior Gestapo agents would not be assigned to watch the wife of a lowly engineer.

"Can I help you, gentlemen?"

The driver stared at him, as if in shock at the gall being displayed. "We are on a mission for the Führer. You will leave at once, and forget you ever saw us."

Vogel smiled. "Of course, of course, though if you are following Frau Lang, she spotted you this morning. If you're expecting her to do anything untoward, I can assure you, you'll be waiting a very long time. She's a loyal citizen, and a friend."

"This is none of your concern."

Vogel nodded. "You're right. The Gestapo's business isn't any of mine. I thought I'd just save you some time. Goodnight, gentlemen." He rose and snapped out a salute. "Heil Hitler!"

He suppressed a smile as the two men instinctively returned the salute awkwardly within the confines of their car. He turned and headed back to his apartment, the sound of the car pulling away confirming Frau Lang's suspicions.

They were following her, and now that they knew she knew, there was little point in remaining.

He tried to read the plate as it pulled away, but with the blackout, there was no hope. He took the steps two at a time, and gently knocked on Frau Lang's door. It was yanked open immediately.

"Was I right?"

Her eyes were wide with panic, and he hesitated to tell her what he had discovered, though the woman deserved the truth. There might be some reason they were following her, and if she thought they weren't, she might continue that activity, forcing the Gestapo to pick her up.

And whatever trivial matter they suspected her of, he was certain didn't merit her facing interrogation and torture.

"I believe so," he said in as calm a voice as possible, gently ushering her inside and into her chair. He sat across from her. "But I wouldn't worry about it. They're gone now."

"Do you think they'll be back?"

"It's possible, but you've done nothing wrong. Just go about your daily business, otherwise they might think you are up to something. We don't know how long they've been watching you, but it's been at least a day, and if they haven't picked you up yet, then I doubt they will. They'll probably move on to someone more interesting shortly, if they haven't already."

This calmed the woman slightly. "But what about my Hermann?"

Vogel smiled reassuringly at her. "I'll tell you what. If he's not here tomorrow morning when I go to work, I'll make some inquiries."

"Not tonight?"

"I'm sorry, but I'm just too exhausted. I've been traveling for two days and am dead tired." He rose, smiling at her. "But I promise, first thing in the morning, all right?"

She was clearly disappointed, but nodded. "Very well." She stood. "Thank you, Herr Vogel."

"No problem." He headed for the door and stepped into the hallway. "Goodnight, Frau Lang."

"Goodnight."

She closed the door, and he stepped inside his own empty, lonely apartment. He pulled off his shoes then dropped onto the bed, his arms spread out to his sides as his muscles ached. It had been a long trip, but he had solved the case, catching the black marketeer red-handed. Yet it was an unsatisfying victory, the operation also netting far too many desperate Germans purchasing his illicit goods out of necessity.

And now they were all in custody.

He sighed.

I can't wait until this war is over and I can just be a police officer again.

He thought of Hermann Lang, and where he might be. His instinct initially had been that he was merely delayed. If anything had happened to him, he was certain they would have notified her already. But with the Gestapo watching her, he had to assume something more was going on here, and now that he had confronted them, he too might be on their radar.

And that was never a good thing.

Yet despite his conscious mind making him worry about the implications, he soon drifted into a deep sleep, the Langs' problems, and perhaps now his, left to wait until morning.

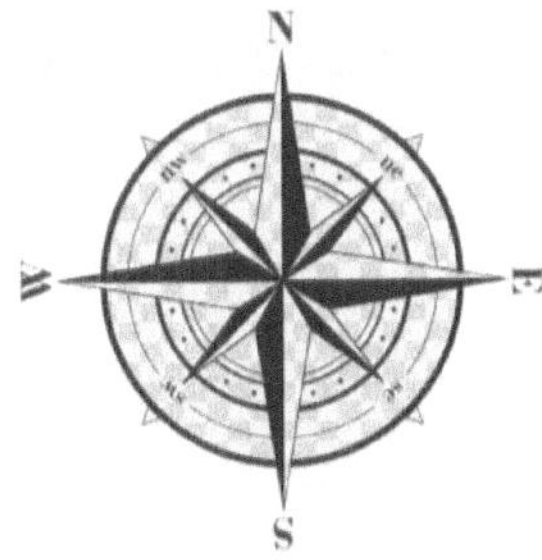

Bosko Residence

Kwidzyn (formerly Marienwerder), Poland

Present Day

Stefan Bosko unlocked the rear door of his apartment, his head pounding, his tongue stuck to the roof of his mouth. He had slept in his car again, though was pleased to see he had made it home without any new damage.

I drive better drunk than sober.

He was convinced of this. It made him pay more attention since he didn't want to get caught, though he could honestly say he had no recollection whatsoever of the drive.

He pushed open the door and kicked off his shoes at the top of the stairs, then began the painful trek to the basement apartment. To call it an apartment might be a stretch, since it was simply his parents' basement, but it had its own door, so he had some privacy if he wanted to bring a chick home.

He scratched the stubble on his chin, wondering when that had last happened.

He heard something.

His eyes narrowed, the sound coming from below, as if from his television.

What the hell?

He hurried down the stairs and rounded the corner to find two men sitting on his couch, one playing Duck Hunt on his vintage Nintendo, and to his horror, both drinking his beer. "What the hell is going on here?"

A throat cleared behind him and he spun around, his heart hammering. He nearly pissed his pants as he noticed the handgun tucked into a shoulder holster, and he wisely kept his mouth shut. An iPad was shoved in his face, his Facebook posting displayed.

Milan was right.

His shoulders slumped as the other two men rose from the couch.

This is gonna hurt.

The man tapped Stefan's head with the iPad. "Tell us everything you know, and you'll live."

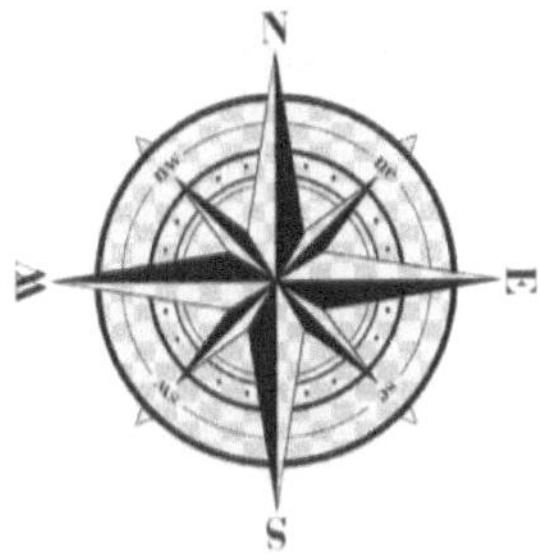

Maier Residence

Berlin, Nazi Germany

January 31, 1945

Dieter Maier pushed his food around his plate with his fork, staring blankly at it as his mind raced. Hermann was a friend, a fairly good one, though it was the wives that were the real friends in the relationship. But, however he felt about the man, he was a good one. A hard worker, loyal, and never one to question authority or the cause.

Like most, he just kept his head down and did his job.

He had seen him a few days ago, both of them eager to return home and see their wives, jokes exchanged about how they didn't plan on leaving the bedroom the entire time.

It had been a friendly moment.

And there had been no indication he had been delayed.

Yet things could change in a heartbeat in today's Germany. It was common knowledge, though not spoken about, that the war was going badly, that the Russians were closing in rapidly from the east, the Americans, Brits, Canadians, and who knew who else, from the west and south.

A simple transport run could result in death, either from above, or a bombed track ahead.

But surely they would have notified her.

Notifications used to be swift, though with the casualties growing rapidly, he had heard of delays, but that would be from the front. Not an engineer on the rail. If a train were attacked, there would be little confusion as to whom the engineer was when identifying the body.

Notice should go out immediately.

Which was why he was certain he hadn't been killed.

Or at least not in the traditional method.

His mind kept returning to the locomotive he had been tasked to recover. It had been attacked, the engineer confirmed dead by the SS colonel, yet he had heard no mention of it when he had returned to the rail yard. Obviously, someone knew the engineer was dead, otherwise he wouldn't have been dispatched, but usually, when one of them died, there was some chatter.

This time there had been none, though he hadn't paid it much mind, instead rushing to catch his transport back to Berlin so he could see his wife.

At the time, he couldn't care less who it was.

But now, he wondered if Hermann had been the victim of the partisans.

Yet that still wouldn't explain why Erika wouldn't have been notified, or why Gestapo would be following her.

"You've barely eaten anything. What's got you so distracted?"

He looked up at his wife. "Huh? Oh, umm, nothing."

She frowned at him, jabbing a fork in the air. "You still haven't given me an explanation for yesterday. You were so rude to Erika! It was inexcusable."

He stared at his plate. "I had my reasons."

"And who are you to tell her to never come back? She's *my* friend! Probably my best friend. God knows she's about the only one I can talk to around here without being worried someone will report me to the Gestapo."

"I wouldn't be so sure about that."

"What do you mean?"

He sighed, putting his fork down and staring at his wife. "Who do you think was in the car following her?"

His wife returned the stare for a moment before her eyes bulged. "You don't think…"

"I *do* think. Which is why I don't want you talking to her ever again. If the Gestapo is watching her, then she's done something wrong."

His wife batted his accusation away with a flick of her wrist. "Nonsense. What could she have ever done wrong?"

"You know her better than I do."

"Exactly, I do. She's a simple, hardworking woman, just like her husband." She put her fork down and wiped the corners of her mouth with a napkin. "And I thought you and Hermann were friends? How could you treat your friend's wife that way?"

"We *were* friends."

"Were?"

He tensed, remembering his final orders from the colonel.

Discuss with no one what you saw here today, or even the fact you were here.

"Leave it."

Her eyes widened. "Leave it? Why? What's going on? What haven't you told me?"

He immediately regretted his words, and searched for something he could say to end the conversation, when an entirely new problem presented itself.

Three firm raps on the door.

His wife turned in her chair, staring toward the entrance. "Who could that be?"

Dieter wiped his mouth on the back of his hand then rose, heading for the door, his heart pounding. Unexpected guests were rare these days, unless the news was bad.

He drew a breath of courage, then opened the door. He paled, his body going weak at the sight of a trenchcoated man in front of him.

"Herr Maier?"

Dieter nodded. "Umm, yes."

"I am Detective Inspector Wolfgang Vogel from the Kriminalpolizei. May I come in?"

Dieter suppressed the sigh of relief as best he could.

Not Gestapo.

And this was confirmed by the fact the man waited patiently for his reply.

Gestapo would have simply entered without waiting.

"Umm, of course." Dieter stepped aside, letting the man into the apartment, then closed the door. "Ahh, what can I do for you?"

Vogel strode through the apartment, his head on a swivel as he took everything in, bowing slightly to Michaella. "Ma'am."

She nodded, clearly terrified as her hands wrung the napkin still clutched in them. "Sir."

Finally, the detective stopped near the window, peering down at the street below. He turned toward them. "You and your wife are friends with Frau Erika Lang?"

"No," replied Dieter on instinct, his wife simultaneously contradicting him. He glared at her.

Vogel smiled. "Well, which is it?"

Dieter held out a finger at his wife, silencing her, he hoped. "We *were* friends, but no longer."

"Oh, why is that?"

Dieter shrugged. "I don't know. Just a falling out. These things happen."

"Did she do something wrong?"

"No."

"Did she say something that made you dislike her?"

Sweat beaded on Dieter's brow as the detective continued to pelt him with questions, the tone thankfully remaining neutral. "Umm, no."

Vogel turned to Michaella. "She was here yesterday, wasn't she?"

"Y-yes."

"So it must have been something that happened during that visit that made you end your friendship. What was it?"

Michaella spun toward Dieter, her hands clasped in front of her chin. "Please, just tell him!"

Dieter glared at his wife as a wave of nausea swept over him. He implored her with his eyes to keep silent, yet it was no use.

The floodgates were open.

Michaella rushed toward the detective. "She's my friend! She still is, but she was being followed yesterday by men in a car. I think it scared my husband. Please forgive him for lying, but he—I mean we—just didn't want to get involved. What's going on? Is her Hermann all right?"

Vogel smiled as Dieter's shoulders slumped, his idiot wife finally sealing their fate. The detective turned toward him.

"You think the men in the car were Gestapo?"

Dieter paled even further, but nodded.

"Then you'd be right."

Dieter almost soiled himself, his knees shaking.

"I confronted them last night out front of Frau Lang's apartment. You were right to be concerned. If she is being watched by them, then you should be careful with your interactions with her, otherwise you too could become of interest to them."

A surge of vindication flowed through him, and he jabbed a finger at his wife. "See! I told you!"

Michaella said nothing, instead staring at her feet.

Vogel jerked a thumb over his shoulder at the window he had looked out earlier. "Unfortunately, it would appear you have already become an item of interest to them."

Dieter paled, his stomach flipping as his eyes darted toward the window. "Wh-why do you say that?"

"There's a car across the street, with two men inside and a pile of cigarette stubs outside each window. They've been here for some time. My guess is since shortly after Frau Lang was here."

Dieter managed to curse through his trembling lips. "I-I knew that woman was going to be trouble."

Vogel stared at him. "Why?"

Dieter had said too much, and joined his wife in staring at the floor as his heart slammed and his ears pounded. The Gestapo was outside, the police were in his apartment, and he was mixed up in something he didn't understand. How he would get out of this, he had no idea. He knew from the stories he had heard, that once you were on the radar of the Gestapo, the only way you left it was death.

He glanced up at his wife, praying they'd leave her alone.

I'll confess to anything they want, as long as they don't touch her.

"You know something, don't you, Herr Maier?"

"No."

"Oh, I think you do, and I think it's about Herr Lang." Vogel stepped closer. "You're aware that he still hasn't returned home."

Dieter shook his head.

"Well, he hasn't, and I believe that his wife deserves an explanation, don't you?"

Dieter glanced up at Vogel, then back at the floor. "I-I can't say."

"You *can't?*"

Dieter cursed to himself for the poor choice of words.

Why did you say, "can't?"

"I…umm, well, it's probably nothing."

Damn!

"If it's nothing, then why can't you tell me?"

Then it dawned on him.

"Orders."

"From whom?"

Does this man ever stop asking questions?

His entire body shook as terror overtook him. "The SS."

Vogel took a step backward, and Dieter stole a glance, taking at least some satisfaction that even this man seemed slightly flustered with the admission. If there was one group that terrified him more than the Gestapo, it was the SS. They were insane. Fanatical.

And not to be trifled with.

Vogel stepped closer, lowering his voice. "An SS officer told you not to say anything?"

Dieter nodded, unable to control the trembling.

"Is it related to Herr Lang?"

Dieter shrugged, not exactly certain. "Possibly." He had his suspicions, yet that was all they were. But Hermann was missing, obviously there had been no notification otherwise this detective wouldn't be here, and now the Gestapo was on their doorstep, something that hadn't begun until Hermann's wife had shown up here, a woman already under surveillance.

It all had to be related.

Vogel lowered his voice further. "Is he dead?"

Dieter's chest tightened as a thought occurred to him. Could the Gestapo be listening to them? He glanced about the apartment, searching for anything out of the ordinary, realizing a bug could have been hidden anywhere, and they wouldn't know it.

And looking for it was out of the question.

It would merely confirm their guilt.

He made a decision.

"I'm sorry, Detective, but I have my orders. I can say nothing to you." He walked toward the door and grabbed a piece of paper and pencil off a side table, quickly scribbling a note as he continued to speak. "Now, I'll have to ask you to leave. We are loyal Germans, loyal to the Reich and the Führer, and I have nothing further to say." He handed the paper to the detective who quickly scanned it, his eyes widening.

"Very well, Herr Maier, I understand completely. If you are under orders not to speak, I cannot compel you. I wish you a good day."

Dieter opened the door, and Vogel bowed to Michaella before leaving. Dieter closed the door and locked it, his entire body shaking.

Michaella rushed forward, opening her mouth to ask him something he was sure would get him shot. He slapped a hand over her mouth, silencing her.

Yet he feared it wouldn't be enough. Whatever had happened last night was serious, and now someone knew that he had a secret.

And the Gestapo was outside, probably listening in to make certain he would keep it.

He again glanced about their humble home, then pulled at his hair as he realized there could be a listening device anywhere, and there was nothing he could do about it. He wanted to search for it, to tear the apartment apart if need be, yet he couldn't.

Innocent men don't worry about being listened to.

Not in today's Germany.

His chest was tight, and he could sense he was about to explode, his hand still over his wife's mouth, a wife who appeared to be getting impatient and scared.

He had to get out of there.

He had to think.

He grabbed his jacket and shrugged it on, shoving his feet into his boots and lacing them up.

"Where are you going?"

"Out."

"Where?"

"Just for a walk. I'll be back shortly."

He unlocked the door and left, leaving his poor, confused wife inside. He buttoned up his jacket as he hurried down the stairs, taking the rear entrance to avoid the Gestapo out front.

Then paused.

Would this make him appear guilty?

He rushed back inside and exited the front of the building, in full view of the car the detective has spotted, and its occupants. He turned left, walking toward the main street, toward the market where he might reasonably be expected to head at this hour, though it would normally be his wife.

But if they were listening in, then they would already know it was a lie.

He used the excuse of crossing the street to check on the car behind him. It was following him, slowly, though that wasn't what had his heart hammering.

It was the two men in leather trench coats that were now crossing the street, making no effort to conceal themselves.

They're going to kill you!

He picked up his pace, and the footfalls behind him did as well. He had nowhere to go. He had to lose them somehow, then get back to the apartment and save his wife.

But how?

They were four men, he was just one.

And they would have weapons.

He spotted an alleyway narrow enough that he could at least eliminate the car from the equation. It opened into another street that if he could just reach it first, he might lose them in the heavy foot traffic.

He bolted.

The engine roared behind him, but it didn't matter. He ducked into the alleyway and sprinted toward the end, checking over his shoulder to see his pursuers close behind.

His foot hit something and he tripped, crying out as he slammed into the cold, hard ground.

And they were on him.

Boots rained down on him, kicking him and stomping him. He curled into a ball, crying out for help, yet no one would come. They'd see who was delivering the beating, then go about their business, terrified they could be next.

A heel crushed the side of his head and he began to pass out, a welcome respite from the excruciating pain.

Please, God, please save my wife!

He opened his eyes for one last look at evil, a heel filling his vision before his world went dark.

Forever.

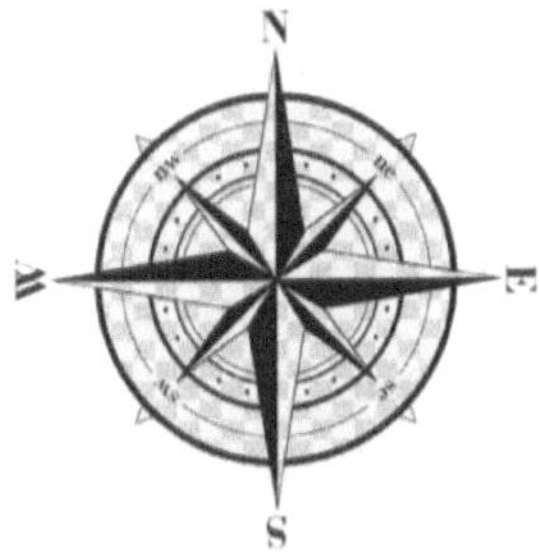

South of Kwidzyn (formerly Marienwerder), Poland

Present Day

Acton stretched with an exaggerated groan, eliciting smiles from those around him. They were all feeling the burn of having worked through most of the night. Two members of the Gdansk University's security team were stationed outside to keep any nosy neighbors out, but beyond being bouncers, they weren't of much use.

Almost a dozen faculty and students from Lisowski's university were now here helping catalog what was turning into an incredible find. Twenty-seven crates, all on the boxcars, were confirmed to contain panels from the Amber Room and nothing else. They had obviously been transported in a hurry, just before this chamber was sealed to the outside world.

After documenting the scene with photographs and video, local officials collected the bodies, some German soldiers, but most appearing to be miners, probably local, finally ready to be reunited with their families.

They had been somber moments, observed by all as each body was removed, reminding him of 9/11 when the entire recovery operation was halted each time another of the fallen heroes was recovered.

He still choked up at the memories.

Working through the night, and with the extra personnel, they had managed to catalog most of the discovery beyond the train. Hundreds of pieces of priceless artwork from paintings to sculptures, had been discovered, many of which they recognized. It was stunning.

And yes, there had been gold.

But despite there being stacks of it, it couldn't compare to the treasure trove of creations from skilled artisans over the centuries.

It was the discovery of a lifetime.

Something echoing from the shaft leading to the entrance had him spinning and raising a hand. "Everyone quiet!"

Everyone froze, and he cocked an ear, not hearing anything else.

"What is it?" asked Laura, tiptoeing beside him.

"I thought I heard something."

"What?"

"I could have sworn it was gunshots."

The room noticeably tensed, even Acton's heart hammering, his encounters with the evil of this world happening far too frequently for his liking, and they were sitting on a find so valuable, that few thieves could resist its lure if they knew it existed.

"I'm going to check it out."

Laura grabbed his arm, holding him back as footfalls echoed from the tunnel, one set joined by another, then another. Soon the chamber was filled with a cacophony of heavy footsteps, sending Acton's heart racing as he held out an arm and gently pushed Laura behind him.

What I'd give for a Glock right now.

Yet even if he were armed, it sounded like there were too many for one person to make a difference.

The first emerged, dressed casually, a submachine gun strapped around his neck, bold as brass as if he had nothing to fear.

And he didn't, not with the three other men behind him, their weapons aimed at the terrified academics.

"Who's in charge here?" asked the man in a thick accent Acton guessed was Russian.

Lisowski stepped forward. "I am."

The man pulled a pistol and shot Lisowski in the thigh. She cried out in agony, collapsing to the ground as Acton and Laura rushed toward her.

"I'll ask again, who's in charge?"

Acton glared up at him as the rest of Lisowski's staff cowered in fear, whimpers and sobs already breaking out. He rose, stepping toward the man.

"You are."

"Exactly." The man eyed him up and down, as if assessing whether Acton was a threat. "Identify yourself."

Acton decided there was no point in lying. "Professor James Acton."

One of the henchmen pulled out a tablet, typing something, then held up the result for the leader to see. He nodded, then looked at Laura, tending to Lisowski's wound. "Then you must be Professor Laura Palmer."

Laura glanced over at him. "I am."

"It says here you are both archaeology professors."

Acton suppressed a frown, his stomach flipping as he realized where this might be heading. "We are."

"Then you are who I need." He motioned to his men. "Tie the rest up." They rushed forward, bundles of zip ties pulled out and tossed to the others.

Laura glared at the man who tossed two zip ties at her. "This woman needs medical attention."

The leader stepped forward. "And she'll get it, as soon as we're gone, so the quicker you cooperate, the quicker we're out of here. Understood?"

Laura turned her head away, likely to hide her disdain for the man. "Yes."

"Excellent." The leader turned toward Acton. "You know what we're here for. Where is it?"

Acton shrugged. "I haven't the slightest idea what you're talking about."

The man shook his head, tapping his watch. "Tick tock, Doc. We're here for the Amber Room. Which crates contain it?"

Acton was tempted to make the man look for it himself, but as the blood continued to pool beside a pale Lisowski, he decided any delaying tactics would merely put his colleague's life at risk. He pointed at the two boxcars. "The entire room is contained in the crates aboard these two boxcars."

"Is there anything else on them?"

Acton shook his head. "No."

The leader climbed into the back, examining several of the opened crates, a smile spreading.

And it enraged Acton to think that after seventy years, what had been thought lost to humanity forever, was about to be lost again. He hated thieves with a passion, and would have no problem if men like this were simply summarily executed for their crimes.

But that was fantasy, and he had to deal with reality.

And that meant asking why the man had said he and Laura were what he needed.

The man hopped down and nodded at another of his team, a radio raised with something said. Engines roared at the opposite end of the tunnel almost immediately. A forklift and small truck appeared moments later, the leader pointing at the two boxcars. "Let's make this quick, gentlemen. We're on a timeline."

Kriminalpolizei Headquarters

Prinz-Albrecht-Straße, Berlin, Nazi Germany

January 31, 1945

Vogel sat at his desk, neatly stacked with papers, his inbox empty, everything he was responsible for already taken care of from a paperwork perspective. He still had open cases. They all did. But in today's Germany, you always made sure your paperwork was up to date.

And there was one piece of paper he wasn't sure what to do with.

His note from Dieter Maier, scribbled in secret in case someone was listening.

What a horrible notion. To fear that one's most private conversations with those closest to you could be listened in upon by strangers was almost unfathomable. If you were a criminal or a traitor, then you should have no expectations of privacy, and probably watched what you said.

But a husband and wife, innocent of all things the state could be concerned about, listened to only because they were friends with someone else of interest?

It was disgusting.

This war can't end soon enough.

He wanted to get back to being a cop again, investigating crimes without worrying about being investigated himself. He missed speaking openly and freely about whatever he wanted, to associate with whoever he wanted to, and to travel without papers. And he was tired of the bombings, of the maimed and starving in the streets, of not being with his family, of wondering if he'd see them again.

And seeing people like Frau Lang wondering what had happened to their husbands.

It was a world gone mad, and he wanted out.

He sighed.

There is no way out.

He reread the scribbled note for the umpteenth time.

In Marienwerder on January 28, Polish partisans attacked train, killing engineer. Might have been Hermann. I brought locomotive back.

There was nothing special about the note. If it were true, it was a tragedy, though not an unfamiliar one. Germany had, after all, invaded Poland, the war was going poorly on both fronts, and partisan activity was picking up across the Reich.

But if this were merely an innocent tragedy, why should the Gestapo be watching the engineer's wife? And more importantly, why, after she visited the wife of the second engineer, was he too put under surveillance?

It made little sense.

A loyal subject of the Reich killed by partisans was a tragedy, though hardly a state secret worthy of two teams of Gestapo. If how he died was an embarrassment to the Reich, then simply tell the wife her husband died in an accident. She'd never know the difference, but she'd have an answer, even if it were a lie. Life would go on.

Surveilling the second engineer was more understandable now that he thought about it. If the first engineer, Hermann Lang, was killed by partisans, and they wanted that fact covered up, Dieter Maier might have been the only one who saw any evidence of how his colleague died when he was sent to retrieve the locomotive. There was no certainty that Lang was indeed the engineer killed, though he wasn't one to put much faith in coincidences.

He could make some calls and try to find out what had happened to Lang. A distraught wife didn't carry any weight with the railroad, but a detective inspector should. All he wanted to know was whether the man was dead. There was no crime committed here, not if it were Polish partisans.

That was war.

He simply wanted to give his neighbor an answer, even if it were bad news.

He took a sip of coffee, only to find his cup empty. He rose and headed for the pot at the far end of the office, two uniformed officers standing nearby, waiting to meet with someone, an animated conversation about a beating victim catching his attention.

"Dead. Beat to a pulp. I haven't seen something like that in quite some time," said the more junior officer.

His older partner laughed. "Not since there were still Jews around to beat."

Junior tossed his head back, roaring with laughter. "Too true, my friend. I doubt there's a single one of them left in the city."

"Not unless they're crawling with the rats."

"Then they must feel right at home!"

More laughter, and the grip on Vogel's coffee cup tightened with the desire to break it over both their heads.

"It's sad, though. Bernauer Street used to be a safe neighborhood."

The senior man agreed. "Nowhere is safe anymore," he whispered, but Vogel was no longer listening. He returned to his desk, his coffee forgotten, and grabbed his jacket, heading for the parking lot. As he drove to the morgue, his gut told him he wouldn't like what he found when he got there. Someone beaten to death was no longer as shocking as it would have been just a year ago, but now, fear and desperation gripped the capital.

Even in decent neighborhoods like the one Dieter Maier lived in.

On Bernauer Street.

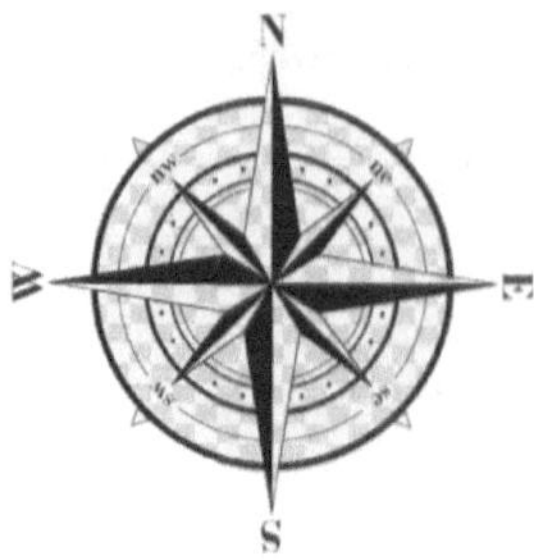

South of Kwidzyn (formerly Marienwerder), Poland

Present Day

Acton's heart sank as the truck and forklift disappeared, the last crate containing the Amber Room offloaded only moments ago. The operation had been executed swiftly, with military precision, and the manner in which these men conducted themselves, despite their attire, suggested they were ex-forces of some type, the accents suggesting to him Spetsnaz.

A terrifying prospect.

Lisowski moaned as Laura loosened the tourniquet, the only treatment they had been able to provide for the poor woman. She was pale and weak, and Acton wasn't sure how much time she had left, though with the operation now complete, he hoped help might be here soon.

He still had no answer to the question of why the leader had said he needed them, and he feared what that answer might be. He decided to risk asking after Lisowski gasped when Laura tightened the tourniquet again. "Now that you've got what you came for, can we call for help?"

The leader addressed the others lined up against the far end of the chamber, their hands and feet zip-tied. "There's a cellphone jammer hidden outside." He dropped a knife next to him, the blade sticking into the dirt beside a pile of confiscated cellphones, Acton's and Laura's purposefully destroyed, perhaps to cause confusion as to where they were. "You'll have to work together to get to this and use it. By then, we'll be gone. Once you free yourselves and walk far enough away from the jammer, you'll be able to get a signal and call for help."

Acton held out his hands, asking a question he feared he already knew the answer to. "Aren't you going to tie us up too?"

The man turned to him. "No, professor, you and your lovely wife are coming with us."

Acton's chest tightened, the answer exactly as he had expected. "Why?"

"We need someone to authenticate the find for our client. He's paying a lot of money, and he's going to want to know he's getting the genuine article before he pays us. Two unwilling professors of archaeology are exactly what I need to do that."

Acton glanced at Laura. "Leave my wife. I'm all you need."

The man chuckled. "So gallant. I do believe you were born in the wrong era, professor. But no, you're both coming with me."

Acton stepped toward him, glaring into his eyes. "I must insist."

The man smiled, tapping his shoulder holster. "Professor, if you continue to insist on delaying me, I *can* allow one of you to remain behind." His smiled disappeared. "Dead."

"It's okay, James."

Acton turned to his wife, feeling helpless. They had no leverage. None. These thieves already had what they had come for, had all the guns, and were in complete control.

The leader held his hand out toward the tunnel, as if inviting them to join him. "Shall we?"

Acton frowned, holding out a hand for Laura. He turned to Lisowski. "Hang in there, Aleksandra. Help will be here soon."

"I-I think I should be telling you the same thing."

Acton smiled then followed the thieves down the tunnel and out into the fresh morning air, his chest aching at the sight of the two unarmed security guards, dead inside the entranceway. He glared at the leader. "Was that really necessary?"

"In the end, no, but we had assumed they were armed."

"And that makes it all right?"

The man shrugged. "Do you really think I care?"

Acton frowned. "I guess not." He stared at two large curtain side transport trucks with a beer company logo emblazoned on their fabric-clad sides, there nothing whatsoever to indicate the actual precious cargo they both contained. Two black SUVs filled with the henchmen pulled out after them, a third with only a driver, waited for the leader of the operation and his two prisoners.

"Get in."

Acton opened the rear door and Laura climbed in, sliding over behind the passenger seat. He followed, closing the door, the leader sitting in the front. He leaned out the window and raised a device that looked suspiciously like a detonator.

Acton gasped as a button was pressed.

A massive explosion erupted behind them, and he and Laura spun in their seats, staring out the rear window dumbfounded at the sight, the entire mine entrance collapsed, and any hope of rescue along with it.

Acton spun toward the man as he motioned for the driver to proceed. "Why the hell did you do that?"

"We can't exactly have your friends telling anyone what just happened, can we?"

"You promised that they would live!"

"And they will. I have no doubt the Polish authorities will be contacted eventually when you miss your next important phone call. They will discover the disaster, dig, and God willing, find your friends alive."

Acton jabbed a finger at him. "You better hope that's how it works out, or there's no way we're cooperating."

The man chuckled, turning in his seat to face them as he drew his MP-443 Grach pistol, pointing it at Acton. "Tough words, professor, but I only need one of you."

Laura squeezed Acton's hand. "Kill him, and I'll tell your client it's a fake."

The man smiled. "Which is why, Professor Palmer, *you* will be the one I kill." He stared at Acton. "So, Professor, if you want your wife to survive the day, you'll cooperate, regardless of what just happened back there. Understood?"

Acton didn't respond, allowing the helpless rage written on his face to do his talking.

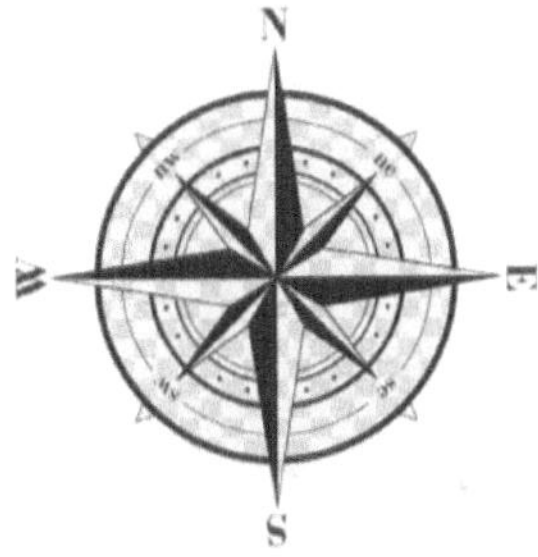

Potsdam, Germany

Tommy Granger drew a deep breath of courage, exchanging a nervous glance with Mai. All of the information he'd found, indicated this house belonged to the daughter of the late Hermann Lang, the train engineer his great-grandfather thought was murdered to cover up what the professors had discovered yesterday.

The Amber Room, plus millions in gold and other priceless works of art.

He had never heard of the Amber Room, though when he looked it up, he had to admit it was impressively gaudy. Definitely not his style, though he could appreciate the craftsmanship that had gone into such a thing, especially the fact it was all designed to be lit by candles.

He loved candles. He wasn't sure why, but he always had one burning in his room, and had been thrilled to discover Mai was also into them, especially the little tealight ones. When she wanted to be romantic, he'd show up at her apartment and find hundreds of the things lit everywhere, with her standing in the middle of the room with something naughty on.

Or nothing.

I am sooo lucky!

She was outwardly shy, though once they had become comfortable with each other, she had opened up in ways he never could have imagined, and they were now almost inseparable. And much to his surprise, he now found himself daydreaming of what life with her would be like. Marriage, children, growing old.

He shivered.

"Are you okay?"

He shrugged, wondering if he'd ever find the courage to tell her how he really felt about her. "Just nervous, I guess."

"Well, let's get it over with."

Tommy sighed then rang the doorbell, a colorful chime echoing on the other side of the door. He heard footsteps, and a woman he'd consider old, though she'd probably take offense if she thought he felt that way, answered the door.

She said something in German, and Tommy's phone translated the inquisitive greeting.

"Umm, sorry, but do you speak English?"

The woman nodded, her eyes narrowing. "Yes, I taught it in school."

Tommy breathed a sigh of relief. "Oh, thank God! My name is Tommy Granger, this is my, umm, friend, Mai Trinh. We were hoping to talk to you about who we think was your father, Hermann Lang."

The women's eyes widened, her jaw dropping slightly. "That was my grandfather." She tilted her head slightly, suspicion on her face. "What is this about?"

"We have possible information on what happened to your grandfather. Apparently, my great-grandfather investigated his disappearance."

The woman's hand darted to her mouth, tears filling her eyes. "You know what happened to my opa?"

Tommy shrugged. "Possibly."

The woman stepped back. "Please, come in. My mother will want to hear this, but she isn't well. Do you mind coming upstairs to see her?"

Tommy shook his head. "Not at all."

He let Mai go ahead, and they both followed the woman up the narrow stairs, the humble home well kept, though with the bones of something that could have pre-dated the war. They were led into a room at the end of the hall, an old lady, a truly old lady, lying in a bed, propped up on pillows, smiling broadly at the prospect of visitors. She appeared frail, though she seemed all there mentally as a brief conversation took place in German between the two women.

The old lady's face brightened considerably at something said, and she turned to Tommy and Mai. "You know what happened to my father?"

Tommy gulped. "Well, we're not sure of all the details, umm…"

Mai saved him, pulling several file folders from her bag, presenting them to the granddaughter. "These are files we found among Tommy's great-grandfather's possessions." She pointed at the top file. "There's a letter in there that he wrote about a case he had been working on before the end of the war. He had hoped to tell the families what he had discovered, but circumstances prevented him."

The old woman beckoned them closer. "Tell me, children, what did he discover?"

Tommy stepped nearer, Mai at his side. "Well, I'm afraid it's bad news. We think your father is dead."

The old woman laughed, her daughter joining in. "I should hope so, young one! If not, he'd be in that record book named after the beer."

Tommy suppressed a smile. "Of course, you're right, I just meant, at the time."

The joy in the room faded, and the woman's daughter sat on the edge of the bed, taking her mother's hand. "Please, tell us what you know."

"My great-grandfather, Detective Inspector Wolfgang Vogel, apparently was neighbors with your family, ma'am. Your mother asked him to investigate the disappearance of your father, and he agreed. In the course of his investigation, he discovered another train engineer— that's what your father was—who was friends with your family, a Dieter Maier—"

"Maier! I remember that name. I used to play with their boys!" The old lady's eyes filled with tears, as if she were reliving a different time.

"Mr. Maier indicated that a train engineer had been killed three nights before, and he had been sent to retrieve the locomotive."

"And you think this dead engineer was my father?"

Mai nodded. "We suspect so, but we haven't confirmed it yet."

"Well, how could you?"

Tommy sucked in a deep breath, and Mai took his hand, squeezing it. "Well, ma'am, we think we may have found your father yesterday."

Both women gasped, clasping at each other. "Where?" asked the daughter.

"Our professors, James Acton and his wife Laura Palmer, are in Poland right now. They followed information found in my great-grandfather's notes, and found treasure buried in an old mineshaft that they think was hidden there by the SS near the end of the war. They think the SS killed your father because he knew of its location."

The old lady's eyes were wide. "Buried treasure?"

Mai smiled, patting Tommy's hand. "Not exactly buried. You'll have to forgive my friend, he's too big a fan of pirates. As I'm sure you're aware, the Nazis stole thousands of pieces of art during the war, and much of it hasn't been found. Over the past seventy years, troves of art have occasionally been found, and yesterday a major discovery was made, along with several dozen bodies, including one wearing a train engineer's uniform. Those bodies have been taken to be identified, and as soon as we have confirmed if the engineer is indeed your father, you will be notified."

"Do you really think it could be him?"

Tommy nodded. "My great-grandfather believed your father was murdered by the SS at this location, and it makes sense that they'd put the bodies inside the mineshaft before sealing it, so they wouldn't have to deal with them."

"This makes sense." The old lady looked up at her daughter, tears filling her eyes. "Wouldn't it be wonderful to finally put your opa to rest beside Oma?"

A sobbing response was all she received as her daughter collapsed into her arms, her shoulders heaving as her mother gently patted her back. A tear rolled down Mai's cheek, and Tommy's throat ached as he resisted the urge to join in.

"I-I'm sorry if I upset you."

Their host rose, shaking her head as she wiped her cheeks dry on the back of her hands. "Oh no, you didn't. These are tears of joy. Our family for three generations has always wondered what happened to my grandfather, and now we may finally have an answer, no matter how tragic."

Tommy said nothing, not sure of what to do now that he had delivered the information. Mai pointed at the folders.

"Those are yours to keep. They are copies of all the original documents kept by Tommy's great-grandfather as they related to your case and that of Mr. Maier's. Our contact information is in there as well, should you have any questions."

The old lady nodded. "Have you spoken to the Maiers yet?"

Tommy shook his head. "No, we're going there next."

She smiled. "They were good friends to the family, that much I remember. Please, if you find them, will you tell them how to reach me? I would love to speak to them if possible."

"Absolutely."

The woman fell back into her pillows, her hand on her chest. "Oh, forgive these old bones. I'm afraid all this excitement has taken it out of me today."

Tommy suddenly felt concerned, stepping closer. "I'm sorry, is there anything I can do?"

She smiled, reaching out for his hand. He took hers, and she squeezed it with surprising strength. "Young man, you have made an old lady very happy today. To finally know what happened to my father is a great comfort. I had always feared he had somehow survived the war, wondering about what had happened to us, and living out his remaining days worrying needlessly. Now I know his life ended tragically, but he did not suffer the pain of losing his family." Her shoulders shook. "I die content now, knowing that I will see him again very soon, and that I didn't fail as a daughter by not finding my papa."

Tommy bowed slightly, again not sure of what to say. Mai saved him once more.

"We'll let you get your rest now. When we know more, we'll contact you."

Pleasantries were exchanged, and Tommy breathed a sigh of relief as the door closed behind them. Mai gave him a big hug. "You did good today."

He hugged her back. "*We* did good today." He smiled down at her. "I don't know what I would have done without you. You're like my rock."

"We make a good team."

His smile widened. "Yes, we do." He led her to the car, opening the door for her.

"Such a gentleman!"

He grinned and closed the door before climbing into the driver's side. He pulled out his phone. "I better call Professor Acton and give him an update."

Mai nodded. "Good idea. Maybe he'll have an ETA on the identification of the remains."

Tommy held the phone to his ear, his eyes narrowing as it went immediately to voicemail. "That's odd."

"What?"

"It's going straight to voicemail."

Mai shrugged. "What's so odd about that? Maybe they don't have a signal inside the mine."

Tommy shook his head. "No, they had set up a relay this morning to make sure they could get a signal while they worked." He dialed Professor Palmer's phone, and it too went straight to voicemail. "I can't reach either of them." He grabbed his laptop and went to work, Mai leaning closer, always fascinated by his skills.

"What are you doing?"

"Accessing the Polish telecom network."

Mai's eyes widened. "Is that wise?"

Tommy laughed. "Probably not, but what are they going to do? We're in Germany, and in a couple of days, we'll be back in the US, and they'll still be looking for someone in Indonesia."

"Huh?"

"I'm bouncing—never mind, I'm in. Look!" He pointed at the map now displayed showing active cellular signals in the area surrounding the mine, his fears confirmed.

"What am I looking at?"

"A dead zone."

"What's that?"

"It's a zone where there are no cellphone signals, and it's surrounding the mine. There's none at all in the entire area."

"Maybe nobody's making a call right now?"

"That's not how cellphones work. They're constantly connecting to the network so that when someone is trying to call a specific number, the network already knows where to route it." He tapped the screen. "But not here. That means either nobody at the mine has a cellphone, or they're all turned off. And neither of those options is likely in today's day and age."

"Or they're all inside, and the booster or whatever you called it, is malfunctioning."

Tommy frowned. "Yeah, I guess that's possible." He gave her a look. "You really know how to suck the fun out of my conspiracy theories."

She patted his leg. "Someone has to keep you grounded."

"I'm glad it's you." He leaned in and gave her a kiss meant to be a peck, but she grabbed the back of his neck and pulled him in, the peck turning into a torrid, passion-filled make-out session igniting the fire down below. He pushed her away, gasping for breath. "We better stop, or we could get arrested."

Her chest was heaving, and she had an animalistic look to her that had excitement surging through him. "Hotel?"

He grinned. "Good idea!" He started the car then paused. "I still think something is wrong in Poland."

"You're just being your usual paranoid self."

He pulled into traffic, pressing the accelerator a little harder, eager to reach the hotel. "You know them. They're always getting into something."

Mai nodded, a hand creeping up his leg, slowly sending his heart racing along with the speedometer. "I tell you what. When we get back to the hotel, you check that map again. If there's still nothing on it, then we'll call Dean Milton. He'll know what to do."

Tommy gasped as her hand struck pay dirt. "Maybe we check the map after we, you know…"

Mai squeezed. "Sounds good to me!"

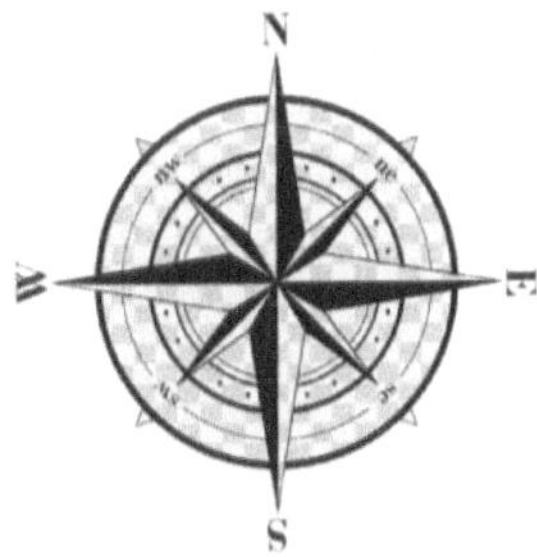

Bosko Residence

Kwidzyn (formerly Marienwerder), Poland

Helena knocked on the basement door leading to her son's apartment, a load of laundry under one arm. "Stefan, are you decent?"

No reply.

She was pretty sure she had heard him stumble in this morning, and his car was parked at an embarrassing angle at the end of the driveway. In fact, she was certain she had heard voices, and video games being played.

She knocked again then opened the door when she still heard nothing.

A wall of stench greeted her. "My God, what have you been doing down here?" It smelled like a backed up sewer, and became progressively stronger as she descended the stairs. She rounded the corner and the laundry basket dropped with her jaw as she saw her precious boy lying on the floor, his hands and feet bound, his mouth covered with tape.

She screamed, then rushed forward. "Oh my God! What happened!" She dropped to her knees beside him, discovering the source of the smell, her poor boy having soiled himself from both ends. "What do I do?"

He stared at her, yelling against his gag, and she decided rather than calling the police right away, she'd better help him breathe. She grabbed a corner of the tape covering his mouth and gently pulled at it. Stefan jerked his head to the side, ripping it off in one swift motion, yelping with pain before dropping his exhausted head to the carpet.

"What happened? Who did this?"

"Nobody. Nobody did anything!"

"Please, Stefan, tell me what's going on!"

Her son's eyes filled with tears and terror as he pleaded with her. "I can't! We can't tell anyone what happened!"

"But why? We need to call the police!"

He shook his head vehemently. "No! Absolutely not! They'll kill us, they'll kill us all!"

Officer Jelen rang the doorbell of the simple home, the cream-colored paint in desperate need of a refresh, whoever lived here apparently either down on their luck, not concerned with appearances, or unable to find someone to do the work.

The door was answered by a larger woman, well-kempt in well-worn clothing, suggesting to him she was struggling to make ends meet, rather than not concerned with appearances.

Her eyes bulged at the sight of his and his partner's uniforms. "Yes?"

Her voice trembled, beyond what he would expect his uniform to produce. Something was definitely wrong here. "Ma'am, I'm Officer Jelen. This is my partner Officer Krakowski. We had several reports from your neighbors that they heard someone scream. Are you all right?"

The woman paled.

Definitely something wrong.

"Y-yes, it was nothing. My son, he, umm, played a practical joke on me. I, umm, don't worry, I scolded him properly. It won't happen again."

Bullshit.

"May we speak to your son?"

"He's in the shower."

"We can wait."

"He-he'll be a while. You know how boys are."

"Uh-huh." A mental image of someone masturbating in the shower flashed, and he pushed it away. "I'm afraid I'll have to insist on speaking with him."

The woman's eyes widened further, but she stepped aside, inviting them inside. "Oh, all right." She closed the door then climbed several steps to the second floor. "Stefan, I need you to come downstairs!"

"Give me a minute, I'm still covered in shit!"

Jelen's eyebrows shot up as he glanced at his partner. "What did he just say?"

The woman was nervous again. "Oh, just an expression."

Jelen was about to dismiss it when he finally noticed the smell.

Shit.

"Do you smell that?"

His partner nodded. "Yup."

"What happened here, ma'am? Please tell us so we can help you."

The woman's hand flew to her forehead before she stepped into her living room and collapsed on the couch. "I-I don't know. He won't tell me. I found him tied up in the basement. Someone had beaten him."

Jelen turned to his partner. "Call it in."

Krakowski pulled out his phone, stepping outside to update their status as footsteps were heard coming down the stairs.

"What is it, Mom?" The young man spotted Jelen, his eyes widening, terror on his face leaving Jelen to worry another eruption of excrement was about to occur. "Wh-what do you want?"

Jelen stared at the swollen face and welts covering the exposed upper torso, only a towel covering the important bits. "What happened to you?"

"Nothing."

"Bullshit. Tell me now, or I take you to the station and you *will* tell me there."

"I've got rights!"

"Yes, you do, but right now, I'm here investigating reports of a woman screaming, I find you beaten up, and your mother telling me you were tied up in the basement."

"Mom!"

"I want answers, and I want them now!"

Stefan was trembling now. "If I tell you, they'll kill me."

"Who?"

"The men who did this."

Jelen lowered his voice, trying to calm the young man down and entice the information he needed from him. "What did they want?"

"What are you, some kind of moron? I just told you that they'll kill me if I tell you!"

Jelen jerked a thumb over his shoulder. "My partner is already calling it in. It's about to be part of the official record. If they really meant what they said, then you better tell me everything you know now, so we can arrest them, or you just may die."

A stream of urine flowed down Stefan's leg, and the story from his mouth.

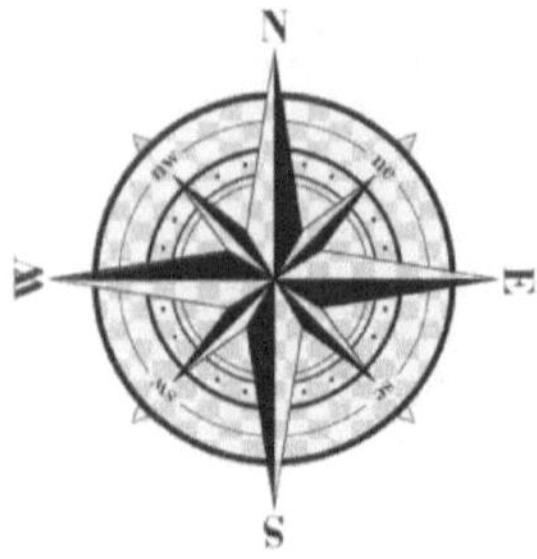

Route A1, Poland

Acton suspected the reason they weren't bound and gagged, and their heads weren't covered, was for the simple fact their captors wanted everything to appear perfectly normal to prying eyes.

And he was taking full advantage of the opportunity.

They were heading south on Route A1, and from the distances displayed to major cities, he suspected they were eventually leaving the country.

Yet that knowledge did them little good, and the fact they were afforded it, and full view of the faces of their captors, had him worried that when their ordeal was complete, they would be dead.

Their captors had already killed two and shot one, then trapped over a dozen inside perhaps to die. They clearly had no scruples that would keep him and his wife alive.

He decided to fish for information, almost nothing said for the last hour of driving. "How long will we be traveling?"

"Shut up."

Acton frowned, this apparently a fruitless endeavor.

Perhaps I can create an opportunity.

"Well, it's just that if we're traveling for too long, we're going to need some pee breaks. I have an overactive bladder, and if I don't pee every two or three hours, I'll be making a mess back here."

"Bullshit."

Acton shrugged. "Your choice. I had asparagus last night, so it's going to get nasty in here."

"If one drop hits this car, I kill your wife."

"Threaten all you want, but we both know that if you touch her, I don't cooperate, and you need me to authenticate things, not her. I'm the expert on the Amber Room, not her. Her specialty is Ancient Egypt."

The man turned in his seat and glared at him. "If you don't shut up, I'll kill the both of you, and find another expert."

Acton stared at him. "Fine, but I'll still need that pee break in about two hours."

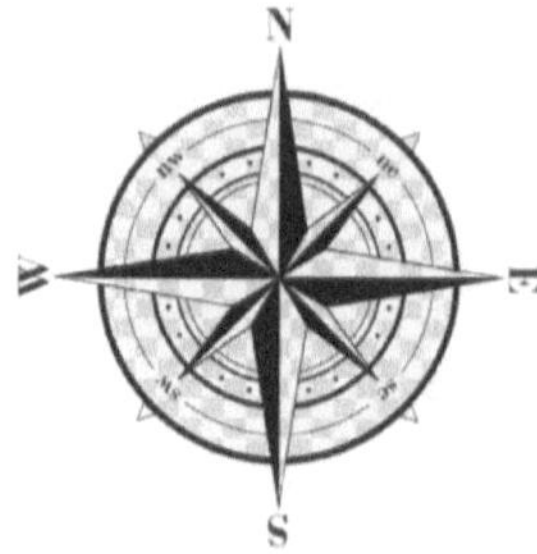

Medical Examiner's Office

Berlin, Nazi Germany

January 31, 1945

Detective Inspector Vogel stared at the almost unrecognizable face of the beating victim spoken of by the two officers at his office. Despite the injuries, there could be no doubt as to whom it was.

Dieter Maier.

Whoever had done this—and he had a pretty good idea who—hadn't wanted the man to be recognizable. While his entire body had sustained significant injuries, and those were likely the cause of death, particular attention had been paid to the face, mostly by shoes and boots.

"So, do you know him?"

Vogel glanced at the Medical Examiner, Hans Naumann. "No, not with that face. He loosely matches a missing persons case I'm working on, but it's the wrong color hair. Any idea who did this?"

Naumann shook his head. "The officers who brought him in said it was most likely Jews. I don't believe that nonsense for a second. Even if there were any left in the city, they wouldn't be targeting innocent people. Not like this." He frowned, staring down at the face. "Somebody didn't want us recognizing this man. The question is why."

"You'll figure it out eventually."

Naumann grunted then covered the body. "Perhaps, but if I don't within the next few months, I think it might be some Russian's job."

Vogel glanced around to make sure they were alone as Naumann sat at his desk, pulling out a lunchbox. He unwrapped a meager looking sandwich and held up half. "Hungry?"

Vogel shook his head. "I don't know how you can eat in here."

Naumann shrugged. "If a little blood and guts got me upset, I'd never eat."

Vogel frowned, gesturing at him. "It looks like you barely do, regardless."

Naumann pulled at his loose clothing. "My wife had to take in my pants a third time just last week. I think I'm down at least ten kilos."

Vogel absentmindedly ran a finger over his chest, his ribcage a little more prominent than it used to be, the rations not enough. "Yet you offer me half your sandwich."

Naumann grinned. "Only because I knew you wouldn't accept!"

Vogel laughed then headed for the door. "I'll see you too soon, my friend."

A mumbled reply was offered, Naumann's mouth full. As Vogel headed for his car, he weaved this new factor into the overall mosaic confronting him. A railway engineer, likely Hermann Lang, was dead, officially shot by partisans, though Vogel had his doubts. If it were the case, then Erika Lang would have been notified. The fact she hadn't been, told him that either it wasn't her husband that was killed, or he wasn't killed by partisans, but by somebody that didn't want questions asked. The fact Hermann Lang was missing, and she was under surveillance by the Gestapo, was proof enough to him that he was indeed the dead engineer that Dieter Maier had referred to.

And now Maier was dead.

There was only one reason he was dead, and that was because he knew something the Gestapo didn't want him knowing. Likely it was linked to the death of Hermann Lang. Maier had been sent to collect a locomotive after its engineer was killed. Whoever was behind this, obviously needed the locomotive returned, and not just anyone could operate one of the massive vehicles.

They needed an engineer.

That would explain why Maier had been exposed to some bit of information that they didn't want out there. Perhaps they had hoped he could be trusted to keep his mouth shut, but the combination of Frau Lang and himself showing up within 24 hours of his return, probably raised alarm bells with those watching them. Or, perhaps they had always intended on killing him, and had simply waited for him to return to Berlin, where it was more plausible for him to be beaten to death in the back alleys of a desperate city, rather than a tightly controlled railyard in Poland.

Either way, one was dead, and he was quite certain so was the other, leaving two widows behind likely in danger too. One had already been under surveillance, probably waiting for her to do something that they could pick her up for, thus preventing uncomfortable questions about her missing husband. The other was probably still under surveillance despite the beating death of her husband, as he was certain the Gestapo would be concerned she had been told something by him.

The bottom line was that both were now in trouble.

And he was sick of innocent lives constantly being destroyed in the final days of a failed empire.

They have to leave Berlin.

The answer was obvious, though not the solution. How could two women escape Berlin? Where would they go? He knew the Langs had sent their child out of the city. Perhaps if Frau Lang were to join her daughter, she would be safe, though it would be the first place the Gestapo would look.

And that was another problem. With the Gestapo watching both, their departures would have to be coordinated, and even if he were inclined to help, he was but one man, and couldn't ask anyone else to risk their lives helping him.

A smile crept up the side of his face as he pulled out onto the street.

Gruber!

Gruber was the exact type of vermin he needed for this situation. The man was a parasite, his father so well connected in the Nazi Party that he was untouchable, despite the fact every law enforcement officer in the city knew he was into human smuggling. Whether it was Jews, homosexuals, or the mentally handicapped, he could move them.

For a price.

A price unaffordable on a detective inspector's salary.

But leverage was valuable. And if Gruber agreed, they would both have leverage over each other, leverage that was only important until the war was over.

Which couldn't come soon enough.

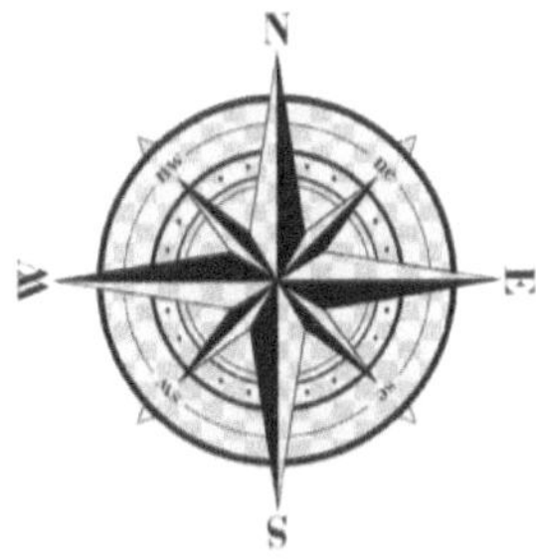

Inselhotel Potsdam

Potsdam, Germany

Present Day

Tommy groaned as Mai wrapped her legs around him, pulling him tighter. He had only been with two other women in his life, neither of whom he had feelings for, and he wondered if that was why it felt so much better.

She was incredible.

Their two bodies meshed so well, it was as if they each knew what the other wanted without having to ask.

Though it hadn't always been that way.

In fact, the first few times had been downright awkward, though now they were like pros.

And it felt so good when you actually knew what you were doing.

He froze in mid-play. "Oh shit, I forgot to check the cellphone signals!"

Mai grabbed his face with both hands, staring into his eyes. "Don't you dare stop!"

"But—!"

"Finish it! Now!"

He grinned and resumed, putting it into high gear, and within minutes, they were both shouting in ecstasy, enough to elicit a pounded wall shared by their bed and another guest. He rolled off her, gasping for breath. "Fast enough for you?"

She lay beside him, her arms and legs spread out like a starfish. "Oh yeah."

"One for the record books?"

"I don't think speed is a record you want to be known for."

He chuckled. "Good point." He drifted off, his body spent and completely content.

"Forgetting something?"

He was suddenly concerned and rolled over. "I'm sorry, did you not…"

She patted his cheek. "Oh, don't worry, I did." She pointed at his laptop.

"Oh shit!" He leaped from the bed and grabbed his computer, returning to bring the map back up. He frowned. "It's still dead. Something is definitely wrong."

Mai sat up beside him, staring at the dead zone. "We better call Dean Milton right away."

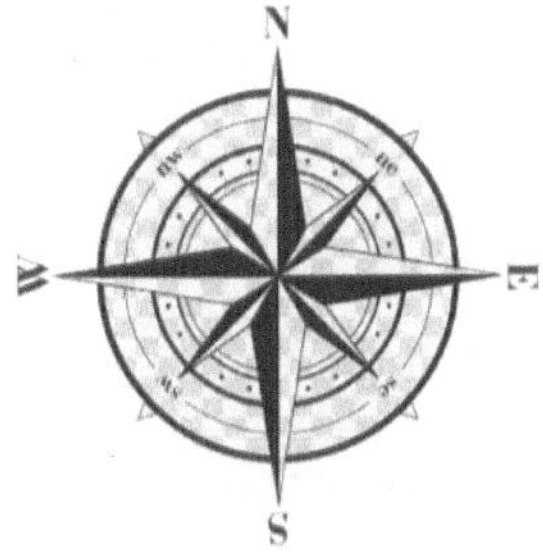

South of Kwidzyn (formerly Marienwerder), Poland

Officer Jelen opened the door before his partner even brought them to a stop, the fact something had happened here, immediately evident. He opened the rear door, letting a much better smelling Stefan out. He had told them everything, showing them the Facebook posting that had apparently led to his assault, and had even offered to show them where it had been taken, something Jelen couldn't pass up.

A chance to see the Amber Room?

He had heard of it, of course, his father a history buff. The man would kill to be here with him, and perhaps he might just find a way for him to experience what Stefan claimed to have seen yesterday.

The young man pointed at what appeared to be a collapsed mine entrance. "I dug that out yesterday. Everything was grown over, and the professors found a cinderblock wall. Look!" He pointed to a pile of debris. "I put that there." His eyes narrowed. "I don't understand. Where is everybody?"

"Look at this."

Jelen rounded the car to join his partner near the entrance, and tensed, immediately spinning on his heel, surveying the area at the sight of at least half a dozen shell casings and some blood.

Something had definitely happened here.

"How many people were working here?"

Stefan shrugged. "Not many when I was here. There might have been a dozen, but they were sending for more from some university."

"Who was in charge of the site?"

Another shrug. "No idea. I was brought in by the city. Maybe they'll know."

Jelen nodded. "Call your supervisor. We're going to need to know who's in charge here."

"Yes, sir." Stefan stepped away to make the call as Jelen returned his attention to the collapsed entrance.

"I really hope nobody was inside when this happened."

"Well, somebody was." Krakowski pointed at two sets of drag marks, likely made by shoe heels. "Looks like two bodies were dragged inside before this was blown."

Jelen cursed. "I think you're right." His eyes narrowed as he spotted something sitting among the debris Stefan claimed credit for. "What's that?" He quickly strode toward what appeared to be an electronic device, suitcase-sized, hiding behind a chunk of cinderblock and rebar. "What do you think this is?"

Krakowski shrugged, taking a knee beside it and pointing to several antennae. "Some sort of cellphone relay for inside?"

Jelen pursed his lips. "Could be." He looked over at the mine entrance. "But wouldn't you put it over there, in plain sight, not hidden away over here?"

Krakowski's eyes narrowed. "Yeah, this doesn't make sense."

"Wait a minute." Jelen pulled out his cellphone. He frowned, holding it up for his partner to see. "No signal. You?"

Krakowski retrieved his cellphone and shook his head. "None."

Stefan walked over, holding up his phone. "I can't get a signal. I've been all around here."

Jelen looked at him. "Were you able to yesterday?"

"Yeah, no problem."

Jelen pointed at the device, a gentle hum suggesting it had a power source of some type. "I think it's this thing." He pointed at a red switch, Russian lettering indicating it was for power. "I wonder what would happen if we turned it off."

His partner reached forward and flipped the switch before he could stop him. The hum died.

"You shouldn't have done that."

Krakowski shrugged then held up his phone. "I've got a signal."

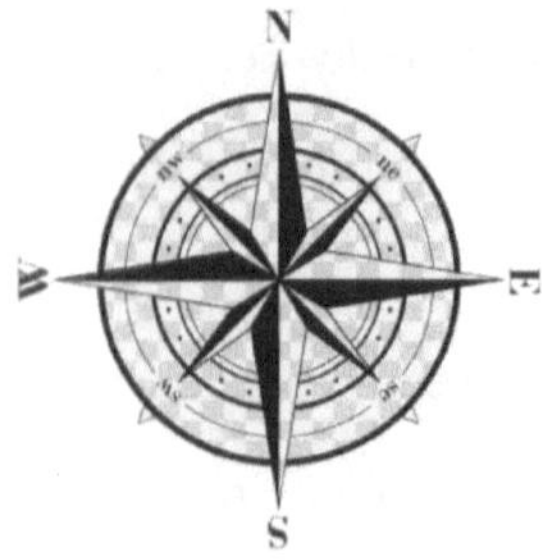

Milton Residence

St. Paul, Maryland

Dean of St. Paul's University, Gregory Milton, moaned as his wife, Sandra, dug her thumbs into the small of his back, his muscles a little tight today, though nothing like the old days, his wheelchair now relegated to the closet, his bedroom once again on the second floor. He was a new man, or at least a renewed one, fully recovered from being shot in the back a few years ago, though his stamina still hadn't returned.

And his doctors were warning him it might never.

Though they were the same ones who had said he'd never walk again.

"Do you want to flip over and let me do your front?"

Milton grinned and flipped over, purposefully yanking the towel aside, someone wagging a hello.

"Huh, I think you were expecting something this entire time."

"Can you blame a guy? His hot wife is rubbing him down with massage oils, what's a man gonna do?"

"Ahh, remember that his daughter is coming home from school at any minute?"

Milton frowned. "Shit, I forgot." He grinned at her. "Quickie?"

She chuckled. "How about we just make this all about you?"

"Steak sauce!"

"Huh?"

"Never mind." He tapped his watch. "Time's a-wastin', hon!"

She laughed and oiled up her hands some more when the phone rang.

"Leave it."

"But I'm expecting a call from Judy."

"Judy can wait. I can't. You've got me so worked up, I could suffer permanent injury."

"Yeah, I heard that one in high school."

"You did this in high school?" He grinned. "I wish I had known you back then."

Sandra wiped her hands quickly on a towel then looked at the phone. "Odd. I think it's Tommy Granger."

Milton's eyes narrowed, Tommy and Mai in Germany while his best friends, Jim and Laura, were in Poland. "Better get it."

She answered the phone as he sat up and swung his legs over the edge of the massage table purchased for his rehabilitation, his wife even getting training on how to deliver the massages so essential to his recovery. "Hi, Tommy? Yes, just a second, he's right here." She gave him the phone and was about to turn away when he grabbed her hand and put it some place safe. He grinned at her.

"Tommy? This is Dean Milton."

"Hi, sir, I'm sorry to call, but, well, I'm here with Mai, and we're concerned something might have happened to Professor Acton. And Professor Palmer."

Milton tensed and Sandra recognized the change, stopping what she was doing. "What makes you think that?"

"We haven't been able to reach them for over an hour, and it looks like there's a dead zone around the site."

"What does that mean?"

"I think there's some sort of cellphone jammer in operation. There are no signals at all from the area surrounding the mine."

"Couldn't it just be a failure with the phone company?"

"No, I don't think so. Their system is indicating everything is fine, but there are no signals at all in just this one area." There was a pause. "Wait a minute, things just came back online. Just a sec."

Milton breathed a sigh of relief as the over anxious students were apparently about to be proven wrong.

"Okay, I've got cellular activity in the area again, but the professors' phones are still offline."

"Maybe they're dead? Low batteries?"

"Both of them? I doubt that."

Milton agreed. "Could they be in the mine?"

"No, I'm picking up a cluster of signals that suggest they're coming from a repeater. Do you have a number for anyone who should be with them?"

Milton stood. "I do. I have the number for their contact there, but I'll have to look it up. I'll call you back." He turned to Sandra then stared at his waning member. "Funs over, big guy."

"What's wrong?"

"Oh, probably nothing, just some overactive imaginations, but I need to make a call." He snapped the towel at her caboose. "Then I'll meet you in the bedroom."

"Our daughter will be home at any minute."

"At which time you will set her up in front of the TV with a snack and a drink, and you and I can squeeze in a few minutes of adult playtime."

She gave him a look. "What's gotten into you today?"

"I think the better question is what's going to be getting—"

She held up a finger, cutting him off while laughing. "Don't you dare finish that sentence, mister."

He grinned. "Save the dirty talk for the bedroom?"

"Exactly." She smiled. "Or the back seat of the car."

His eyes widened. "Ooh, it's been awhile since we've done it there!"

The door downstairs opened, the alarm chiming.

"Mommy! Daddy! I'm home!"

Sandra turned toward the hallway. "Just a second, dear!" She gave junior a squeeze. "I'll see you in a few minutes."

Milton wrapped the towel around himself, then headed for his office with a smile of anticipation. He called the number for Professor Lisowski, and it rang several times before going to voicemail. He frowned, trying it again, sighing in relief as this time it was answered on the third ring.

"*Halo?*"

"Hi, can I talk to Aleksandra Lisowski? This is—"

"Oh, thank God! We thought the phones weren't working! Aleksandra has been shot, and we're trapped! We need help!"

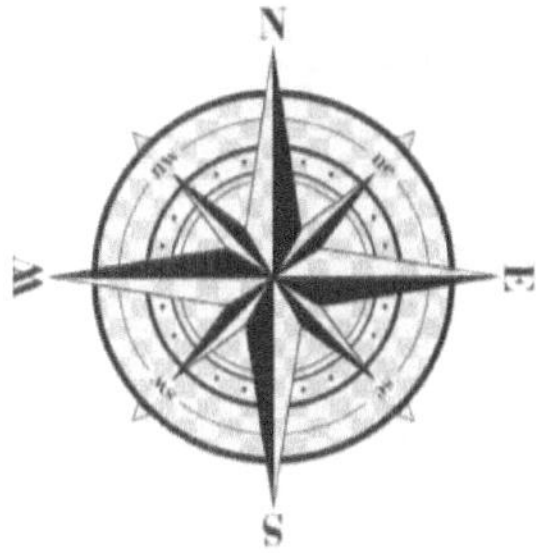

Inselhotel

Potsdam, Germany

"You were right to be concerned."

Tommy gulped at Dean Milton's statement, Mai's eyes widening beside him as they both listened on speaker. "We were?"

"Yes, something has happened. According to someone I just talked to, they've all been trapped inside the mine since a group of armed men stole the Amber Room crates. They kidnapped Jim and Laura, then blew the mine entrance. And they shot and wounded their Polish contact, Professor Lisowski."

Mai gasped. "Oh my God! What are we going to do?"

"I've reached out to the university where Aleksandra works, but there's no answer. I've left messages, but these people are running out of air and need help."

Tommy stared at the screen of his laptop. "I'm showing cellphone signals outside."

"If only we had one of their phone numbers, we could call them."

Tommy chuckled. "Who needs numbers? I can connect to them right now."

"You can?"

"Sure, all I need to do is—"

"I don't need a technical explanation, I just need results. Can you patch me through to someone?"

Mai pressed against him, a smile on her face, and he stared into her eyes for a moment, then sighed. "Just a second." He tapped away at his keyboard, and a phone rang, something in Polish said. "Go ahead, Dean."

"Hello? Do you speak English?"

"Yes, some," was the heavily accented reply.

"Good! My name is Greg Milton. I am the Dean of St. Paul's University in Maryland, in the United States. Who am I speaking to?"

"This is Officer Jelen of the Polish Police."

"Oh, thank God, a police officer! Listen, I just got off the phone with a group of people who are trapped inside an old mine that I believe you are standing outside of—"

"Wait. How did you get this number?"

"That's not important. There is a woman inside who has been shot, and the others are running out of air. If you don't start a rescue operation immediately, they will all suffocate to death."

"Give me your number, and the number you spoke to inside."

Milton quickly relayed the numbers.

"Very good. I will call you back shortly."

The call ended, and Tommy leaned closer to the phone. "What do we do now, sir?"

"Wait."

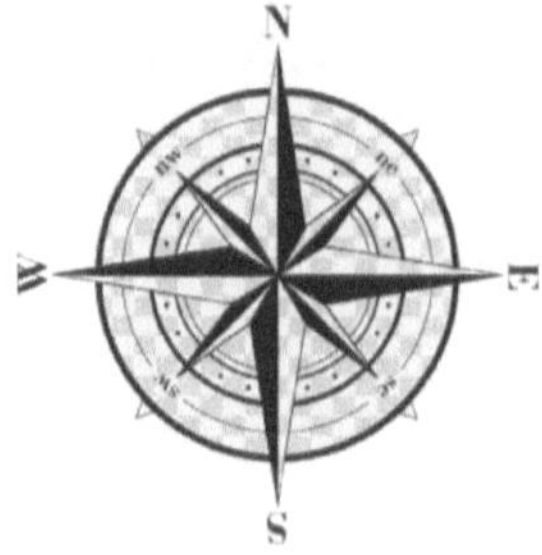

South of Kwidzyn (formerly Marienwerder), Poland

Jelen ended the call from the American and pointed at a nearby backhoe while turning to Stefan. "You said you were a heavy equipment operator?"

Stefan nodded.

"Then start digging! We might have people trapped inside!"

Stefan's eyes bulged. "Yes, sir!" He sprinted for the backhoe as Jelen relayed the conversation he had just had to his partner while dialing the number he had received for a phone inside.

Someone answered.

"Hello, this is Officer Jelen. Who am I speaking to?"

"Daniel Marek! Please help us! We're trapped inside!"

Jelen snapped his fingers at Krakowski, who immediately dialed his phone, the situation about to escalate far beyond a potential domestic violence call. His heart hammered as he realized this was the biggest case of his career.

And he was about to have it taken away.

He refocused on the panicked victim on the other end of the line.

"Tell me everything, from the beginning."

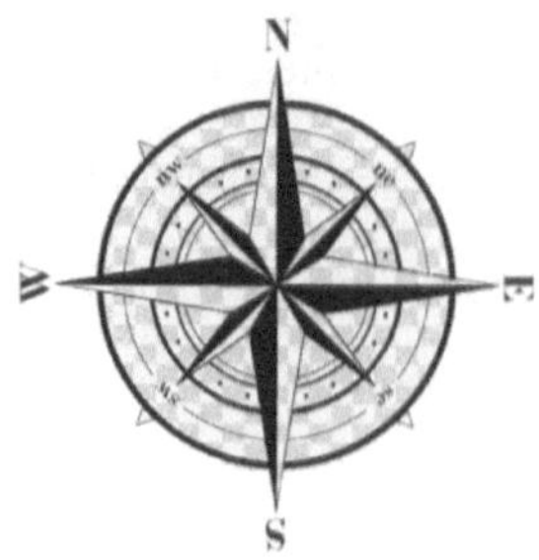

Gruber Residence

Berlin, Nazi Germany

January 31, 1945

"Detective Inspector Vogel, I can honestly say that when I woke up this morning, I never would have guessed that *you* would be honoring me with a visit."

Vogel forced a smile as the portly man extended a swollen hand, a large gold ring with a diamond-encrusted swastika making its presence felt as the hand was shaken. "Nor I, I assure you."

"Are you here in an official capacity?" Gruber leaned over in his chair, staring past Vogel. "I see you've come alone."

Vogel took a chair in front of Gruber's ornate desk. "I'm alone, and I'm not here officially."

Gruber smiled. "My favorite kind of visit from a Kriminalpolizei officer." He flicked a hand at one of his men standing behind Vogel at the door. "Cigars and cognac for our guest."

Vogel decided it best not to refuse. "Thank you, you are most generous."

"To my friends."

Vogel knew what that meant. It meant Gruber knew why he was here. Not the specifics, just that a favor was about to be asked, and something would be expected in return.

Gruber lit his cigar, dipping the other end in the cognac. "What is it I can do for you, my friend?"

Vogel puffed on his cigar as Gruber's henchman bent over with the match, patiently waiting for Vogel to signal success. Vogel leaned back, then took a sip of the cognac, the bite sweet, an almost forgotten experience, most alcohol today little better than furniture polish. "I need a favor."

"I suspected as much. What is it?"

"I need two women smuggled out of Berlin, reunited with their families, then both families taken some place safe to wait out the war."

Gruber chuckled, then much to Vogel's horror, the chuckle turned into outright laughter, his men joining in. "Is *that* all?"

Vogel nodded, knowing full well it was a rhetorical question. "Yes."

Gruber leaned forward, jabbing the air between them with his cigar. "You want me, as a favor, to get two women out of the city, reunite them with their families, then find some safe haven for both to ride out the war."

"Yes. And they're both under surveillance by the Gestapo."

Gruber tossed his head back, roaring with laughter again. "Oh, God, this just keeps getting better." He calmed himself, taking a sip of his cognac, leaving his face to linger in the snifter. He swallowed then sighed, finally staring at Vogel. "Why?"

"Because they're innocent, and don't deserve to die."

Gruber pursed his lips. "Why should they die?"

"Because their husbands were mixed up in something. What, I don't know, but something that wasn't their fault, and now they're dead. Their wives don't deserve the same fate."

Gruber sighed. "And what's in it for me?"

"I'll tip you off to any raids that might be planned for your operation."

Gruber dismissed the offer with the bat of a hand. "I've got people for that. And besides, you know who my father is."

Vogel's mind raced. Gruber was right. His offer was worthless. He eyed the Nazi Party pin on Gruber's jacket when an idea came to him. "The war is almost over."

"Yes."

"And what do you think will happen when it is?"

Gruber shrugged. "I've hidden my assets around the country. I'll ride out the rough patch, then when things settle down, enjoy my spoils."

"A good plan in theory. But what do you really think is going to happen?"

"I'm not sure I understand what you're getting at."

Vogel leaned forward, pointing at the pin with his cigar. "What do you think the Allies are going to do to those who were Party members?"

Gruber glanced at the pin, then chewed at his lip. "What do *you* think they're going to do?"

"I get to hear the reports that you don't, that the public doesn't. The Allies are already planning on trials. They've already got a plan for when Germany falls. They are going to track down every single Nazi they can, and put him on trial. And you know what that means."

Gruber paled slightly. "What?"

"The noose."

Gruber gulped, staring at Vogel, his eyes slightly wider than moments ago. "All right, so you seem to know my future. How does helping you today, save me from that fate?"

"When the time comes, I'll testify that yes you were a human smuggler, a piece of shit in many police officers' books, but in fact, you were doing your part to help save the lives of those the Reich deemed enemies. Thanks to your unselfish efforts, hundreds of Jews and traitors alike were saved from certain death."

A smile slowly spread on Gruber's face. "You would do this for me?"

Vogel shook his head. "No. I'd do it for these two innocent widows."

Gruber rose, extending a hand. "We have a deal."

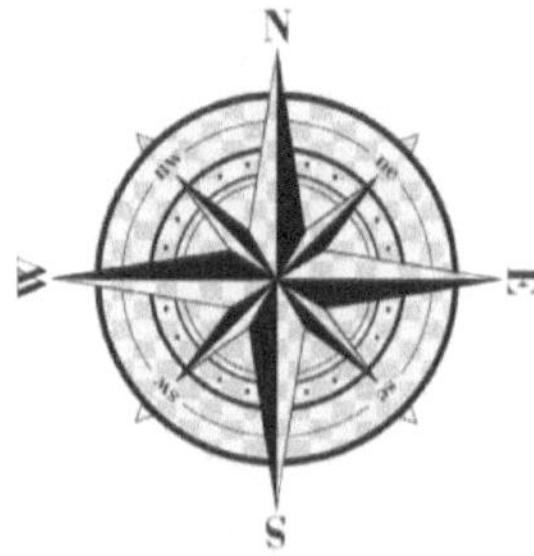

Fairfax Towers

Falls Church, Virginia

Present Day

Oh God, I love it when she comes back from assignment!

They hadn't even made it up to their apartment. In fact, they hadn't even made it out of the car. When Chris Leroux had opened up the rear door to get his girlfriend's luggage, Sherrie White had shoved him into the back seat and jumped him, closing the door behind her. The windows were now fogged up, and the shocks had been receiving a workout for the past ten minutes as the love of his life burned off the pent up energy she always returned with after an op.

She was CIA. An agent like his best friend Dylan Kane, though he was a Special Agent.

But none of that mattered right now, as he held on for dear life as her 8-seconds style of riding passed the ten-minute mark, and he fought to outlast her. She was particularly insatiable tonight, and fortunately for them, their assigned parking spot under their apartment building was fairly secluded, though not completely, and that distraction was helping him hold out a little longer, thinking about baseball not necessary tonight.

As he sensed her impending release, he gripped her shoulders as they both strove for that simultaneous climax they enjoyed so much. They were seconds away, and it would be so good—

His phone vibrated from somewhere underneath him.

"Oh God, don't you dare answer that!"

"I-I won't."

But her moans each time the vibrations traveled through him and into her suggested she had an entirely different reason for him not answering.

She tipped.

And he raced to catch up as she shook all over, her moans probably reaching the stairwell.

Then she collapsed as his phone indicated a voicemail had been left, his final efforts leaving him gasping in exquisite release as he held the love of his life tight, and thanking all that was holy for bringing the two of them together.

He was a changed man, and it was all because of her. Shy, awkward, with no ambition, she had turned him into a much less self-conscious man, hints of confidence making their presence known, and he was now an analyst supervisor at the CIA. His life, as far as he was concerned, was near perfect, and it was all thanks to Sherrie White.

She sat up and ground her hips into him.

"Don't you dare start again. Let's get dressed and upstairs before someone finds us."

Sherrie gave a pout but swung off him, eliciting a final groan from both of them. He pulled his pants up and awkwardly zipped them as she dressed. She smiled at him. "Ready?"

"I hope so."

Sherrie opened the door and stepped out, straightening her blouse as he stumbled out beside her, tucking his shirt into his pants.

Someone started to clap behind them, and they both spun toward the intruder.

"Encore! Encore!"

Leroux flushed. "Dylan! What the hell? How long were you there?"

"Long enough to get a little worked up myself."

Leroux burned even hotter, though Sherrie seemed unaffected as she adjusted her bra. He had to remember sometimes that she had been trained by the CIA to handle situations like this, and didn't embarrass easily. In fact, he was pretty certain he had never seen her even flustered.

"So, umm, what are you doing here?"

"Ahhh, I live here now, remember?"

Leroux gave him a look. "I know that. I mean, what are you doing *here*, in the parking garage, in the middle of the night?"

Kane grinned. "Watching my best friend get it on!"

Leroux shook his head, but smiled.

Best friend.

He loved that he actually had one. Life had been tough when he was young, especially during high school. Kane had been the jock, and he the geek, fate bringing them together, Kane providing his tutor a brief reprieve from the bullying he had suffered for years. They were unlikely friends, and he was sure if it weren't for their accidental encounter at Langley, where they discovered they both worked for the spy agency, he never would have seen him again.

He was thankful he had, and they were now great friends. Great friends who rarely saw each other. Special Agent Dylan Kane was one of the agency's top operators, the real world's James Bond.

Just American, and a little rougher around the edges.

Leroux led them toward the elevator, Kane still grinning at him. His buddy offered up a fist bump, and Leroux glanced at Sherrie.

"Oh, go ahead, you know you want to."

He grinned and bumped Kane's fist.

"My man! If only those bastards in high school could see you now!"

Leroux's chest ached at the thought of those years, and Sherrie's hand gripped his, squeezing it tight as if she knew the pain he was feeling.

If only.

"Did you check your messages?" she asked, and Leroux cursed, fishing his phone out of his pocket as they boarded the elevator.

"Forgot."

Sherrie turned to Kane as he pressed the floors for their apartments. "Are you in town for long? Last night Fang said she didn't know when you were due back."

"Just a couple of days. I surprised her last night when she got back from your place." His tone softened with the mention of his girlfriend, Lee Fang, an ex-Chinese Special Forces exile in hiding from her government, and the first woman Kane had ever loved. "Listen, thanks again to both of you for helping her out. She's been so much happier since we moved into the building."

Sherrie smiled. "It's been our pleasure. Fang is wonderful. And funny too!"

Leroux tuned out of the conversation as he listened to the voicemail left by one of his analysts, Randy Child. He frowned, waving the phone at the others. "Sorry, I've gotta take this." He dialed the office, Child answering.

"Hi, sir, sorry to bother you at this hour, but I've got something here I figured you'd want to know about."

"What is it?"

"Well, our intrepid professors are at it again."

"Acton and Palmer?" This silenced the conversation, both Sherrie and Kane turning their attention to him.

"Yes."

"What is it this time?"

"A flash just went out from the Polish Police. Apparently, they've been kidnapped."

Leroux sighed, shaking his head. "Those two shouldn't be allowed out of the country. Does the chief know?"

"Not yet, I figured I'd see what you wanted to do first."

Leroux stared at Sherrie, already regretting the fun he was about to miss out on. "I'll be there shortly. Let the chief's office know what's going on, then start pulling any intel you can find on the situation. And call in the rest of the team. I have a funny feeling we're going to be busy."

"Yes, sir."

Leroux ended the call and gently slammed his head against the mirrored wall behind him.

Kane broke the silence. "What's happened to my former prof?"

"He and his wife have been kidnapped in Poland."

Kane's eyes widened. "Poland? Who the hell gets kidnapped in Poland?"

Leroux shrugged. "They do, apparently. I have to go in."

Kane frowned. "I'll go with you. Just let me tell Fang."

Leroux shook his head. "No, there's nothing you can do from here to help them, and you've only got two days with her. If I need you, I'll call."

Kane chewed his lip then nodded. "You're right. I'd just be a third wheel or fifth wheel, whatever the damned expression is."

Sherrie patted his arm. "I think you mean pain in the ass."

"Hawhaw. And here I thought I liked you."

The doors opened to Leroux and Sherrie's floor, and Sherrie grabbed him by the arm, hauling him into the hallway. "Say hi to Fang for us!"

Kane waved at them as the doors closed. "Will do!"

Sherrie dragged him toward their apartment door.

"What's the rush?"

"You've gotta go to the office, and I need one last jolly rogering before you do."

Leroux chuckled as her key hit the lock. "Was your last assignment in the UK?"

She grinned.

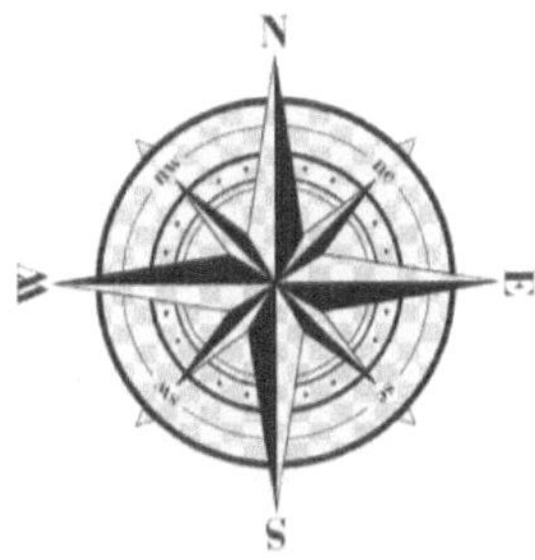

Route A1, Poland

Alexie Tankov glanced back at his prisoners, the arrogant American professor tapping his crotch.

"Getting close."

Tankov ignored him, the man just baiting him. The situation was curious. Neither of these two people were reacting the way he would have expected. Neither appeared scared, in fact, more angry than anything else. In the past, anyone he had placed in a similar situation would have been begging for their lives, yet this one just complained he needed to pee, and his wife merely sat silently, watching out the window.

As if gathering intel.

Who were these people? The fact they were acting so strangely, so atypical, had him thinking it might be safest to simply kill them and find someone else to authenticate the find. Yet that would delay things. He wanted this cargo delivered as quickly as possible, not only so he could get his money, but so he could transfer the responsibility of such a valuable, priceless find, to someone else.

The more he read about the Amber Room, the more he regretted not asking for $200 million. The sheik would have given it to him, he was sure. But what was done, was done. He was never one to change a deal. It made for bad business. And anyone who changed one on him, he never did business with again.

And sometimes they never did business with anybody again.

Especially if that betrayal cost one of his team.

His comms beeped, and he activated it. "Go ahead."

"We're in position."

"Take your time and make sure you find good matches. There's nothing on the scanners yet, so I don't think they have any idea what to look for."

"Copy that."

Tankov pointed at a rest stop ahead. "Let's pull over there." He turned in his seat. "My partner is going to take you to the bathroom. If you try anything, I kill her."

Laura Palmer grimaced. "But I need to go too!"

He growled. "One at a time!"

He faced forward, debating whether bullets or adult diapers would be preferable to the current situation.

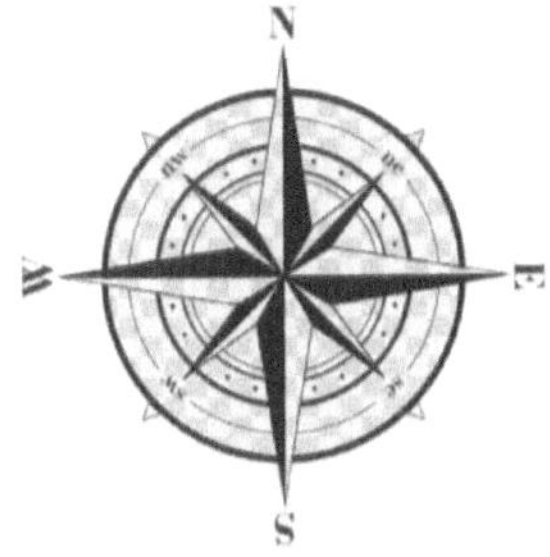

Vogel Residence

Berlin, Nazi Germany

January 31, 1945

Vogel sat in the chair normally reserved for him in his lonely apartment, the Allies pounding the city once again in the distance. The darkness he sat in was complete, the blackout curtains doing their job. He fished out an extra cigar Gruber had given him, and a box of matches. Striking one of the sticks in the dark, the flare briefly illuminated the room, and he lit the cigar, shaking out the matchstick before tossing it on the side table, something his wife would have snapped at him for if she were here.

But she wasn't.

This isn't living. It's existing.

He was still doing his job, and it was an important one when times were normal. But now, with people desperate for food, terrified of what was soon to come, he wondered if the crimes he still investigated were of any importance.

They had to be.

Crime was crime, and the victims deserved justice.

Victims like Lang and Maier, and the other victims like their wives and now fatherless children.

He sighed, wishing he had some of Gruber's cognac to enjoy. He had made a deal with the devil, though he was quite certain he'd never be called upon to deliver. He'd be dead before the war was over, and if he weren't, Gruber would be. The Russians were coming, and he had little doubt anyone associated with the Reich, whether a Party member or not, would be executed.

He stared into the darkness at the closet containing his uniforms, now rarely worn.

Will they spare me because I was just a police officer doing his duty?

He doubted it, not if the broadcasts were to be believed.

He flinched as someone knocked on the door.

"Herr Vogel?"

It was Erika Lang.

He ignored her, as she was ignoring the note he had slipped under her door. It had explicitly said to talk to no one, including him. It was a set of instructions telling her exactly what to do and when, a nearly identical note slipped by him under Frau Maier's door earlier in the evening.

Gruber was extracting them tonight, right under the noses of the Gestapo, then he would likely never see them again. He just prayed it was because they were safe.

Perhaps after the war.

There was no reason. He wasn't sure if he'd like to know what really happened to them. If he never knew, he could imagine they were reunited with their families, and had survived the war, living out their days in peace.

But should he find out differently?

He'd rather live with the fantasy.

He had already sent his family to southwestern Germany, where the Americans and their side of the fight would be arriving shortly, not the bloodthirsty Russians. He hoped once Germany was liberated, he'd join them should he survive the final onslaught.

Liberated.

It was an odd word to associate with the conquering of one's country, yet it was how he felt. At first, he had supported Hitler, like most had, but then it had turned to something different than simple national pride. It had become a cult of personality that he simply couldn't support.

He had kept his mouth shut, said and did what was expected of him, though had stayed in the job he had always wanted, avoiding military service, or any form of supporting the Party.

He was there to serve the people, and he had done so faithfully throughout the war.

A final knock from Frau Lang was followed by a loudly whispered, "Thank you, but I can't go." Footsteps receded to her apartment as he cursed, leaping from his chair. He yanked the door open, and Erika spun on her heel, her eyes wide with shock. He put a finger to his lips and grabbed her by the arm, hauling her into the dark abyss that was his apartment, before closing the door.

"What do you mean you can't go?"

"I have to wait for my Hermann."

Vogel closed his eyes, frustration building. He opened them, staring into the darkness. "He's dead."

She cried out, and he slapped a hand over her mouth.

"You must be quiet, understood?"

She nodded, and he removed his hand. "A-are you sure?"

"Yes." He decided a lie was better than giving her some false sense of hope to cling to. He needed her to leave, and as long as there was some remote possibility Hermann might be returning, he'd never get her to go, and she'd be dead at the Gestapo's hands, possibly tomorrow, perhaps tonight.

She collapsed in his arms and quietly sobbed. He gave her a few moments before gently pushing her away, keeping both hands on her shoulders. "You read the note?"

"Yes."

"Will you be ready?"

There was a pause in the dark, then she finally replied. "Yes."

"Good. Then go back to your apartment and say nothing—it could be bugged. Don't leave a note for anyone, don't leave anything that might suggest what is going on. Take the note I left with you, and give it to the men you will meet. At exactly eleven o'clock, be at the rear entrance. A car will pick you up and take you to your daughter. You will then be taken to a location even I don't know."

"But what if you're wrong, and Hermann is alive?"

"I'm not, but if I somehow am, I will have him sent to join you. Understood?"

She trembled. "Yes."

"Good. Then go, stay quiet, and pack nothing. Just be outside, at the rear entrance, at eleven o'clock."

"All right." She hugged him, gripping him tightly as she shook in his arms. "Thank you so much. I don't know how I can ever repay you."

"Just stay safe, and survive. That's all the payment I need."

She reached up and patted his cheek. "You're a good man, Herr Vogel. I hope you see your wife and children soon."

"So do I."

He opened the door and ushered her out, a final quiet look exchanged before he closed the door and sighed. Sobs escaped her, heard through the door, and he just prayed the neighbors didn't take an interest. She had been clinging to the hope that her husband would show up, but he was never going to.

Yes, he wasn't certain that he was dead, but it had been three days with no word, and everything pointed to him being the dead engineer referred to by Maier.

And on the off chance he did show up, he would indeed try to reunite him with his wife.

But there was no chance of that.

At least, however, she now had a chance. If Gruber held up his end of the bargain, Erika and Michaella would survive the war, then everyone could be reunited to mourn their losses, and get on with their lives.

He stepped over to the window and pulled open the blackout curtain slightly. As expected, a car was parked across the street, two cigarette cherries burning brightly. When he had returned home, he had checked the back alley, and there appeared to be no surveillance set up. The Gestapo didn't seem too concerned with the possibility that Frau Lang might flee. After all, she would have no money, and nowhere to go.

But they hadn't counted on the involvement of a kriminalinspektor, a detective inspector with connections and favors owed.

He returned to his chair and closed his eyes as the air raid continued to hammer the city. This area had been mostly spared so far, though eventually it would become a target. He held out some small hope it might be left alone, since it was nowhere near any factories or military and government facilities, though in reality, he didn't care anymore.

If he died, he died, though he would like to see his family again.

Berlin would be overrun by the Soviets soon.

Very soon.

It would be every man for himself.

The Reich was desperate now, enlisting children to do the fighting, and without a doubt, the police like him would be put on the front lines should it become necessary.

And it would.

And the Soviets would show no mercy, killing every one of them to a man, if need be. All he could hope for was to somehow allow himself to be captured, and survive the day, this a country he was no longer willing to fight for.

He had supported Hitler once, but not when he had turned into a warmonger. He had agreed with taking back the lands stolen after the Great War, he had even agreed with annexing Austria and Czechoslovakia, all accomplished without firing a shot.

But Poland?

That had been a stretch, though reunifying territorially with Prussia made sense, and it had been Polish troops that had attacked first, though he had heard rumors that this wasn't actually true.

But to keep going? To take all of Western Europe, Scandinavia, North Africa?

And what of all the disappearances? He was no fan of the Jews, though they had never wronged him in any way he could think of. They were a convenient scapegoat for the problems of the twenties and thirties, though the real criminals were the French, British, and Americans for imposing the onerous Treaty of Versailles upon them, punishing the German people rather than their leaders, and guaranteeing a meagre existence with the bulk of the country's revenues going toward war reparations.

What had the Allies expected? Of course the people were going to revolt. They merely needed a charismatic leader to organize them, and convince them that enough was enough, and that it wasn't their responsibility to continue to pay for past mistakes made by unelected leaders.

He wondered, when this war was over, would the Allies have learned from their mistakes, and allow the country to rebuild, or would they once again punish the populace with crippling sanctions, thus setting up the continent for a third war, one he feared would be the last ever fought by man.

He sighed, wishing he were in the southwest with his family, away from the madness of Berlin and the mighty Red Army.

The door across the hall clicked shut and a key turned. He steadied his breathing, listening to the footsteps of Frau Lang as she headed for the stairwell. They eventually faded, and he strained to hear past the pounding bombs, praying he didn't hear any shouts of the Gestapo, or screams of a woman.

He heard nothing, though couldn't be sure that meant anything, uncertain as to whether he would ever know if she had been picked up and delivered to safety as promised, or arrested and sent to some Gestapo torture chamber for interrogation before execution.

Perhaps after the war, he would know what happened to the two women, one a neighbor of at least ten years, the other a woman he had never met until this morning.

He drifted off, the rhythmic pounding of the Allied bombs oddly relaxing, a smile on his face as he pictured his two young children and his beautiful wife, none of whom he had seen in months, and none of whom he expected to see again.

And made one last fateful decision before finally giving in to sleep.

He had to make sure Hermann Lang was dead.

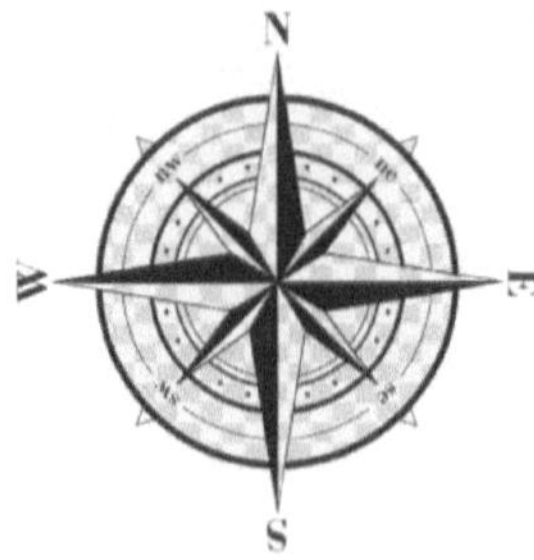

South of Kwidzyn (formerly Marienwerder), Poland

Present Day

"I'm through!"

Officer Jelen rushed toward the entrance of the mineshaft, but was stopped by Inspector Filip Zabek, a new arrival who now had command of the scene.

"Let the engineers make sure it's safe," said Zabek. "The last thing we need is more people killed."

Jelen paced as the crew approached the entrance, but it didn't matter, those inside already emerging from the darkness. He sprinted past the overcautious inspector, and joined the paramedics as they rushed to treat the survivors. A woman carried between two men looked as if she could die at any moment, and the paramedics attended to her first, a gurney brought forward then loaded into the rear of a waiting ambulance, the vehicle pulling away within minutes.

"Which one of you is Daniel Marek?"

A man held up his hand. "That's me."

Jelen stepped over to the man he had spoken to earlier. "Is this everybody?" he asked as he did a quick headcount.

"Yes. Thank God you're here. Where are the professors? Did you find them?"

The man now in charge interrupted. "I'm Inspector Zabek. We're searching for them now. What can you tell us?"

"Nothing much beyond what I said in our conversation. These men arrived, heavily armed and well equipped. They took the crates containing the Amber Room using a forklift and a truck, all equipment they brought with them, then took the professors."

"Why do you think they took them?"

"They needed them to authenticate the find with whoever their buyer was."

Zabek frowned. "And they took nothing else?"

"No, just the Amber Room."

"And this Amber Room, it's valuable?"

Marek exchanged an exasperated look with Jelen. "I should say so! Depending on who you talk to, anywhere from one hundred million to half a billion Euros. Easily."

"And what about the other stuff they didn't take. Is it valuable?"

"Very. Collectively, hundreds of millions as well, probably. But they didn't seem interested. They only seemed to care about the Amber Room. They asked for it specifically, and took only it, despite there being crates filled with gold and other precious artwork."

Zabek scribbled notes as Marek spoke. "And these professors. Why were they here?"

"Professor Acton and his wife, Professor Palmer, are world-renowned in their field, and actually were the ones who made the discovery based upon some old letters found recently by one of their students."

"Both American?"

"No, he's American, she's British, though I think she lives and works in America now that they're married."

"Okay, I'll have the American and British embassies contacted." He motioned toward the paramedics. "Thank you for your help. Please join the others."

"Please find them. If it weren't for them, Professor Lisowski would probably be dead."

"Don't worry, we'll find them."

Marek left to join the others, and Zabek turned to survey the scene, Jelen beside him.

"What now?"

Zabek pointed at several deep tire tracks. "They left in two transport trucks, by the looks of it. I've got a team coming in who should be able to help narrow down what we're searching for. Have your men canvass the area. Talk to everybody along the routes from here to any major highway, see if they saw anything."

"Yes, sir."

"I'm going to contact Interpol and have our professors put out on the wire. I'm afraid if we don't find them soon, we never will."

Interpol Liaison Office, National Crime Agency

London, England

Interpol Agent Hugh Reading pulled at his hair, trying to stay awake as he sat at his desk, bored to tears. Every day he spent here was sucking the life out of him, and he knew he should retire, but he just couldn't bring himself to do it.

I'd go batty stuck in my apartment.

About the only excitement he had in his life was provided by his best friends, Jim Acton and Laura Palmer. They often invited him on their exotic vacations, paying his way, something it had taken some time for him to become comfortable with. He had finally settled on the analogy that due to Laura's extreme wealth thanks to her late brother's Internet business, her buying him a luxury vacation was equivalent to him buying them a fancy cup of coffee.

Something he wouldn't hesitate to do.

Though vacations weren't the only way they provided excitement.

They had a knack for getting into trouble, their recent escapades in the south of France with the Templars nearly getting them all killed, including his son, Spencer.

He smiled at the picture of his son sitting on the corner of his desk. Their trip to Spain, the first as father and son, their relationship strained for over a decade after the divorce, had been interrupted by the troubles in France, but the experience had brought them closer together than ever before, his son confessing he wanted to be a police officer.

It had been the proudest moment of his life when he dropped him off at Hendon Police College last week. It had taken a lot of convincing to get his mother to support the decision, but she had eventually come around. Reading had his suspicions it was mostly because she didn't want to be on the opposite side of the choice as he was, when it was clear Spencer would join regardless of what she said.

These were dangerous times, but if no one let their sons and daughters join the fight, then all would be lost.

His computer beeped at him, and he snapped out of his reverie, grabbing the mouse and clicking on the keyword alert notification in his inbox.

And cursed.

It was from the Interpol office in Warsaw, an alert issued about the possible kidnapping of one American, and one Brit.

His friends.

Not again!

He grabbed his phone, dialing Acton as he read the rest of the notification. It went directly to voicemail. He dialed Laura with the same result. He sat for a moment, wondering who to call next that might actually know something, then smiled. He pulled up the number for Acton's best friend, Gregory Milton, and dialed.

"Hello?"

"Hi Greg, it's Hugh Reading."

"Oh, God, Hugh, have you heard?"

"I just saw a notice. So it's true?"

"Yes. It looks like they were kidnapped sometime this morning, their time, and nobody has seen them since."

"Why them?"

"As far as I can gather, they were taken so that they could authenticate the find when the thieves delivered the Amber Room to their buyer."

Reading scribbled notes the old-fashioned way, as his mind raced. "This 'room,' is it big?"

"Very."

"So not something you just toss in the back of a truck."

"According to Jim, it was contained on two boxcars, so I would suspect you'd need at least one, if not two transport trucks to move it. Can you help?"

"I don't know, but I can bloody well try. I'll have to figure out a way to get to Poland."

"Just use the account, that's what it's there for."

Reading paused. Milton was right. He had access to an emergency fund, Laura having given him all the information he would require should there be a need. He didn't know how much it contained, but it was millions. And he also had permission to make use of their personal travel agent, who arranged pretty much any kind of transport, including access to their private jet network.

And he hated using it, every single time.

He sighed. "I can't believe we have friends that have a bank account with millions of dollars in it just in case they get kidnapped and need to be rescued by their friends."

"It is rather fantastic, isn't it?"

"That's putting it mildly." He blasted some air through his pursed lips, then nodded. "Okay, fine, I'll use the account. I'll contact you later with an update."

"Thanks, Hugh, and good luck. Oh, wait!"

Reading pressed the phone back against his ear. "What?"

"Tommy Granger and Mai Trinh are in Germany. I'll text you their contact info. Tommy's a whiz on computers. He might be able to help you."

"Thanks, I'll keep that in mind." He ended the call and headed for his boss' office, knowing full well how the conversation he was about to have would go. He tapped on the glass, and Betty Richard waved him in.

"Hi, Hugh, what can I do for you?"

Reading closed the door. "An alert has been issued. Professor James Acton and his wife, a British citizen, Professor Laura Palmer, have been kidnapped in Poland."

"Yes, I saw that."

"I want to be assigned to the case."

She shook her head. "I'm sorry, Hugh, I need you here."

"But these are my friends. I have to help them."

Richard motioned to an empty chair. "I'm sorry, Hugh, but we've got that human trafficking operation tomorrow, and you're key."

Reading remained standing. "Bollocks! Anyone can handle that. Give it to Michelle. She's fully briefed, and twenty years younger than me. She can handle it."

"I'm sorry, Hugh, but the discussion is over."

Reading cursed. "Fine!" He pulled out his ID and dropped it on her desk. "I quit!"

Richard's eyes widened. "You can't just quit! You have responsibilities! Obligations!"

"Yes, I do. To my friends. These people have saved my life on too many bloody occasions to leave them hanging, and frankly, they've saved thousands of lives if not more, over the years doing things you'll never know about. I *am* going to help them. I'd prefer to do it with my position intact and the resources of the agency, but if that's not possible, then so be it."

Richard sighed, then chuckled as she shook her head. "Hugh, you're a pain in my bloody ass." She reached forward and grabbed his ID, tossing it at him. "Consider yourself reassigned. Just try not to kill anyone this time."

Reading grinned. "No promises."

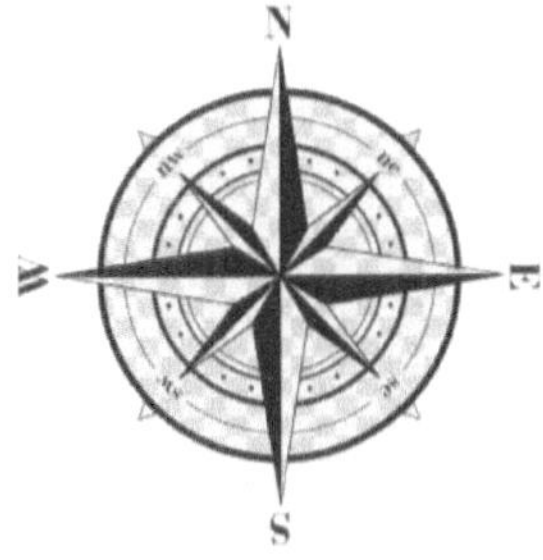

Inselhotel

Potsdam, Germany

"What should we do?"

Tommy rolled over to face Mai, brushing some stray strands of hair from her face, though it was merely an excuse to touch her. "I don't know." He thought for a moment. "What would the professors want us to do?"

Mai shrugged. "They'd want us to stay safe."

Tommy grunted. "Well, that should be fairly easy. We're in Germany, and they're in Poland."

"Are they? We really have no idea where they're taking them, do we?"

Tommy's eyes widened. "You're right." He brought up a map of Europe, pointing at Poland. "They could be heading in pretty much any direction, even Russia."

Mai propped herself up so she could get a better look. "I doubt that. They'd have to go through Belarus or Ukraine, and those are controlled borders."

"Aren't they all?"

"No, not in Europe. Most countries are part of the Schengen Agreement, which means open borders. No passports required."

Tommy was once again impressed with how smart his girlfriend was. "So they could be traveling almost anywhere within the European Union."

"Yes, but let's think about this. They won't head east, because those are all controlled borders. They could head north to the Baltic Sea, but those ports are going to be watched closely." She pointed at the map. "They could head west to Germany, or south to the Czech Republic or Slovakia."

Tommy scrolled the map. "You know, if they went south, they could stay in the former East Bloc countries. Things aren't as tight there as they would be in Germany or France."

Mai nodded. "True, but really, except for heading east, I don't think we've completely ruled anything out."

Tommy growled in frustration. "And we can't even be sure they didn't go east, because maybe these guys have bribed someone to let them through."

Mai sighed. "If only we had some clue as to which way they headed."

Tommy's eyes widened. "Maybe we do!"

"How?"

"The cellphones! There would be a record of the phones the network connected to, and where. If these guys had even one cellphone turned on before they activated the jammer, we might be able to track it!"

"You can do that?"

Tommy stuck his hand out. "Hi, Tommy Granger, hacker extraordinaire. Nice to meet you."

Mai giggled. "I know, I know, I should never doubt you when it comes to computers. It's one of the things I love about you."

He paused, his stomach flipping. "Love?"

Mai blushed and turned away. "Sorry, I shouldn't have said that."

Tommy smiled, his heart hammering. "Do you, umm, love me?"

She stole a glance. "I, ahh, I…"

He grabbed her by the shoulders and stared into her eyes. "I love you too!"

Her face brightened, making her more beautiful than ever, her smile almost stopping his hammering heart. "I love *you!*" She wrapped her arms around him and hugged him hard before finding his lips and dropping a kiss on him that removed any doubt about how she felt.

She pushed him away. "The professors," she gasped, and he groaned in response, adjusting his shorts.

"Right, I almost forgot." He sneaked one last peck.

She loves me!

Operations Center 3, CIA Headquarters

Langley, Virginia

Analyst Supervisor Chris Leroux suppressed a smile as he entered the operations center, lest his well-trained team figure out their boss had got some before arriving for work.

Twice!

"Status?"

Randy Child, their youngest team member and brilliant on the tech side of things, spun in his chair. "Not much yet, beyond confirming that the professors were indeed kidnapped. Interpol has been notified, and the appropriate embassies along with every other law enforcement agency out there. The Poles are handling this by the book."

Sonya Tong, another of his crack analysts, and one with an inappropriate crush on her boss that he was aware of, though he hoped she wasn't, raised a hand. "They've apparently freed those trapped inside the mine. One was shot, but she's stable and at the hospital."

"And we have no idea who took them?"

Tong shook her head. "None."

"Any satellite images of the area?"

Child grunted. "We're working on it, but apparently the primary bird for that area was retasked at the time. I guess nobody's really concerned what happens in Poland these days."

Leroux sat in his chair. "How times have changed. World War Two started there, it's where the Germans and Russians first went to war, it's where the Red Army rolled through to get to Germany, it's where the Solidarity Movement started that helped trigger the collapse of the Soviet Union, and it was one of the first former Warsaw Pact countries to join NATO. And now no one cares."

"I care, boss."

Leroux gave Child a look. "Thanks, Randy, that's helpful."

Randy grinned, giving a thumbs-up, eliciting a snicker from Tong.

The door swung open and their boss, National Clandestine Service Chief Leif Morrison, strode in, waving a greeting to the room. "Good morning, everyone. Status?"

Leroux leaped to his feet before his boss could stop him. "We're trying to track the Actons now, though without knowing what to look for since we didn't have satellite coverage over that area, there's not much we can do until we get a lead. We'll run their faces through every camera in the area, see if we get lucky. They have to have used trucks for all those crates, so we might spot something there."

Child cleared his throat. "Doubt it, boss, there's a major transport route near the mine. My guess is they just blended."

Leroux frowned. "Well, we'll try anyway."

Morrison shook his head. "I hate to do this, but State says they want the Europeans to handle this on their own."

Leroux's eyebrows shot up. "What? Why?"

Morrison shrugged. "Hey, I'm just the messenger here. With things so delicate right now, we don't want the Europeans thinking we're spying on them, so CIA is out"—he raised a finger, cutting off Leroux's imminent protest—"of *Europe*. If you can find anything *outside* of Europe, like who the guys behind this are, who their buyer might be, or if they leave the continent, then we're back in the game. But for now, we aren't allowed to access any European system that we don't already have an open agreement for."

Child cursed, and Leroux almost joined him. "Okay, that ties our hands. We'll look for any reference to this Amber Room in the past couple of days. Maybe that will lead us somewhere."

Morrison headed for the door. "Good luck."

Leroux frowned. "We're not the ones that need it. It's the professors that do."

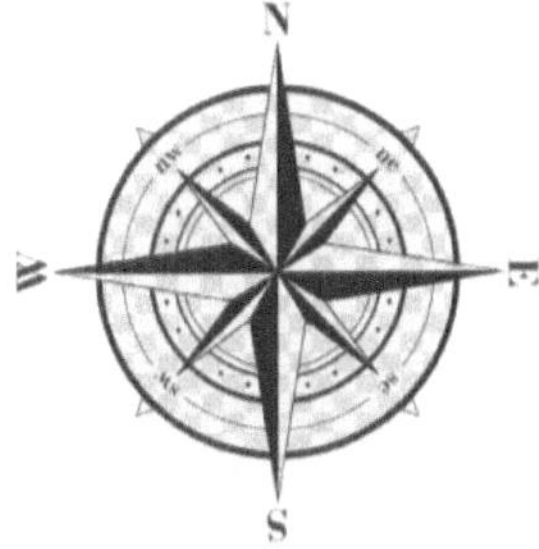

Route A1, Poland

Acton listened to everything said in the car, even if it was only one side of the conversation. Though he gleaned little, he gathered at least some additional intel. He knew there was at least one other team out there still involved, which made sense. There had been three SUVs at the mine when they left, along with the two transport trucks.

He also knew the second team was looking for some type of match for something, and that they had succeeded. The only problem with that little tidbit, was he had no clue whatsoever as to what they were talking about.

At this moment, there was no indication anybody was even searching for them, and if they were, these men seemed unconcerned with the prospect, especially after notification had been received that 'matches' had been found. For now, the real hope was that someone would figure out what trucks had been used, then those trucks would be found on the traffic cameras, a much better prospect than his own face being captured, though he hoped they both had got on some camera at their last bathroom break.

The immediate problem was that everybody at the mine had been in the chamber, so nobody except for them saw the trucks used. Unless there had been a stray sighting, there might be no hope of ever being found. Perhaps someone had witnessed the trucks and thought nothing of it at the time, but would make the connection when the news broke.

It was a possibility, but he wasn't willing to hang their lives on that faint hope. They had to escape somehow. These men were professionals, and their demeanor suggested military backgrounds, and their accents suggested at least the occupants of this vehicle were Russian, though they were speaking English consistently, perhaps in an effort to disguise that fact.

I wonder if they're Spetsnaz.

If they were, they wouldn't hesitate to kill them. He'd have to be a little more careful with his provocations, though he feared that once this was all over, and they had played their part, they'd be killed regardless. They were witnesses who had seen faces.

If they were to escape, then he had to figure out some way to communicate with Laura. Their first bathroom break had provided no opportunity for both of them to escape, their captors only letting them go one at a time, and escorted.

Though there had only been opportunities for one of them to get away.

The rest stops were very busy with plenty of witnesses. He didn't care what happened to him, but Laura had to escape at the next opportunity, as they had no idea how many more they would get. But he needed to somehow convey this to her. His finger tapped on his knee, and he wished they both knew Morse code.

He suppressed a smile as he realized there was one code that they both would know from their pre-smartphone days. He placed his hand on her leg then tapped his index finger, then his middle finger, then his ring finger, then bent his wrist upward, repeated the process, then bent his wrist even further, tapping each finger once again. A total of nine times. He repeated this process once more then exchanged an innocent glance with Laura, who looked at him, her eyes suggesting she had no idea what he was trying to communicate.

He leaned forward. "Can I borrow your phone? I need to text our cleaning lady to let her know we're going to be late."

The man growled at him, but said nothing. Acton sat back and made eye contact once again as he repeated his finger tapping. Laura's eyes suddenly widened and she nodded slightly.

He typed a word out on her leg, purposefully positioning each finger as the nine keys on a phone, 2 through 9 each assigned three to four letters.

It was time to go old school. He tapped.

U-N-D-E-R-S-T-A-N-D.

She shrugged slightly. He repeated the message, slower, and her eyes widened slightly. She placed her hand on his leg and typed out a message.

Y-E-S.

He suppressed a relieved sigh. It would be slow, each letter having to be thought out as he struggled to remember the old style of texting, but it was something that would work, and could be done without their captors knowing.

WILL KILL US.

She nodded.

MUST ESCAPE.

HOW?

IF OUT CAR RUN IF CHANCE.

YOU TOO.

He shook his head.

Her lips thinned. YES. She jabbed her finger hard into his thigh on the last letter.

He frowned. OK.

Though he had no intention of following through on that. He watched as they pulled in behind their two trucks, and he again wondered what was meant by finding matches, matches that had been apparently found. They entered a tunnel, and he made a point of leaning against the window, hoping a traffic camera might pick up an image of his face, then leaned back toward Laura before he was noticed.

As they emerged from the tunnel, his eyes narrowed, something different about the two trucks ahead as they took a slight bend to the right, revealing the fabric-clad sides.

What happened to the beer bottles?

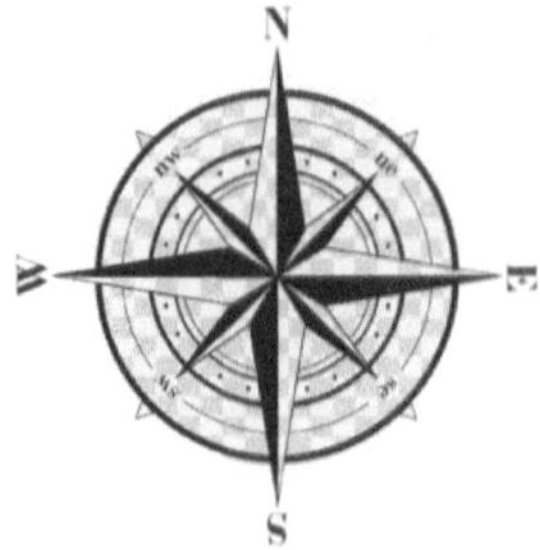

South of Kwidzyn (formerly Marienwerder), Poland

"We're looking for two large trucks."

Officer Jelen gave the tech a look. "No shit. I think we're going to need more than that."

A flurry of technical data, including number of axles, tires, tire types, estimated vehicle length, width, and more, was spat at him as if to make a point. Then a tablet was shoved in front of his face, showing a Mercedes transport truck.

"We're looking for two of these."

Inspector Zabek had a slight smile. "You're sure?"

"Well, there's some guesswork involved, but I'm fairly confident."

"And the other vehicles?"

"Three SUVs, but we're not sure the type. They seem to be much heavier than an SUV should be."

Zabek's eyes narrowed. "Could they have loaded some of the cargo in them?"

"I doubt it. The crates the witnesses described were pretty big. And this was pretty evenly distributed."

"What does your guesswork tell you?"

The tech hesitated. "Well, *if* I had to hazard a guess, I'd say they've been modified."

"In what way?"

"Armored in some way."

Zabek cursed. "Which means they're expecting trouble, and ready for it."

Jelen took a more cooperative tack. "So, is there anything else you can tell us about the SUVs?"

"Nothing except that they're all probably identical."

Zabek frowned. "That's not going to really help us much unless they stay together, which I doubt."

The tech shrugged. "Sorry, that's the best we can do. We'll take all the data back to the lab and continue working on it."

"Okay, let's start pulling footage, see if we get lucky."

"Sir!" One of Jelen's fellow officers rushed over, unsure of who to address. Jelen motioned toward Zabek. "Sir, I just spoke to a farmer down the road. He said he saw two large trucks leaving here this morning. Beer trucks."

Zabek's eyes narrowed. "Beer?"

"Yes."

Zabek looked at the tech. "That doesn't really match what we're looking for, does it?"

The tech shook his head. "No, not really. I'm quite confident we're looking for curtain side transport trucks, not local beer delivery trucks. We're talking long distance, heavy loads."

Jelen tapped his chin. "Maybe the witness was confused."

Zabek turned toward him. "Explain."

"Maybe they just had beer company advertising on the sides."

Zabek nodded. "That would explain it." He pointed at the cop. "Go find out if that's what he meant."

"Yes, sir!"

"And get a notice out that we're looking for two curtain side trucks with possible beer logos on the sides."

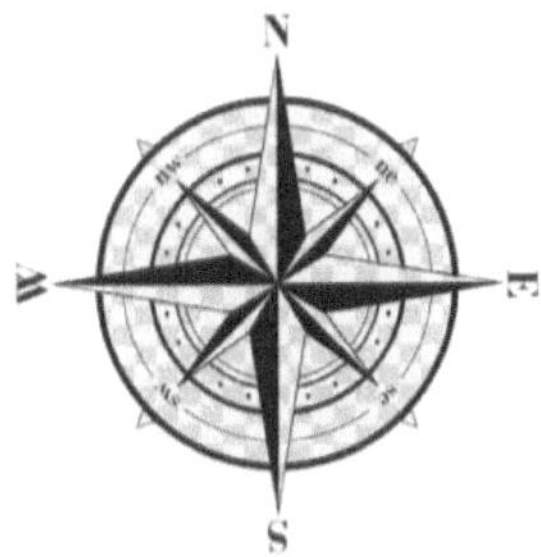

Inselhotel Potsdam

Potsdam, Germany

Mai Trinh stared dreamily at Tommy as he hammered away at the keyboard. She had never told anyone that she loved them before, and had certainly never had anyone tell her the same. *This* was what it felt like to be a woman. She was in love, and her entire life had changed in an instant with a few simple words.

She just wished she could share the news with her family.

She was still in contact with them through social media, though she had to be careful about what she said. She wasn't worried that the Vietnamese government might target her in America where she now called home—they weren't China. Vietnam was a poor country, probably happy to have their "dissidents" outside of their borders, as long as they kept quiet.

Which she did.

Her concerns were entirely centered on her family, especially her father. Her mother was dead, and her brother was a petty criminal, making his problems his own.

But her father was innocent.

Their messages were passed through friends, computers never something he had shown any interest or aptitude in, though she was hoping he'd someday embrace a smartphone so they could at least text.

One day.

Her eyes glistened with the knowledge that she would probably never see him again, and he would never get to meet his son-in-law should they get married.

Her heart skipped a beat.

Married!

She smiled at Tommy as her heart raced with the idea. She had daydreamed of the possibility, of course. What woman didn't? But to actually face the prospect, was an entirely different thing. Two years ago, she never would have dreamed she'd be dating, let alone contemplating marrying a white guy, yet here she was, lying in bed with him, neither with a stitch of clothing on, working to save the two people who had brought them together.

She sighed.

"You okay?"

Her smile broadened. "Perfect."

Tommy paused, staring into her eyes for a moment. "I love you."

Her stomach flipped. "I don't think I'll ever get tired of hearing that."

He leaned in and gave her a quick kiss, then gestured at the laptop. "I think I've got it."

"What?"

He pointed at a red blip on a map. "A cellphone entered the area just before the jammer was activated, and now it's a couple of hundred miles south. All of the other signals that were present before this new signal arrived, are either still there, or off."

"So you know where the bad guys are?"

Tommy grinned. "Yup!"

"We need to tell someone."

"Didn't Dean Milton say that Agent Reading was now involved?"

"Yes! Can we call him?"

"I don't have his number."

Mai grabbed the phone. "I'll call the dean. He'll have it."

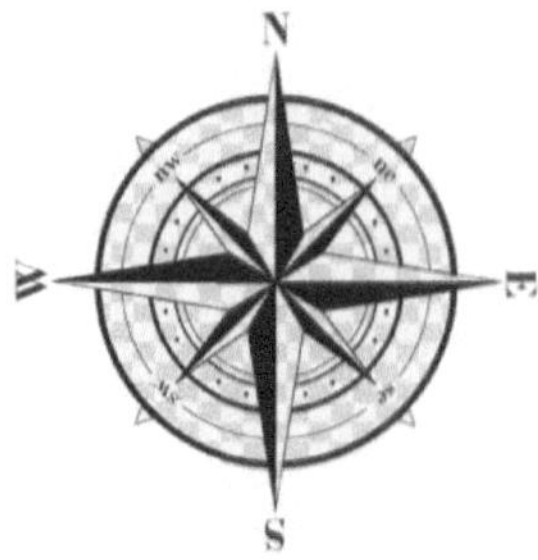

Route A1, Poland

"Sir, our monitors are showing your cellphone has been compromised."

Alexie Tankov cursed at the message received through his comms as he retrieved his cellphone from his jacket pocket. He removed the SIM card and hit the button to lower the window. He snapped the phone over the car door, then tossed the device onto the road, eliciting a few honked horns, soon silenced as the window closed.

"By who?"

"Unknown, sir. We just know it's been pinged several times, unauthorized. Probably CIA or another state's equivalent."

Tankov frowned. "Then that means they'll be able to backtrack us on camera. If they've got my phone, then they might have others. Everyone, scrap your phones and switch to backups. Team Two, find us two new matches."

"Roger that."

His driver, Arseny Utkin, handed him his phone and Tankov repeated the process, disposing of the device before pulling two new phones from the glove compartment. They had been shut off since they were configured at the start of the mission, so there was no way they could have been compromised.

Someone must have figured out his phone had been at the mine. They were clever, though it was a possibility they had planned for. The order had been that all phones were to be turned off ten minutes before reaching the mine, but he had turned his on to test the jammer.

A jammer that hadn't been powered up properly.

He belted Utkin on the shoulder.

"Hey, what was that for?" he protested as their vehicle swerved slightly.

"For messing up the jammer."

Utkin frowned. "Yeah, that one's on me."

"Damn right it is."

The screw up had meant his phone was on the cellular network for several seconds.

Apparently, enough for somebody to figure out it shouldn't have been there.

Very clever.

"I need another pee break."

"Hold it."

"I'm serious. Your guy was watching me last time like he was interested in making Jim, Jr.'s acquaintance. I've got a shy bladder."

Tankov glared at him, though the man was lucky this time.

He had to go as well.

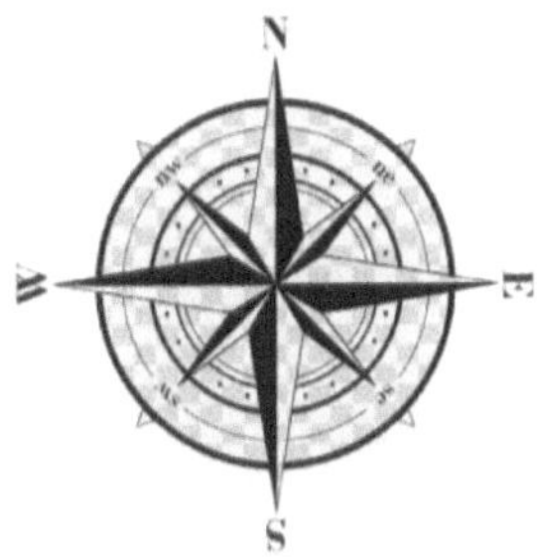

Somewhere over Europe

Agent Hugh Reading had raided the proverbial kitty, and was feeling guilty about it as he usually did, despite the fact the only reason he was on this luxury Gulf V was that his friends paying for it were missing, and now confirmed, without a doubt, kidnapped.

The flight attendant, a statuesque blonde who would look at home on any fashion runway in Europe, strode toward him, her form-fitting blue uniform a constant distraction, despite her age being less than half his.

And she was the source of most of his guilt.

A dedicated flight attendant, just for me.

"You really don't have to be waiting on me. I'm not rich."

She flashed a Hollywood smile. "My job is to serve you. I come with the plane whether you need me or not."

"Huh. Next time can I specify no flight attendant?"

"Sorry, it's required in case there's an emergency."

Reading frowned, though did feel slightly better knowing that she wasn't an option he had forgotten to tick off while making the reservation.

"Are you sure I can't get you anything?"

Reading sighed.

You might as well let the poor girl work. She'll be bored otherwise.

"Just a Diet Coke if you've got it."

"Of course." She smiled. "Can I add a splash of something in there for you?"

He shook his head. "No, I'm on duty."

As if on cue, his laptop beeped at him with a notification about the vehicles the Polish now suspected were involved.

Finally, a lead!

His drink was delivered with a smile and a gleam, and he had to resist the urge to lean out into the aisle as she walked away.

You're a dirty old man.

His phone rang, startling him, and he almost spilled his drink. He put it on the table in front of him and took the call. "Reading."

"Oh, hi, Agent Reading, this is Tommy Granger, from Prof—"

"I know who you are. Have you found something new?"

"Umm, yes, sir. I was able to track one of the bad guy's phones."

Reading chuckled.

'Bad guys.'

"Excellent work. I won't bother asking how. Where is it?"

"Until a few minutes ago, it was heading south on the A1 highway in Poland, approaching the Czech Republic. I lost contact with it just a few minutes ago. It might have gone offline, or they might have figured out they were being tracked."

"Do you have the number?"

"Yes, sir. I'll send it to you right away."

"Good. I'll see if Interpol can find out anything about it. Anything else?"

"Well, we'd like to help."

"I'm not sure what more you can do."

There was a pause. "Well, umm, let's just say that I'm very good at accessing things I'm not supposed to. I was thinking that since we know where they've been traveling the past several hours, maybe I could give the traffic cameras a go."

Reading smiled. "That would be illegal."

"Only if I'm caught."

He frowned. "With an attitude like that, one day you will be."

"Okay, I understand."

He shook his head. "You're going to do it, anyway, aren't you?"

"Ahh, yes?"

"Fine, I just don't want to know about it unless you find something. And make sure you don't get caught."

"I never do!"

He ended the call and sighed.

Kids!

His phone vibrated with the suspect's number, and he forwarded it to his partner at Interpol, then pulled up a map on his laptop. He followed the A1 south, picking a spot a couple of hours ahead of their suspects' current location, then waved the flight attendant over.

"Yes, sir?"

"Tell the pilot to reroute to Krakow."

"Right away, sir."

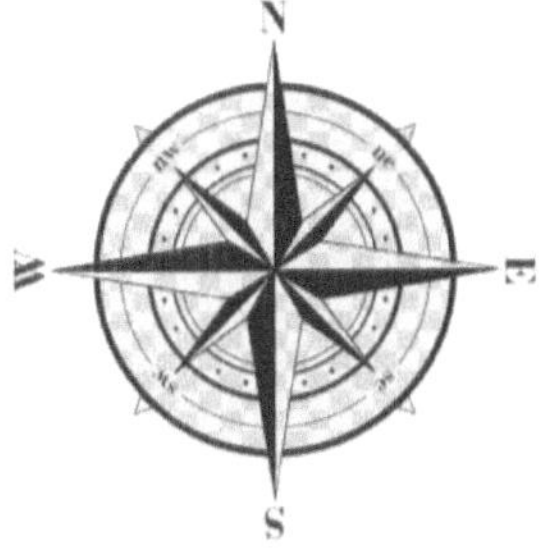

South of Kwidzyn (formerly Marienwerder), Poland

Officer Jelen listened to the update provided by one of his fellow officers, Inspector Zabek graciously allowing him to remain involved, mostly as a liaison between him and the locals he was familiar with.

"The old farmer has confirmed it was two trucks with beer company advertising, *not* beer trucks like he originally said."

Zabek nodded. "Good work. Traffic cameras caught two trucks matching the description coming onto the A1. We're setting up roadblocks at the border as we speak."

Jelen's eyebrows popped. "That far?"

"They're over four hours ahead. That's almost five-hundred-kilometers they could have traveled."

The sound of a helicopter approaching had Jelen turning along with the dozens of personnel now on scene.

"That's my ride," said Zabek, heading toward the landing zone nearby. He pointed at Jelen. "I want you to come with me. You can still serve as my liaison."

Jelen grinned at Krakowski. "Yes, sir!" He rushed after Zabek then climbed in the chopper, this the first time he had been in one. Zabek showed him how to strap in, then handed him a headset as they lifted off. He put the headphones over his ears, the din of the rotors cut, and positioned the mic in front of his mouth as they lifted off.

He watched his colleagues below shrink to ants as they rose, the entire area crawling with police as well as academics from Gdansk and Warsaw, there to document the massive treasure trove discovered inside the old abandoned mine.

I wonder how many other locations like this are hidden around Europe.

He stared at the scarred hillside, its secret finally revealed.

And why, whoever buried these things, never came back for them.

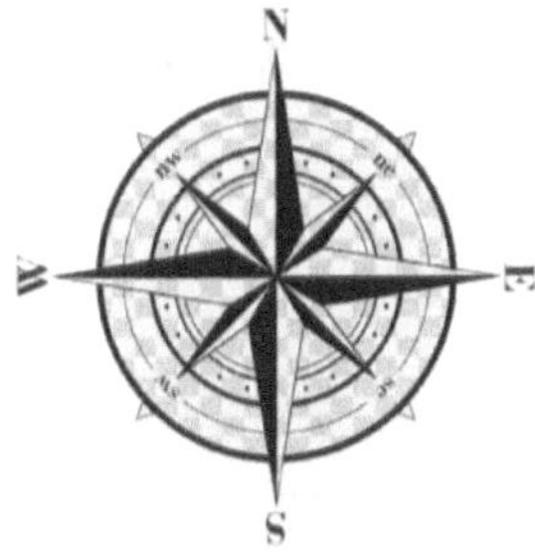

South of Marienwerder, West Prussia

Nazi Germany

February 3, 1945

Vogel sat in the back of the car assigned to him, his driver silently carrying out his duty, a duty Vogel wasn't happy about. It had taken several days to get the permits to travel to Marienwerder, the location provided by the late Dieter Maier for the locomotive he had picked up, but one of the stipulations was that he had to take a driver familiar with the roads.

Command claimed they were concerned he might get lost and fall into Russian hands. It was more likely they feared he was making a run for it to rejoin his family. The thought had occurred to him, though traveling across Germany without being picked up would be impossible.

At least without the help of criminals like Gruber.

"We're here."

Vogel leaned forward, his eyes narrowing at the sight before him. There were several transport trucks being loaded by a dozen men operating heavy equipment, one truck stacked with what appeared to be railroad tracks.

What's going on here?

They passed through what at one time must have been a gate, but the fence that surrounded the area was gone, only the posts remaining, and those were being removed. He surveyed the hill ahead of them, then pointed to the left, something appearing off. The driver stopped about fifty yards from the hillside, and Vogel climbed out, approaching what appeared to be a carefully disguised collapsed tunnel entrance. He had little doubt that given a few weeks, perhaps months, no one would even know there had been something here.

He turned and scanned the area, whoever was in charge clearly attempting to remove all evidence that anything had ever happened here. He knew from the records it was a mine, and that it was due to be shut down. So why would they hide any evidence it had been there? Perhaps if there was still something here to be mined by the enemy, but why the subterfuge? Just blow the tunnels, making it impossible to work.

None of this made sense.

Unless they're hiding something else.

The locomotive had been here, he could even see where there used to be tracks leading to the disguised entrance, crews raking out the ground as he watched. The locomotive wouldn't be here for no reason.

It had obviously delivered something. The question was what. It was a question that would probably go unanswered, though whatever the answer was, it was worth killing for to protect.

He was convinced now more than ever that Hermann Lang had been killed here after delivering a secret cargo, then Dieter Maier was sent to collect the locomotive, and killed for what he had seen.

Nobody could know something was hidden here, and secrets that deep were held by organizations like the Gestapo.

Or the SS, like the colonel now marching quickly toward him.

"Who are you? Why are you here?"

Vogel kept his immediate uneasiness hidden, or at least he hoped he had. An angry SS colonel was dangerous. Extremely dangerous, especially outside of Berlin, where he at least had some protections.

Vogel presented his ID. "Detective Inspector Vogel, Kriminalpolizei. I'm investigating a missing person's case." He decided a bit of the truth might get him out of this, but he had to be careful.

"Who are you looking for?"

"A train engineer named Hermann Lang. One of his colleagues said he might have been killed here by partisans. I was just hoping to confirm the story so his wife can stop wondering what happened."

The colonel's eyes flared. "This is military property, under the direct control of the SS. You have no permission to be here. You are under arrest!"

Vogel raised his identification and travel permits once again as his heart slammed.

He was about to die.

"I have the proper travel permits, and you have no authority over me." He motioned to his driver to bring the car around. "I am, however, perfectly willing to discuss this with our superiors in Berlin." He opened the rear door and climbed in. He leaned out. "Do you want to travel in my car, or do you have your own?"

The colonel glared at him, clearly unsure of what to do, no one probably having challenged his authority before.

Vogel couldn't wait, as at least half a dozen guards were strolling over.

"Very well, I'll see you in Berlin." He shut the door. "Drive."

His driver stared in the rearview mirror for a moment, unsure of what to do.

"Now, if you want to make it out of here alive," hissed Vogel.

The man shook out a terrified nod then hit the gas, sending them toward the entrance a little too quickly.

"Slow down, or they'll open fire."

The gas was eased off, and Vogel resisted the urge to check behind them and see what was happening. As they cleared the gate without incident, he breathed a little easier.

"Are they following us?"

The driver glanced in the mirror then paled. "I-I think so. There's a car pulling through the gate."

"All right, just stay calm. Set a good pace as if you're in a hurry to get back to Berlin, but not a crazy pace like you're trying to escape someone."

The accelerator was pressed, pushing Vogel into his seat.

"Easy."

"Sorry, sir. It's just that I'm about to piss my pants."

Vogel laughed, trying to make the man at ease while he too struggled to control his full bladder. He had little doubt this SS colonel intended to kill them both to preserve whatever secret was hidden in the former mine.

What didn't make sense to him was the location. Why hide something of obvious importance to the Reich, where the Russians would soon be arriving? It made no sense.

His jaw nearly dropped as he realized what must be going on.

They were planning for *after* the war.

Was it weapons for an armed resistance? It was possible, though again, why here? Wouldn't the resistance be in Germany?

Gold to finance the resistance? Again, why here? And if it were just gold, why not transport it to Germany? Even if the train were hit by the Allies, it was just gold. Pick it up, load it on another train, and continue on.

What if it's something fragile?

He chewed his cheek. If it was fragile, the only thing he could think of was weapons. Ammunitions, bombs—that he could understand, again for some type of resistance.

And again he returned to the question of why locate it here and not Germany?

He sighed. Whatever it was, it was important to someone, and important to the SS. And the Gestapo.

And now they knew, without a doubt, he was involved.

Even if he made it to Berlin somehow, he wouldn't be allowed to remain alive. They were killing all the witnesses, and he had known that, yet his ridiculous notion of justice had sealed his fate, and that of this innocent driver.

They were both already dead.

They rounded a bend, and he saw no one ahead, a decision made. "Stop here. Quickly."

"Why?" asked his terrified driver.

"I have to use the bathroom. Quickly!"

The driver slammed on his brakes and Vogel stepped out before they had even come to a halt. The car carrying the SS colonel rounded the bend and skidded to a stop, the SS colonel leaning out his window.

"What is going on here?"

"Bathroom break!" replied Vogel as he relieved himself.

"Hurry up!"

Vogel glanced over his shoulder at the impatient Colonel, wondering if the man might just kill him here and now, though counting on him not wanting to shoot a man in the back while he relieved himself. "The more you yell at me, the longer this is going to take." He finished, then drew his sidearm, stepping through the brush lining the road with it behind his back.

"It's about time!"

Vogel nodded. "I agree." He pumped two rounds into the colonel, then two more into the man's driver. He double-checked that they were dead, then reached into the shoulder pocket of the colonel, retrieving a notepad he had seen him making notes in, just in case he had recorded the name of the detective inspector that had visited the mine.

Vogel's driver ran toward him, his hands on top of his head, his mouth agape. "Are you insane? What were you thinking?"

Vogel leaned in and put the car in neutral. "That if we reached Berlin with him, we'd both be dead."

The driver froze. "Why? What have you gotten me into?"

"Nothing you need concern yourself with. You are *my* driver. You were following my orders, and I had all the proper paperwork for this journey. You did nothing wrong. When we arrive in Berlin, you will drop me off, then immediately report to your superiors exactly what has happened here."

"They'll kill you for sure!"

Vogel nodded. "Yes, I'm sure they will." He pushed the car toward a nearby farmer's access road. "Don't just stand there, help me push this thing out of sight before someone finds us."

"Y-yes, sir!"

As they pushed the car out of sight, Vogel realized he had now transitioned from loyal detective, to traitorous murderer, and every one of his colleagues across the Reich would now be searching for him.

And he could think of only one way out of his predicament.

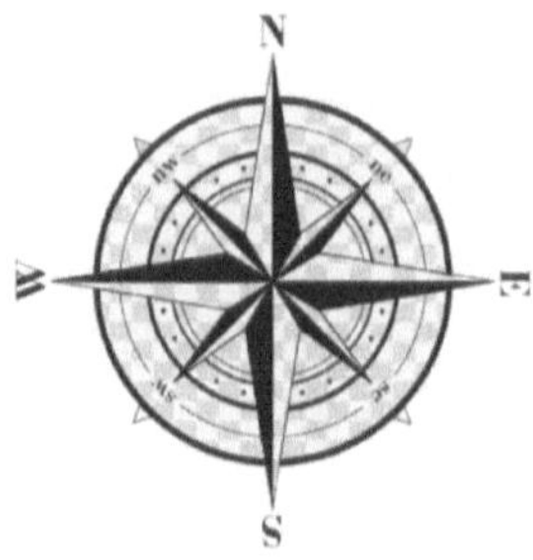

Route A1, Poland

Present Day

Acton had had too many opportunities to escape, but there was no way he would do it. Not with Laura still in the car. If he got away, he had no idea what they'd do to her, and he couldn't risk it. Yet it also gave him hope that she could succeed where he had intentionally failed.

She had received the same training he had, knew what to do in these situations, and was the strongest woman he had ever met. If anyone could do it, she could.

He climbed back in the car, the door slammed shut behind him, then their captor rounded the rear of the vehicle and opened the opposite door.

"Let's go."

Laura flashed him a smile, and he gave her an almost imperceptible nod, his eyes imploring her to follow through on their plan. The door closed and he watched them head for the bathrooms. A crowd of tourists approached, and he suppressed a gasp when Laura whipped around, grabbing her captor's wrist and bending it down, the expression on his face revealing his intense pain. She booted him in the head then sprinted, screaming something and pointing at the downed man, a large crowd converging on the area.

The driver cursed and threw his door open. Acton reached forward and grabbed him by the back of the shirt, holding him in place, then dragged him into the back seat so he could inflict some real damage.

The door opened and a gun pressed against his temple.

"I'll kindly ask you to stop that, Professor."

Acton let go, cursing, their captor already returned. The door slammed shut once again, and within moments, they were underway.

Yet it didn't matter.

Laura had escaped, and now, should he die, he could die knowing that she was safe and among friends who loved her.

Laura sprinted toward the largest group of men she could see, a football team from the looks of it. She glanced over her shoulder to see her captor climbing into their SUV and leaving, her beloved James still in the back seat, staring at her.

But she was free, their captors gone, and now it was up to her to save him.

She knew him so well, she hadn't been surprised when he had returned from the bathroom. There was no way he would be the one who escaped—it was always going to be her. He was too chivalrous to leave her behind.

And now that she was free, she had to be as calm as possible, as smart as possible. Calling local police would just delay things, and probably prevent her from making further calls for perhaps hours. She had to call someone who would believe her immediately, and would know who to call to take action.

Hugh!

Reading was one of her best friends, Interpol, and was the exact person she needed to contact. One of the men asked her something in Polish, concern on his face. She waved him off, feeling safe now, and not wanting to draw any more attention to herself now that her captors had left.

"Are you okay?" he asked in English.

"Yes, thank you. I guess you should never accept rides from strangers."

The man nodded, along with the others. "Especially as a woman. Can we help? Do you need a ride?"

She smiled. "That would just be getting a ride from more strangers, now, wouldn't it?"

His jaw dropped, the poor man uncertain of what to say.

She laughed. "I'm just joking with you. I'm okay, you don't need to worry about me. I'm just going to call for a friend to pick me up. Thank you."

She hurried toward a small restaurant, spotting a payphone in a hallway to the left. She picked up the receiver and dialed the operator, shaking with relief as her ordeal was finally over, and, she feared, her husband's was only about to get worse.

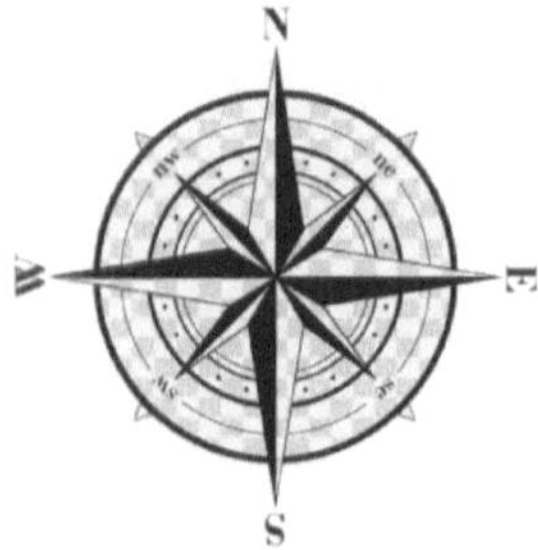

Gruber Residence

Berlin, Nazi Germany

February 3, 1945

Vogel found himself once again sitting across from Gruber, but this time there were no cigars, no snifters of cognac. Instead, he had the distinct impression Gruber might direct his men to carry out the orders probably already issued to every Gestapo agent in the Reich.

Kill Detective Inspector Wolfgang Vogel.

"There are a lot of people looking for you." Gruber leaned back in his chair. "I must admit, I never thought you had it in you. Murder! Two men, including an SS colonel, no less!"

Vogel was impressed at how well informed Gruber was, though he shouldn't have been surprised. The man had his fingers in so many pies, so many people on his payroll, he doubted there was little that went on in the Reich without his knowledge.

Though perhaps there was one thing.

"I had no choice. It was him or me."

"And why was that?"

"Because I saw something I wasn't supposed to."

"And *what* was that?"

He had no idea, but he couldn't let Gruber know that. It was the only card he held. "I'll tell you when I'm with my family."

Gruber chuckled. "I've already moved two people for you, with what is now a worthless promise. You'll be dead before the war is out, and dead men don't make good witnesses at trials."

"Only if I'm caught. If you get me to my family, then I'll still be alive to testify on your behalf."

"You shot an SS colonel. If I'm caught trying to move you, not even my father will be able to protect me." Gruber shook his head. "No, you're too hot. In fact, I think it's best I build a little more goodwill." He flicked his wrist. "Take him to Gestapo headquarters."

Two of Gruber's men stepped forward, hauling him out of his seat.

"Wait! Don't you want to know what I found?"

"Not interested."

The men continued to drag him toward the door, Gruber already turning his back on him. "A train full of gold!"

Gruber's chair stopped spinning and he raised a hand, his men pausing. "How much gold?"

Vogel shook the two men off, returning to his chair, resting his hands on the back as he leaned in toward a reengaged Gruber. "At least an entire boxcar worth, probably more. I only had time to see the one before the colonel caught me."

"And why should I believe you?"

"Why else would the SS want me dead?"

"Because you killed one of their own!"

"No, the only reason I killed him was because he *already* wanted me dead. Like I said before, it was him or me. I killed him to save my own life, and he wanted me dead because I found his gold."

"Where?"

Vogel smiled. "Get me to my family, and I'll give you the location. You'll be richer than you could have ever imagined."

Gruber leaned back in his chair, then clapped, slowly, deliberately, shaking his head. He rose and extended a hand. "Well played, Detective Inspector. *Very* well played."

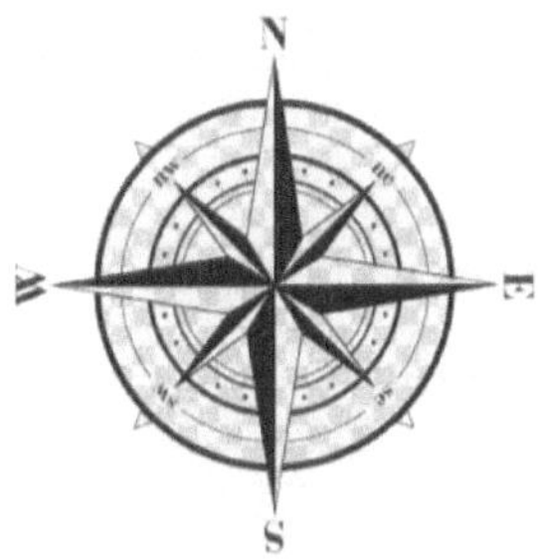

Route A1, Poland

Present Day

"We've got a roadblock ahead. Looks like they're pulling over all the trucks."

Tankov cursed at the update from Team Two. "Okay, they must have discovered what happened at the mine and somehow figured out we were heading south."

Utkin nodded. "Probably whoever hacked your phone."

Tankov gave him a look. "Remind me to give you a good beating when this is all over."

Utkin grunted. "Yeah, I'll be sure to."

Tankov laughed. "Team Two, what can you tell me? Are they searching everyone?"

Laughter replied. "Only those advertising beer!"

He smiled. *"Please* tell me our new matches aren't advertising anything that could be remotely mistaken for beer."

"Nope. One's got a tasty looking soup, the other a grocery chain. No way they'll be mistaken for beer."

Tankov breathed a sigh of relief, the one part of their plan not completely under their control, working for the moment. "Excellent. Let me know as soon as they're through."

"Roger that."

They rapidly approached a long line of trucks, dozens of police vehicles ahead dividing the traffic between transport trucks and smaller vehicles like their SUV. They approached the normally ceremonial border, the Schengen Agreement giving passport-free access throughout the European Union. He spotted their two vehicles in the mix, and smiled.

Perfect.

The tech they were using was highly advanced and extremely expensive. It was essentially a highly flexible television screen, or more accurately, a grid of them, covering both sides of their curtain side trucks. It was treated to give any image it projected a matte appearance with no backlighting, and as long as no one touched them, or examined them too closely, they'd never know what they were seeing was actually a computer-generated image from scans his second team had made of actual vehicles on the road with them.

It was incredible tech they had used several times before on operations throughout Europe, and it was only a matter of time before it was legitimately rolled out to trucks around the continent for rotating advertising, once the costs had come down.

What an incredible time to be alive.

He glanced at Acton in the back seat, the man quiet since his wife had made her escape. He was curious to see if the man's bladder problems continued, or if he had somehow made a miraculous recovery.

Professor Palmer's moves were impressive. It was clear she had received self-defense training from someone, her moves not something taught at the local women's center, but military.

Special Forces.

They were executed with precision and decisiveness, something most civilians failed at. They might know the moves, but once in the situation, they couldn't execute them, immediately doubting their abilities, and scared to actually inflict harm.

This woman had none of those qualms.

She had disarmed him and inflicted excruciating pain within seconds, catching him completely off guard. It was his fault she had escaped and drawn attention to them, and he had no doubt reports were already going out over the wire to watch for their vehicle.

A helicopter landing to his right caught his attention, a man climbing out who appeared like he owned the place, clearly some government official in charge, and probably the man now pursuing him.

"Hello, Czech Republic!"

He smiled at Utkin's declaration as they cleared the border, and this new arrival's jurisdiction. He activated his comms. "Time to switch vehicles."

The acknowledgments came in, and Utkin changed lanes in anticipation of their exit. They had eight more hours of travel, then they'd be safe, but until then, they'd have to be a lot more careful than they had been.

Tracked cellphones and an escape were not the way things were supposed to be playing out.

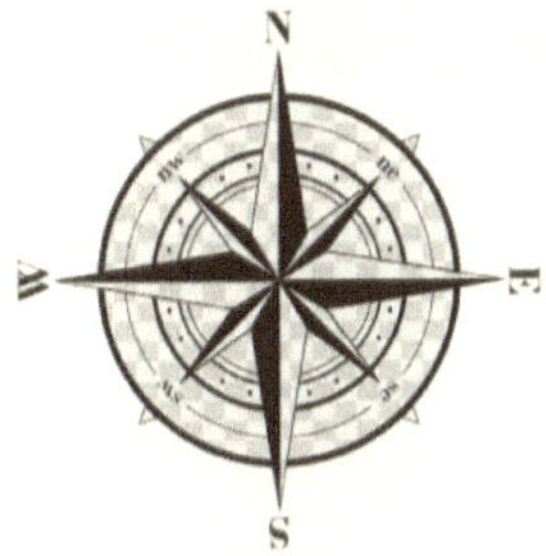

Inselhotel Potsdam

Potsdam, Germany

"Wait! Look!"

Mai pointed at the screen and Tommy tapped a key, halting the footage racing forward as they tried to track the two trucks involved in the professors' kidnapping. They had quickly found them once they knew where and what to look for, but they were hours behind, and now had to perform the painstaking task of following them past each traffic camera. Skipping ahead could have them missing a turn-off, or misjudging the speed and assuming they had turned off when they hadn't.

Slow and steady would win this, and they were quickly gaining back the time lost.

Like now.

Mai had been correct, the two trucks, beer logos emblazoned on their sides, had entered a tunnel about three hours ago.

"Check out that black SUV behind them. Can you zoom in on the driver's side rear window?"

Tommy dragged the mouse pointer, the image zooming in, his software smoothing it out somewhat. "Holy crap! That's Professor Acton!"

Mai tossed her head back. "Thank God, he's alive! Can you see Professor Palmer?"

Tommy ran the zoomed image forward and back, but they could see no one except the two men in the front seats, and the brief moment where Acton had leaned against the window. "I think he did that on purpose."

Mai nodded. "He's a very smart man." She leaned in. "Can you get the license plate?"

"Should be able to." Moments later, he had it.

"We should get that and this image of the two in the front seat to Agent Reading."

Tommy agreed, already sending the info as he called the agent.

"Reading."

"Hello, sir, it's Tommy. I've found him, or at least where he was a few hours ago."

"I thought we already knew that?"

Tommy gulped, the man gruffer than he was used to, and his British accent intimidating. "Well, we did, but I mean, I have an image showing Professor Acton in the back of an SUV."

"What?" This excited the man. "They're not in the trucks?"

"No. Well, I don't know about Professor Palmer, but—" His eyes narrowed as he noticed something on his laptop, the footage continuing forward on the camera at the tunnel exit. "Wait, something's wrong."

"Are you okay?" Reading sounded concerned for their safety.

"No, I mean, yeah, just a sec." He backed up the footage, and he spotted the SUV following the two transport trucks, two trucks that had beer logos on their sides when they entered. "Holy shit!"

"What?"

"The trucks! They've changed their side panels!"

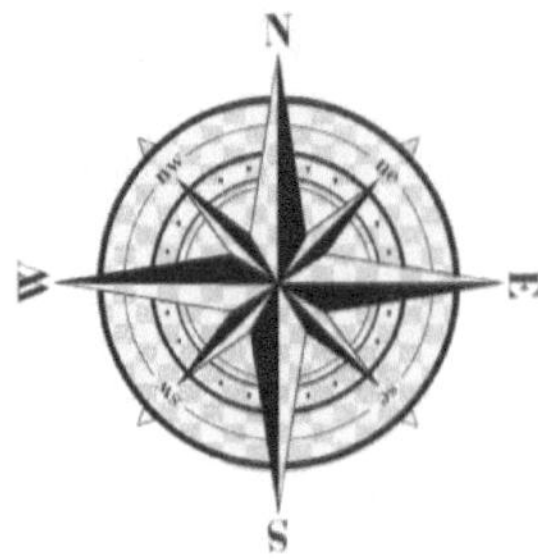

Polish-Czech Republic Border

Officer Jelen stood uselessly on the side of the road, watching truck after truck get waved through, those with anything that remotely appeared to be a beer company logo, including soft drinks or alcohol, pulled over and searched.

Nothing had turned up so far, and he had a feeling nothing would.

These guys were too good to be caught at a roadblock. They would have planned for this eventuality, and figured out a strategy against it. Most likely they had already left the road, traveling west toward Germany, though if they had, it had to have been recently, as they had been caught on camera north of here a couple of hours ago, though they had been lost after that.

And that had him concerned. Could they have offloaded the cargo to different vehicles? It was a possibility, but he doubted it. It would take too long, and they could be discovered, unless they did it inside, away from prying eyes. And if they had a facility to do the switch, wouldn't it be wiser to just sit pat and wait until things cooled down?

He wouldn't.

Europe wasn't like most other parts of the world. It was fairly small, especially when you discounted Scandinavia. The United States was almost three times the geographic area, and there were no longer any guarded interior borders. Their suspects could travel from Poland to the Baltic Sea, the Atlantic Ocean, or the Mediterranean if they wanted, unimpeded.

Or simply to another country within the union, if that was their final destination.

And they could do it all in less than a day.

They were already almost six hours into their journey, so if they were leaving Poland, they probably had already done so, and they were too late.

He watched a truck pass advertising soup, and his stomach grumbled, downright gurgling as another advertising a grocery store followed, delicious baked goods displayed on its side that had his mouth watering, then his jaw dropping.

"Stop those two trucks!"

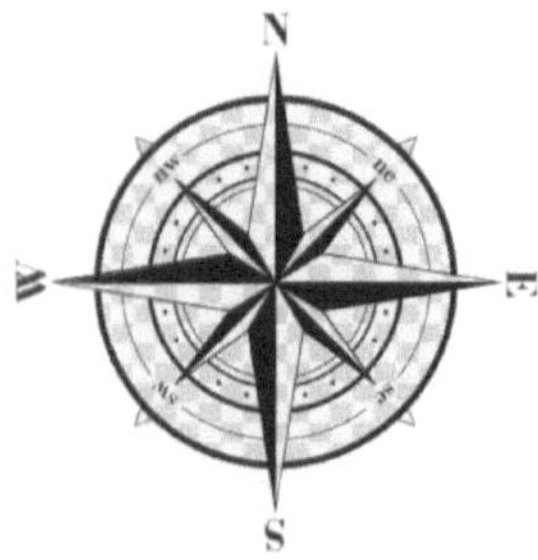

Operations Center 3, CIA Headquarters

Langley, Virginia

"So, I think I've figured out what's going on."

The room, including Leroux, turned toward Child. "Explain."

"I found this." Child tapped at his keyboard, then motioned toward the large set of screens curving across the front of the operations center. A photo of an opened crate with an unfortunately unattractive face blocking half of it, was displayed as part of a Facebook page.

"What is that? Polish?"

"Yup. This guy is bragging that he discovered the Amber Room yesterday."

Leroux's eyes narrowed as he rose, stepping closer to the screen, trying to pick out details in the background. "Who is he?"

"A nobody, as far as I can tell. I ran him through the standard searches, and beyond a few petty arrests in Poland, mostly disturbing the peace and public drunkenness, he's never really been on the radar. I found a license for him, though. He's apparently a heavy equipment operator living in Kwidzyn, a town just north of the kidnapping site."

Leroux grunted. "Which would have required heavy equipment to excavate."

"Which would need licensed operators." Child spun in his chair, staring at the ceiling. "I'm guessing he was hired to do some work, took a photo he wasn't supposed to, then posted it on Facebook like a Millennial tool."

Leroux glanced at him. "Aren't you a Millennial?"

Child grinned. "I may be a Millennial, but I ain't no tool!"

Sonya Tong snorted, muttering something that Leroux suspected was a contradiction to the statement. Child laughed in her direction, apparently having heard her.

"You might be right!" He turned back to Leroux. "*Anyway*, as most tools, he has his privacy settings wide open so that the world can see all his posts, probably because he hopes to attract more followers and satiate his desperate need for validation through strangers 'liking' his posts. I'm guessing this is how word got out about the Amber Room's discovery."

Leroux's head bobbed slowly as he returned to his station. "Makes sense, and fits the facts. Now we need to figure out *who* found out."

Tong cleared her throat. "I've been combing the Dark Web. There are a few known hangouts for collectors of stolen art, relics, whatnot, and there was one reference to the Amber Room on a forum yesterday.

All it had was a message that said, 'Amber room found? Probably BS. PM me if interested.'"

Leroux stared at the posting Tong had put up on the display. "Anybody respond?"

"Nobody publicly, though they might have personally messaged him like he requested. I'm trying to pull any information I can on the poster. If we can find him, then maybe we can grab him and interrogate him."

Leroux frowned. "I doubt *we'll* be able to do that, but somebody might. Let's find him first, then worry about who gets to have all the fun."

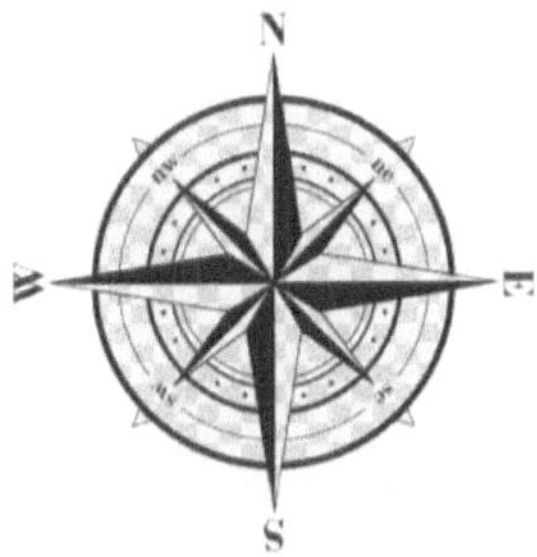

Polish-Czech Republic Border

"Why did you think these were the trucks?"

Officer Jelen frowned as he watched the vehicles pull away, their cargo verified as perishable goods, no stolen art contained within. He turned to Inspector Zabek. "I'm positive I saw those same two trucks go through here since we arrived. I'm sure of it."

Zabek's eyes narrowed. "That doesn't make sense. Why would they go through twice?"

"Exactly. It *doesn't* make sense, but I'm sure they did." He looked about. "We're taping everything that goes through, right?"

"Yes."

"Let's review the footage. We'd just arrived when I saw them."

"What makes you so sure?"

"Because I'm starving, and when I saw them the first time, my stomach grumbled just like it did the second time."

Zabek chuckled, waving over one of the officers recording the proceedings. "I think this redefines 'gut instinct.'" He turned to the man with the camera. "I need to see the footage from about fifteen minutes ago."

He was handed a tablet from a bag slung over his shoulder. "Everything is on here." The man resumed taping, and Zabek brought up the footage, dragging his finger to back up to the time index where they first arrived.

"There!" Jelen jabbed a finger at the tablet, and Zabek lifted his finger, the footage rolling forward at normal speed. "That's them. See, the exact same advertising. Check the plates."

Zabek zoomed in, and Jelen jotted down the plates from both trucks, then compared them to the two that had just left.

They didn't match.

Though he wasn't exactly surprised at that. There was no possible reason he could think of for the trucks in question to have gone through the border crossing twice.

"So it's not them," said Zabek.

"Yeah, but what are the chances that two trucks that match the description of the vehicles we're looking for, with the exact same corporate advertising on their sides, both traveling together, pass through the same border crossing as two other vehicles, less than fifteen minutes ahead of them?"

Zabek chewed his cheek for a moment. "Slim to none would be my guess."

"That's exactly what I'm thinking." He pointed at the image on the screen. "These are the trucks. I know it!"

Zabek sighed, staring at the border. "But they're in the Czech Republic now, and out of our jurisdiction. I'll notify Warsaw so they can get the Czechs involved, but if you're right, I think we're done."

Ostrava, Czech Republic

Acton sat quietly in the back seat as he took in everything he could about their new surroundings. They had pulled off the highway and into the city of Ostrava, several turns made before they had arrived in an alleyway, two white SUVs parked ahead of them, along with a black one that matched theirs.

I wonder where the third one is.

His captor turned to his driver. "Let's do the switch fast." He looked back at Acton. "Professor, cooperate, or you die."

Acton kept his mouth shut, realizing this might be his only chance now of escape, his captors unlikely to allow him a bathroom break again.

It was now or never.

The man exited the vehicle, joining several others already at the new SUVs, as the driver stepped out and opened the rear door. Acton climbed out, and as soon as the door was out of his way, punched the man in the throat as hard as he could, then kneed him in the groin. The man doubled over, his crushed windpipe not allowing him to deliver a warning. Acton grabbed the man's weapon from his shoulder holster, and the keys still gripped in his hand, then jumped into the driver's seat before the others could react.

He shoved the key in the dash and started the engine as the hostiles drew their weapons. He slammed it into reverse and bent over as gunshots erupted. Using the rearview camera, he gunned it out of the alleyway then jerked the wheel to the right and out of the line of fire. Popping up, he put it in drive and hammered on the gas, pulling a U-turn as several of his captors emerged from the alleyway, holding their fire. He took another quick turn, reorienting himself with the landmarks he had spotted upon their arrival, wondering what to do next.

John Paul II International Airport

Balice, Poland

Reading stared at the map as the Gulf V was refueled, the notice about the trucks having new paneling and crossing into the Czech Republic just received. It confirmed what Tommy had suspected.

The lad is good.

And it also meant he was too far north, the trucks now at least half an hour into Czech territory. The authorities there had been notified, but he was quite confident the trucks had already changed their side paneling again somehow, and their plates, Tommy confirming they had changed the last time the advertising had.

The Czechs would be chasing ghosts.

He debated having the pilot skip farther south, but without a specific destination, there was little point in hopscotching across the continent. Every traffic camera in the Czech Republic would be monitored now for the two trucks, and hopefully, they'd get lucky, catching them somehow despite their changed appearance. As soon as he had word of an arrest, he'd fly in.

What had him curious, was how they were redoing the trucks. These were curtain side vehicles, their siding made of fabric. That would make it theoretically possible to change them fairly easily to some other random logo, but that wasn't the case here. They had changed the siding to match other vehicles on the road, traveling only minutes behind them.

It was as if they had either known what trucks would be on the road with them in advance, which he doubted, or they were somehow able to print off new sides, which seemed unlikely. How they were doing it wasn't important for now, it was the fact they *could* do it that was his concern.

He cursed.

These bastards are good.

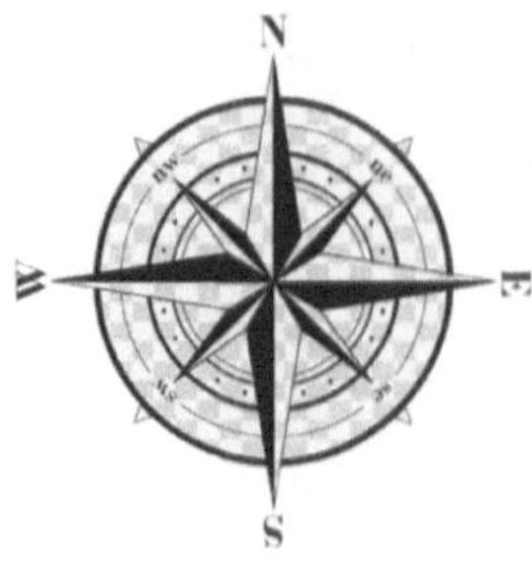

Ostrava, Czech Republic

Acton pulled into the parking lot of a grocery store, taking a moment to assess the situation. The windshield had half a dozen splintered impact sites, the glass clearly bullet-resistant, which meant it could still be driven with hopefully little attention drawn to it, especially on the highway.

Though that wasn't what he should be doing. He should be going to the nearest police station and reporting what happened. Yet that wasn't a good idea, as it could take hours before he might get in touch with the right people, and the Amber Room would be lost forever.

He needed to phone Reading. He'd know what to do. Unfortunately, he had no phone, and if he went to find one, the trucks again could be lost.

But they already are!

The two transport trucks had continued down the highway when they had pulled off to switch vehicles. He had no way of finding them.

Unless you follow the new vehicles.

His decision was made. Laura was safe, and now he had to protect this precious find. He pulled out of the parking lot and hammered on the gas, knowing this could be a colossally stupid move, but determined not to let one of the greatest finds in modern history be lost to a bunch of thieves.

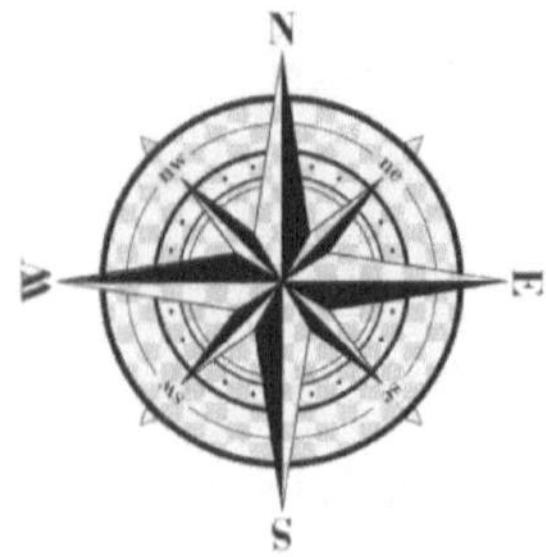

Operations Center 3, CIA Headquarters

Langley, Virginia

"I think I found him."

Leroux turned to Tong. "Who is he?"

Tong motioned to the display, a man badly in need of a haircut shown. "If he's who I think he is, he's a Danish citizen living in Copenhagen, working for a local newspaper. His Dark Web profile seems to suggest he fancies himself a bit of a player, but from what I can tell, he just puts up posts claiming to have information on things that other users claim never pan out."

"But this one might have."

Tong nodded. "Yup."

Child spun. "But how did you make the link to the real world?"

Tong shrugged. "Easy. He's an idiot."

Leroux chuckled. "Explain."

"He uses the same handle on the Dark Web as he does on Twitter. His Twitter profile links to his Facebook profile, and he liked the damned photo our Polish heavy equipment operator posted."

Leroux laughed, shaking his head. "A true genius. If only they were all so easy to find. Do you have an address on him?"

"Yes, sir. Are we going to pick him up?"

Leroux shook his head. "Not our job. Pass it on to Agent Reading. He'll make sure it gets followed up on."

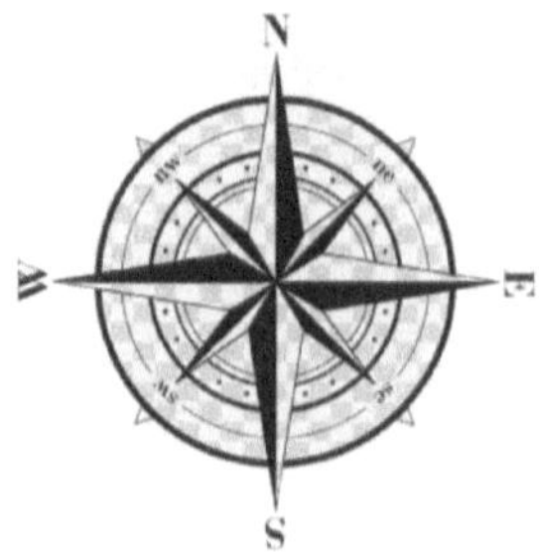

Inselhotel Potsdam

Potsdam, Germany

"I'm so glad you told me."

Tommy tore his eyes away from his laptop. "What? That I love you?"

"Yes. It takes away so much of the pressure."

"Yeah, I know! I mean, I feel so much better now that that's out of the way."

Mai smiled. "I know, but…"

Tommy tensed. "What?"

"Well, I don't know what to do now."

His eyes narrowed. "What do you mean?"

She stared at the bedspread. "Well, umm, I've never really loved anyone before."

Tommy laughed, his tension relieved. "Me neither!" He paused, then decided to go for broke. "You know, umm, I've been thinking of getting my own place. I'm making some coin now, and I think it's time."

Mai continued to stare at the bedding. "You could, you know, move in with me."

Tommy's heart hammered and his eyes shot wide. "Really! I mean, you don't think it's too fast?"

Mai shrugged. "I don't know, maybe it is, but it feels right."

He grabbed her and hugged her. "I love you so much!"

She laughed, finally making eye contact again. "I love you too!"

He kissed her, gently, enjoying her soft lips, then opened his mouth slightly, gripping the back of her head with his hand as he pulled her tighter against him, the kiss building into something more urgent, more demanding. He reached down and drew her closer to him, grinding his hips into hers, and they both groaned.

And the laptop beeped.

He growled in frustration.

"What is it?"

He rolled away and checked the laptop, his eyes widening. "We've got a match to the plate from the SUV I pulled earlier. The one that Professor Acton was in when he entered the tunnel. It was spotted in Ostrava."

He tapped at the computer, bringing up the footage and playing it from the time index indicated by his alert.

And gasped.

"Isn't that Professor Acton driving!"

Ostrava, Czech Republic

Acton followed the two white SUVs as they headed toward the highway. They had driven right by him mere minutes after he had made his decision to pursue them, and he had left several cars between them and him, hoping they wouldn't notice him in their rearview mirrors. One of the vehicles turned onto the onramp, the other continuing past, filling him with doubt as to what was going on, and who to follow.

He made a split-second decision, not knowing which contained the man who seemed to be the leader of this operation.

Though it didn't matter.

He jerked his wheel to the right, onto the onramp, committing. Who was in the vehicle in front of him was irrelevant. He knew they'd be eventually meeting up with the trucks. All he had to do was sit back in traffic, remain unnoticed, and eventually they'd lead him to the Amber Room.

And hopefully Laura had already contacted the authorities, and by then they would have found him, since he planned on sticking his face out the window at every camera he spotted.

He glanced in his rearview mirror and gasped as a white SUV rushed toward him then slammed into his rear end, sending him careening across his lane and sideswiping another vehicle. Brakes locked up all around him, but he resisted the urge, instead hammering on the gas and surging the SUV out of the chaos.

He checked his rearview mirror and spotted the white SUV emerging behind him, much slower, and cursed. He checked his gauges, and everything seemed in order, the vehicle clearly customized so that rear-end collisions didn't trigger a fuel cutoff like so many vehicles did today.

It was designed for this.

And it made him thankful he had stolen it, rather than a civilian vehicle.

The SUV he had been following slowed, the man who had held him and Laura, leaning out the passenger side window, a submachine gun in his hand, the muzzle flashing. The windshield and hood took several rounds before he jerked to the left, out of the field of fire, only to be rammed again from behind.

"Piss off!"

He jerked the wheel to the right then slammed on the brakes, his pursuer shooting past him. He hammered on the gas, quickly closing the gap as it tried to get in front of him. He shifted to the right and floored it, slamming into the passenger side rear bumper, sending the

SUV into a spin. He aimed square at it and braced as he accelerated. He smashed into the passenger side, sending it skidding ahead of him before the wheels caught, flipping it several times.

Acton swerved around it and checked his rearview mirror to see a notorious British-made car slam into them, sending both vehicles spinning in opposite directions, the convertible coming to a stop against the guardrail, its driver stunned, and perhaps thankful his ownership experience was over.

Acton focused ahead, those behind him no longer in the game, and rushed after the trucks containing the priceless Amber Room. Something thundered overhead, and he leaned forward to catch a glimpse when a helicopter blasted past him, banking sharply, the harsh white on blue *Policie* label clearly visible, something in Czech blared at him.

It was over.

He took his foot off the gas, slamming his fists into the steering wheel as he came to a halt, his mission to save the half-billion dollar artifact a failure.

He sighed.

At least everyone is safe now.

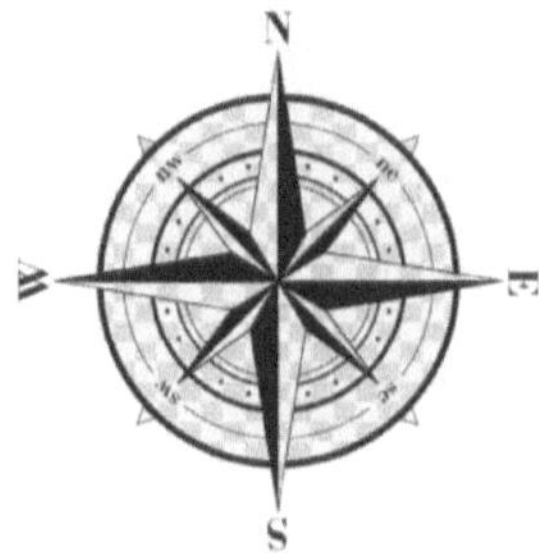

Polish-Czech Republic Border

Officer Jelen listened in on the call Inspector Zabek had graciously put on speaker so he could be kept in the loop. Though the search was ongoing, those participating were now convinced they had missed the trucks, or they had rerouted at the last minute, making the search fruitless.

Though still the most exciting thing he had ever done.

"They've arrested a suspect."

Jelen and Zabek exchanged excited glances.

"Where?"

"Outside Ostrava. They're holding him for questioning, but he says he's innocent."

Jelen grunted. "They all do."

"This one claims he's Professor Acton, but he has no ID on him."

Zabek rolled his eyes. "Well, does he match the photo we have?"

"I haven't got word yet. I'm trying to get through, but the local police chief is refusing to take calls. The peon that I've managed to talk to, says the chief doesn't care if the guy is innocent of the theft, he's guilty of causing havoc on the highway. He's planning on charging him for that, and for possession of an illegal firearm! Can you believe it?"

Zabek shook his head, his face red with anger. "Keep trying to get through. We need to find out if this is indeed Professor Acton, and what happened to his captors and the stolen artifact!"

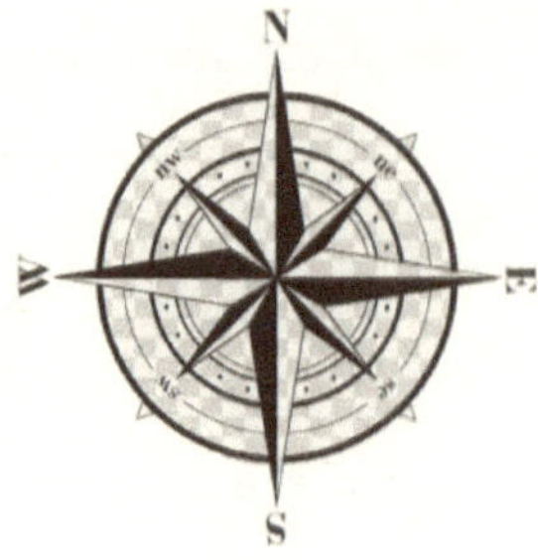

John Paul II International Airport

Balice, Poland

If there was one thing Reading hated, it was waiting. And that's all he had been doing for hours. He was still sitting on the runway in Krakow, in the wrong country, but there was still no point in flying to the Czech Republic. The pilot had explained that if they landed somewhere and needed to take off again, it would take longer to file the flight plan and wait their turn, than it would to simply wait and make a single trip.

It made sense.

He was still waiting for information on the hit Tommy had showing what appeared to him to be Acton driving the SUV he had been kidnapped in.

It made no sense.

If he had escaped, why hadn't he gone to the authorities for help?

Reading shook his head.

Knowing him, he's chasing the Amber Room.

And then there was the matter of—

His phone rang and he took the call, the display indicating it was his partner back in England. "Hey, Michelle, give me good news."

"Well, I'm not sure if it's good news, but it's news at least."

Reading tensed. "What's happened?"

"Your friend, Professor Acton, has been arrested."

"What! Are you serious?"

"Yeah. I'm looking at the report right now. He's been charged with all kinds of traffic violations, and possession of an illegal firearm. It looks like they're throwing the book at him."

"Who?"

"The local police in Ostrava."

Reading shook his head, beckoning the flight attendant to join him. "Don't they know who he is? That he's the victim?"

"All we know is that they responded electronically to our notice that we put out on him, and that's it. Nobody can reach the station where he's being held."

Reading cursed. "Do we have a local agent there?"

"No. We're sending someone from Prague, but he won't be there for at least an hour."

"Okay, keep me posted. I'll be there as soon as I can."

"Understood."

Reading ended the call and turned to the flight attendant. "Tell the pilot we need to get to Ostrava in the Czech Republic as quickly as possible."

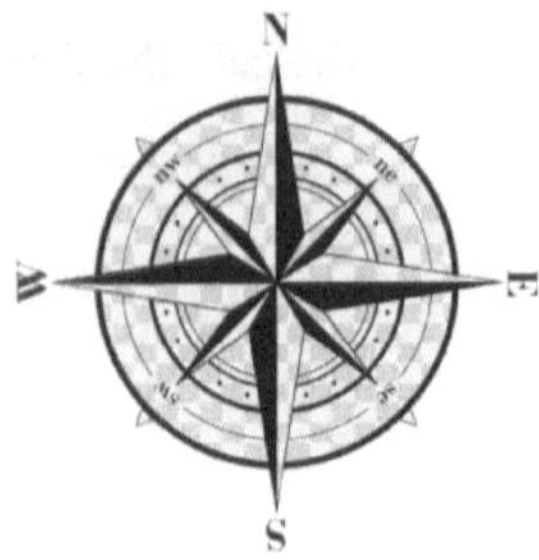

South of Marienwerder, West Prussia

Nazi Germany

February 7, 1945

Gruber stared ahead, unable to check the excitement he now felt. He had done his part, delivering Vogel to his family, and the man had been true to his word, delivering the exact location of what should be so much gold, he could shut down his entire operation, move out of the way of the Russians, and sit out the war in some small town unlikely to draw any attention from the Americans when they rolled through.

In fact, leaving the country after the war might be a good idea. There would be little left of Germany by then, and why be a rich man in a poor country? Life in America with millions in gold would be bliss.

New York City!

He closed his eyes, imagining what it would be like living the high life on the streets of the city that never slept.

"We're here, sir."

Travel permits had been easy with his connections, his small convoy of cars and trucks passing through the checkpoints unchallenged, though with each passing, the warnings of what lay ahead became more dire. The front was close, which meant little time. This wasn't an exploratory mission to see if Vogel had been telling the truth, this was a mission to retrieve as much as they could before it was too late.

He leaned out his window, taking in the sight, his chest tightening as he cursed. The car came to a halt and he stepped out, surveying the area, his hands on his hips as his heart hammered at the betrayal.

"There's nothing here!" He kicked at the snow-covered dirt, his men mingling about, afraid to say anything as his rage built. "The bastard lied to me! I want him dead! I want his family dead! And find those two women I moved for him! I want them dead too!"

"Sir!"

He turned toward the call, spotting one of his men kicking at something. "What is it?"

"I'm not sure, but something *was* here."

Gruber quickly joined his man pointing at a square in the ground. "What's that?"

"I'm not sure."

"There's another one over here."

Gruber joined his other man, finding an identical square in the ground about ten paces from the first.

"Here's another!"

Gruber smiled. "It's a fence. Or at least it was." He stared at their surroundings. "Something *was* here, and they tried to hide it."

"But why would they leave these here? Why not remove the posts?"

Gruber kicked the ground with the toe of his shoe. "It's frozen solid. Have you ever tried to remove a fence post frozen in place?" He didn't wait for an answer. "All they could do was cut them off at the base, and hope no one would find them." He waved his arm around him. "Search everywhere." He jabbed a finger at the hillside in front of them. "Especially there. That's where I think we'll find our gold."

His men were powered by greed and excitement now, the cold forgotten as they eagerly spread out, most heading for the hillside with shovels. He heard a buzzing sound in the distance, but ignored it, his ears pounding with excitement as his men attacked the frozen hillside.

All of his avarice filled dreams were about to come true.

The buzz grew louder.

He stared toward where the sound was coming from, but saw nothing. It sounded like an engine of some sort. He stared down the road, a sudden fear gripping him that the SS might be returning to make sure their gold was safe, when one of his men pointed.

"Look!"

He turned and the blood drained from his face as he spotted two planes racing toward them. He looked about, yet there was nowhere to hide, only the vehicles. He ran toward the car, cursing his overweight bulk as he searched for his driver. He spotted him at the hillside. "Get me out of here!"

His driver spotted the planes and froze for a moment, their distant buzz now a high-pitched wail, their pilots obviously having spotted a target of opportunity. He yanked open the rear door and climbed in as his driver reached him. The door slammed shut and his driver took his seat, cranking the engine, gunfire erupting from the Allied fighters as it roared to life.

His driver floored it, and Gruber watched in horror as his men scrambled, at least half a dozen felled by the first volley.

Then his bladder gave way as his ears filled with the high-pitched wail of a bomb dropping.

Ending his parasitic existence.

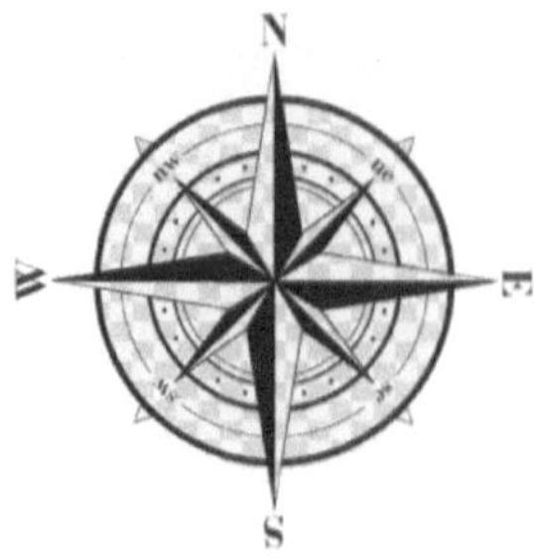

Police of the Czech Republic - Transport Inspectorate

Ostrava, Czech Republic

Present Day

Acton was beyond frustrated. He had been sitting in the small interrogation room for hours, nobody having even offered him a glass of water or a bathroom break since he had arrived. His wrists were handcuffed to the metal table, and the only thing of interest was the clock on the wall, its hands slowly ticking by, showing the minutes then hours waste away.

He yelled at the door for the umpteenth time, and again, no one came. He was being treated as the criminal, arrested when the police had arrived, brought in alone, the occupants of the rolled SUV apparently gone.

And with each passing minute, the trucks containing the stolen Amber Room continued to roll toward their destination.

It was frustrating.

At least you're alive and free.

He just wanted to get out of here, call Laura, and tell her he was okay. She had to be worried sick.

I wonder if she even knows I've escaped.

She would have called Reading, that was an absolute certainty, and with him part of Interpol, Acton was sure he'd have found out about the arrest, and knowing him, he was already on his way here, perhaps with Laura.

It's just a matter of time.

He wasn't worried about the arrest, though the police were excited by the fact he had the liberated handgun on him. Once someone told them what had happened, and who he was—the victim—things would be smoothed over and he'd be released.

But in the meantime, the thieves were getting away, and he was helpless to do anything about it.

The door suddenly opened and he leaped to his feet, rage in his heart, when he dropped back down, sighing with relief at the sight of one of his best friends.

"Hugh! Thank God!"

Reading entered the room, a broad smile on his face. "I understand you've been a bad boy."

Acton chuckled. "I've done nothing you wouldn't do."

"Yes, but I'm a copper, you're not."

Acton shrugged. "In my heart, I know I was always meant to be one."

"Bollocks!" Reading pointed toward the handcuffs, and an officer stepped forward, unlocking them. Acton rubbed his wrists, exhaling loudly.

"Does this mean I can go?"

"Yes, eventually. I've got a Polish investigator on his way who wants to debrief you, and the locals will want to listen in and may have questions of their own, but don't worry, all charges have been dropped."

Acton's shoulders slumped in relief. "Well, that's good to know." He leaned over. "Where's Laura?"

Reading shook his head. "We haven't found her yet, but don't worry, we won't stop looking."

Acton's heart hammered as the room closed in on him. He gasped, sucking in a deep breath. "What do you mean? She didn't call you?"

Reading's eyes narrowed. "What do you mean? Isn't she still with the kidnappers?"

Acton's jaw dropped. "No! She escaped hours ago in Poland! She never called you?"

Reading's face went red as he dropped into a chair opposite Acton. "I haven't heard anything from her. Nobody has."

Acton stared about the room, gripping the table as panic set in. "Oh my God, they must have recaptured her! And those trucks are hours from here!"

Reading pulled out his cellphone, quickly dialing. "Don't worry, Jim, we'll find her."

But Acton wasn't listening anymore. His wife was missing, obviously either recaptured or dead, and after his recent actions, he might have sealed her fate. He stared at Reading, talking rapidly into his phone, the conversation a million miles away.

Laura!

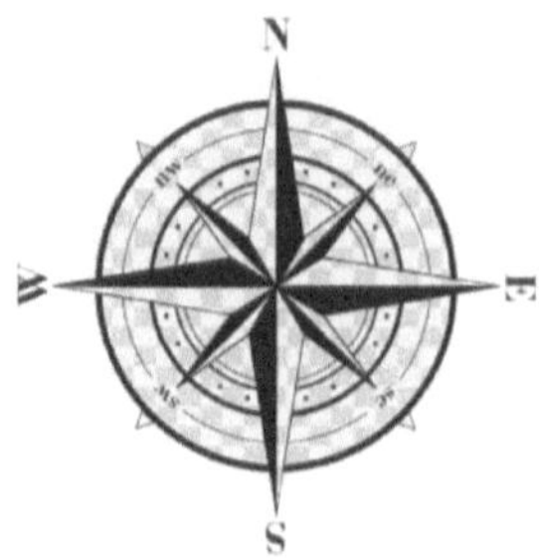

Inselhotel Potsdam

Potsdam, Germany

Tommy's eyes glazed over then his head drooped. He jerked awake and cursed, tapping the keyboard, Mai passed out beside him. They had been going through footage for hours after receiving word that Professor Palmer was still missing. As soon as he had heard that Acton had been "arrested," he had assumed the ordeal was over.

And he and Mai had celebrated.

Twice.

He barely had any time to rest before he received the call, and after being wired the night before about this morning's visit to the Lang residence, he was working off about three hours sleep in the past 48.

It was too much.

But he couldn't give up. It was Professor Palmer that was missing. He liked to think he would put in the effort for anyone, even a stranger, though he knew that wasn't true. He knew this woman, knew her husband, and knew everything they had done for Mai since she had been forced to flee to the United States.

If it weren't for the professors, the woman he hoped to spend the rest of his life with, would be a stranger.

There was nothing he wouldn't do for those two, or the woman who slept beside him this very moment.

Finding the trucks in question that they assumed had not only the art, but the professor on board as well, was fairly easy, since he knew exactly when Acton had been arrested. He watched the footage of the incident on the highway in the Czech Republic in awe—Acton never ceasing to amaze him.

I wish I was that brave.

When he heard about some of the things the professors had done, he often daydreamed of being in their shoes, playing the hero, killing the bad guys, and knew deep down that there was no way in hell he'd match them in any way, shape, or form.

They were simply exceptional people, and the fact they had found each other was a miracle.

They are so suited for each other.

Watching Acton swerving in and out of traffic, avoiding bullets, then forcing one of the SUVs to flip and intentionally ramming it to make sure they were out of the game, still had his heart racing. He had found the trucks, their logos once again changed, and had managed to follow them through the Czech Republic and into Slovakia, skirting the border with Austria, then finally into Hungary.

He zoomed out on Google Maps, and examined the route they had taken the entire way. It was clear they were heading south. They had intentionally avoided a shorter route through Austria that would have taken them through Vienna, a highly risky move.

Shorter route.

It was only shorter depending on their destination. He pursed his lips, spinning his finger on the trackpad, his mouse pointer looping about the screen as he thought. If they kept going directly south, they'd hit Croatia, and he knew from bringing up a map of the Schengen Agreement countries that Mai had referred to, that Croatia wasn't participating, though they were supposed to be.

That meant a guarded border.

I can't see them risking that.

If they wanted to avoid borders, they would be forced to head into Slovenia, and then they'd only have access to a borderless Italy.

He smiled.

Or the Adriatic Sea.

He zoomed in on the tiny sliver of Slovenian coastline, finding the only city with a port.

And his gut told him this was exactly where the kidnappers were heading.

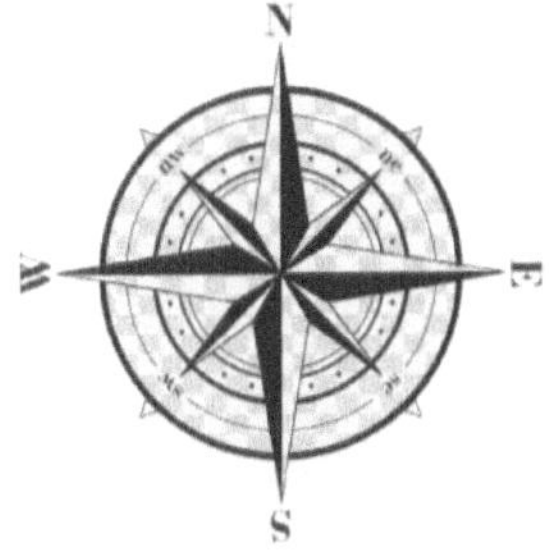

Port of Koper

Koper, Slovenia

Alexie Tankov watched with satisfaction and a hint of impatience as the last of the crates were offloaded from the rear of their two transport trucks. It was a swift operation, though they were still on a deadline.

The captain of their hired cargo ship, a man he had worked with on several occasions before, strolled over, cigar clamped in his mouth, a white peaked captain's hat tipped sloppily to the side, the caricature of what one might expect an unscrupulous freighter captain to be.

He couldn't stand the man, but he was as trustworthy as they came in this business.

Probably because he knew if he betrayed Tankov and his men, he'd be dead before the sun rose the next day.

"We should be underway in less than half an hour. Everything has been arranged, the appropriate palms greased."

Tankov nodded. "Good. We can't afford any delays. I want the ship in international waters as quickly as possible. You get paid the rest of your money when you reach Tripoli. Understood?"

"No problem. We'll make it. We always do."

Tankov ignored the arrogance. "You've got the extra men I requested?"

The cigar was jabbed toward the ship. "Two dozen, heavily armed and experienced. Most of them have fought in the civil war for years. This is a vacation for them!" He laughed then stuffed the cigar back in his mouth. "If anyone tries to stop us, they'll be in for one hell of a surprise."

Tankov allowed himself a slight smile. "I expect so."

Utkin walked over as the trucks behind him were closed up. "Everything is loaded. We're done here."

Tankov turned toward him. "Good. And our troublesome professor?"

"Still sedated."

"Good. Let's move, there's no time to waste."

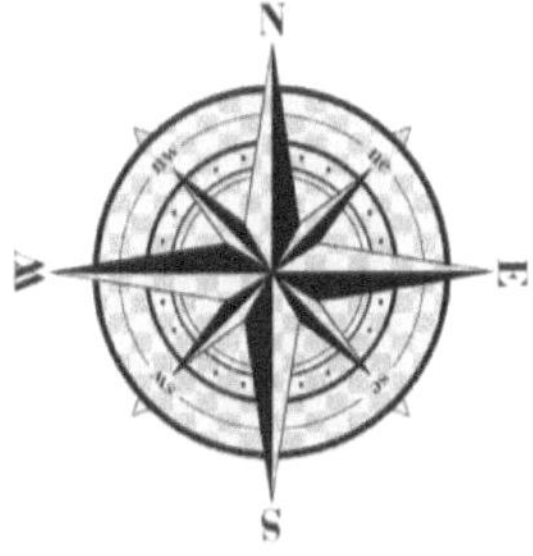

Somewhere over Slovenia

Acton checked his lap belt as the flight attendant indicated they were about to land. It had been a quick jaunt to get to where Tommy and Interpol had confirmed the trucks had offloaded their cargo. Nobody had caught Laura on camera, but he had to assume she was on the ship, a ship apparently already in international waters.

And nobody seemed willing to do anything about it.

At least not yet.

And he wasn't willing to wait.

"You're sure you want to do this?"

He gripped the armrests as he looked over at Reading, his friend finally freeing him after hours more of interrogation. "Absolutely. But I'll understand—"

"Bollocks! Don't even suggest I stay behind."

Acton chuckled. "I figured you wouldn't, but I was giving you an out. You're getting old, you know."

"Sod off! Old my ass. Kick your ass any day," muttered his friend.

Acton laughed. "I have no doubt."

Reading turned in his seat. "In all seriousness, I'd love to know what your plan is if we actually catch up to them in this boat you've rented."

Acton frowned. He had contacted their travel agent to book a high-speed boat in Koper, and as usual, she had come through, the boat already waiting, as well as a ride from the airport to the port. It had been the logical thing for him to do. He had to catch up to the ship and rescue Laura.

But Reading was right.

He had no plan.

"I have no idea. Exchange her for me?"

"They could very well take us both hostage."

Acton jabbed a finger at him. "Which is why I told you to stay behind."

"Not bloody likely."

Acton sighed. "Well, if the Slovenians actually act, they should have the ship in custody by the time we get there."

"And if they don't?"

Acton growled in frustration. "Why wouldn't they? I can't understand why we haven't heard back yet!"

Reading smiled slightly. "Maybe I should have said, 'if they can't.'"

"Then it will be up to us to find them and track them, at a minimum. Surely somebody will eventually help."

Reading stared at him, serious. "So now we're just tracking them, not exchanging your life for Laura's?"

Acton sighed. "Okay, okay, I have *no* idea what I'm doing. All I know is that I'm going after her."

"Damn the torpedoes?"

Acton groaned. "Let's just hope there's none of those!"

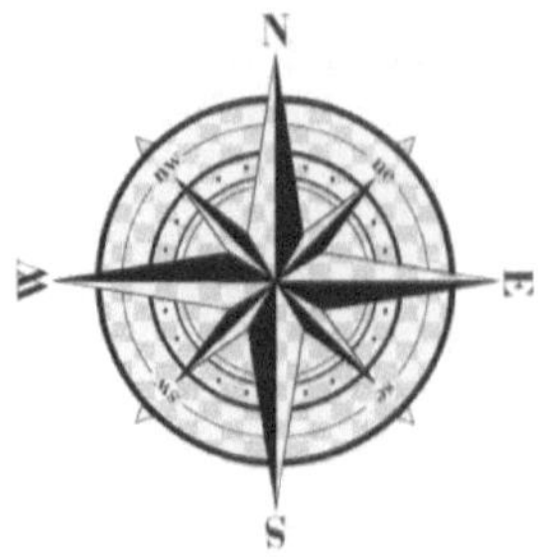

Operations Center 3, CIA Headquarters

Langley, Virginia

"Sir, I just got a hit."

Leroux stifled a yawn, his only rack time in the past two days, a couple of hours squeezed in earlier. Since they were restricted by what they could do, they were reliant upon gleaning information from legitimate sources, or sources outside the European Union. There had been jubilation at the word of Acton's arrest, though short-lived once they realized Laura was still missing.

According to Interpol, a ship had sailed from the Slovenian port of Koper not even an hour ago, and governments were figuring out what to do now that it was in international waters.

He gave up and yawned. "What did you find?" he asked Sonya Tong.

"Laura Palmer just rented a high-speed boat in Slovenia."

Leroux's eyes narrowed as he sat up straight. "Huh? Did she escape?"

Tong shook her head. "No, it looks like it was done through an agency in London, with instructions that it would be picked up by Professor Acton."

Child laughed as he spun in his chair. "That crazy bastard is going after her! He's certifiable!"

Leroux agreed. "He is that."

The door opened and Director Morrison entered, waving everybody off as they were about to rise. "Sit, I'm not the president." He dropped in a seat across from Leroux. "We've got a complication."

Leroux tensed. "What?"

"The Russians are coming."

Leroux frowned as he processed this new bit of intel. "Let me guess. They want their Amber Room back, and will stop at nothing to get it?"

"Something like that. They caught wind through Interpol, and know about the ship that we think is carrying it. Are our guys still inbound?"

Leroux leaned over and looked at Tong who nodded. "Yes, sir. They just landed at Aviano, Italy. They're deploying any minute now."

Morrison pursed his lips, staring at the displays showing a map of where the boat was, the government's response to the state of affairs, and the pesky Professor Acton about to insert his nose into another dangerous situation, something Leroux was quite certain his boss didn't know about. "Okay, we're just observers on this one, so let's hope the timing works out. The Slovenians agreed to let the boat head into international waters so our guys can hit it."

"No surprise there," muttered Child. "They're probably happy to be rid of it."

Morrison grunted. "Exactly. The nearest Russian assets are at least an hour out, so if everything goes smoothly, we should get there first."

Leroux cleared his throat, squirming slightly in his chair. "Umm, I'd hate to throw a wrinkle into the plan, but…"

Morrison closed his eyes, exhaling. "What has Professor Acton done now?"

Leroux was impressed his boss immediately made the leap. "He just rented himself a high-speed boat, and is in the air right now—"

"He's landed," interrupted Tong.

"—and has just landed, and is on his way to pick it up."

Morrison cursed. "He could come up on the boat when our guys are assaulting it."

Leroux frowned. "Or worse, he could show up when the Russians do."

Morrison shook his head then rose. "Well, like I said, not our show, but pass that on to Washington so they can decide what to do with it."

"Yes, sir."

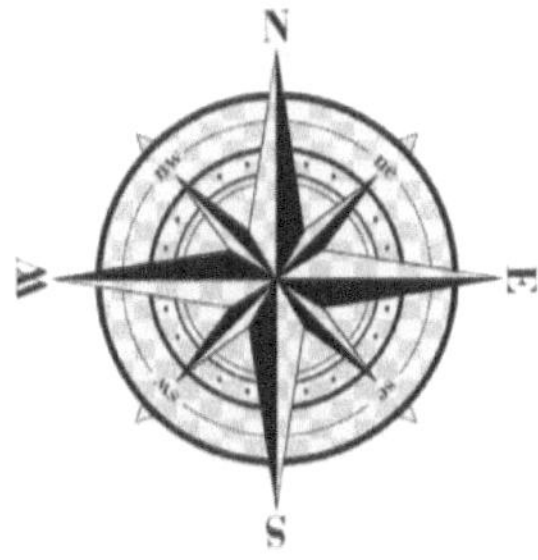

International Waters

The Adriatic Sea, off the coast of Croatia

"You know how to drive this thing?"

Acton gave Reading a look. "I don't think you drive a boat. You pilot it."

"You don't *think*?" Reading growled. "Now I really feel confident in your abilities to *pilot*"—he delivered air quotes—"this thing."

Acton chuckled as he peered ahead into the darkness, wishing he could just gun it, but nervous about hitting something else out on the water. "Just sit back and get comfortable. I have no idea how long it will take to catch up to them."

"*If* we ever catch them. We have no idea where they're going."

Acton agreed. "Yes, but this is the Adriatic, not the Mediterranean. It's only a hundred or so miles wide, and I'm guessing they'll stay on the eastern side, away from Italy."

"You've thought this through, haven't you?"

Acton grinned. "Nope, just making it up as I go along, but someone has to keep you feeling warm and fuzzy. Just keep your eyes peeled. It's a big ocean, and I don't want to miss them."

"Sea."

"Potayto, potawto." He checked his compass, making sure they were still on course. "According to the last update from Tommy, they should be on this course. I can't see them mixing it up much. That would just waste time, and I'm sure they're in a hurry."

"At this speed, we're liable to run right into the back of them."

Acton shrugged. "Well, I did ask for a high-speed boat. Just be thankful she didn't rent us a cigarette boat."

"Is that one of those really long things?"

"Yup. No need for that though, we're just chasing a cargo ship, so it can't move that fast."

Reading stared into the dark. "And again I ask, when we get there, what the hell are we going to do?"

Acton smiled, patting his pocket. "We use the satellite phone to call in its position, then wait for the cavalry."

Reading grunted. "Well, I'm glad you've thought this through at least partway."

Acton's eyes narrowed, stealing a glance at his friend. "Partway?"

"Yes, partway. You are aware that modern ships have radar?"

Acton tapped his. "Yup. Got one right here."

"Right. So don't you think they'll get a little suspicious when they pick us up on radar, then hold position?"

Acton tensed, his eyes narrowing as a frown spread. "Huh. Hadn't thought of that. I figured we'd just stay well away from them."

"In the dark? If they don't have their lights on, you won't see them until we're on top of them."

"The radar will spot them."

"Yes, and if *you* can see them, then *they* can see you too. You'll have to—"

Reading was drowned out by a thundering sound overhead, a bright light suddenly illuminating them from bow to stern.

"What the bloody hell is that?" cried Reading as he leaped to his feet, shielding his eyes.

"I think it's a chopper."

"Of course it's a bloody chopper, it's not a UFO!"

Acton struggled to hear what was now being said over a speaker, but couldn't make it out."

"Cut the engine."

Acton's eyes went wide at Reading's suggestion. "Are you kidding me? They could be hostile!"

"If they're hostile, they'll just open fire. If they're not, but they think we are because we don't obey their orders, they might open fire regardless."

Acton cursed and cut the engines. "Good point." As they came to a halt, he and Reading stepped out of the cabin and onto the aft deck, where he could finally hear what was being said.

And it shocked the hell out of him.

"Professor Acton, prepare to be brought aboard."

He turned to Reading. "Umm, did he just say what I think he said?"

A harness lowered toward them, answering the question for Reading. "I guess so. Who the bloody hell is it?"

Acton shrugged. "No idea, but they sounded American at least, so I guess we can trust them."

Reading eyed him. "Right, because there are no bad Americans."

Acton grinned. "Glad you finally realized that!" He reached up and grabbed the harness. "Umm, you first?"

"Kiss my ass."

"Sorry, I'm married." He fit himself into the harness, then gave the line a tug, saying a silent prayer that this wasn't a huge mistake. He was lifted off the deck and swung away from the boat, sending a surge of adrenaline through his system. He wasn't sure who would be at the end of this line, though he had his suspicions.

He just hoped they proved correct.

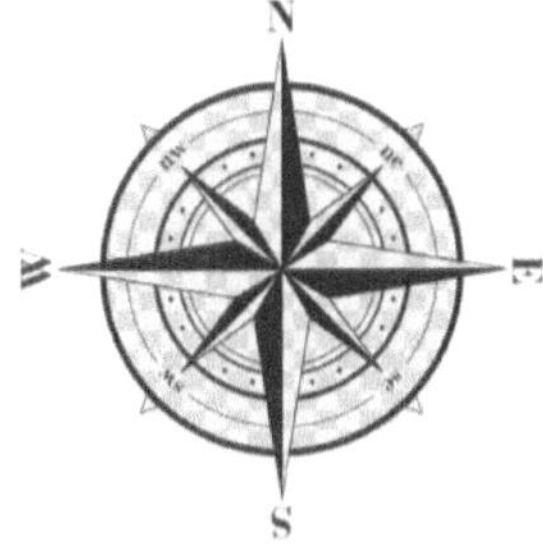

Over International Waters

The Adriatic Sea, off the coast of Croatia

Command Sergeant Major Burt "Big Dog" Dawson steadied the line as he watched the man he had once tried to kill, smile up at him. If he were now asked to define their relationship, he would say Acton was a friend he usually saw on the battlefield. A comrade-in-arms on too many occasions.

A man he still owed to this day.

And would continue to owe until the day he died.

He was the leader of Bravo Team, in his opinion, and many others, the toughest bunch of Special Forces operators in the elite Delta Force, officially 1st Special Forces Operational Detachment-Delta. And they had been duped into killing a group of innocents that still haunted them all to this day.

Which was why, when Acton or his wife needed help, they would always try to be there, though tonight they would have been here regardless.

He pulled a grinning Acton inside.

"I had a feeling it was you guys."

Dawson smiled as he shook the professor's hand. "You're lucky it was. We've got Russians inbound."

"What are you doing here?" asked Acton as he shook hands with the rest of the team, all familiar faces to the man.

"Langley let us know where you were, so we figured we better pick you up before you got in the way." He peered down at the boat. "I assume that's Agent Reading down there."

"You assume correctly."

"Should we get him?"

Acton laughed. "You better, otherwise he's going to be impossible in the morning."

Dawson chuckled then handed the harness over to Sergeant Carl "Niner" Sung. "You do the honors while I brief our guest."

"Yes'm!" Niner leaned out, taking over the recovery operation.

Acton peered over the edge at the boat. "Umm, are we just going to leave it there?"

Niner glanced over his shoulder. "What, Doc, you didn't take the insurance when you rented her?"

Acton gave him a look. "Not exactly a car rental."

"So that would be a *no*."

Master Sergeant Mike "Red" Belme laughed. "Lifestyles of the rich and famous."

Acton patted the fuselage. "Not exactly a cheap chariot you're in either, Sergeant."

Red rubbed the seat. "No leather here, Doc."

"Uh huh."

Dawson leaned over to see Reading fitting himself into the harness. "Don't worry, Doc, we'll send someone to pick it up as soon as the mission is over." He turned to Sergeant Leon "Atlas" James. "Call in the coordinates so I'm not made a liar. I'd hate to lose the professor's yacht."

"I'd hardly call it a yacht."

Atlas' impossibly deep voice rumbled through the cabin. "No, *you* wouldn't. Millions would, but *you* wouldn't."

Reading was hauled inside and stumbled into a seat between Sergeants Will "Spock" Lightman and Gerry "Jimmy Olsen" Hudson, cursing the entire time. He looked about. "I was hoping it was you lot. What are you doing here?"

Dawson signaled the all-clear to Sergeant Zach "Wings" Hauser, piloting the Black Hawk, and the chopper dipped forward as they resumed course for their target. Niner slid the door closed, reducing the noise level considerably.

"Agent Reading, good to see you." Dawson exchanged a handshake. "The Russians caught wind that the Amber Room was discovered, and they're laying claim to it. Through their liaison connections with

Interpol, they found out about the ship it's on, and have sent a team to retrieve it."

"Lovely."

"Exactly what Washington was thinking."

"So why are you here? America isn't exactly involved in this."

"The Poles say it's theirs, since it was found on their soil, and they asked us, as in the US, to intervene on their behalf the moment it hit international waters. *We* happened to be returning from an op, so were tasked with the recovery operation."

Acton leaned forward to be heard. "How far are we from the ship?"

"About fifteen minutes."

"And the Russians?" asked Reading.

"Thirty."

"Lovely."

Acton shook his head. "So we need to secure the boat before they arrive."

Dawson nodded. "Exactly. If we don't, they're probably going to open fire and kill everything in sight."

Acton's face slackened. "Including Laura."

Dawson's face was grim. "I'm afraid that's a possibility."

Acton gripped his seat. "Can't this thing go any faster!"

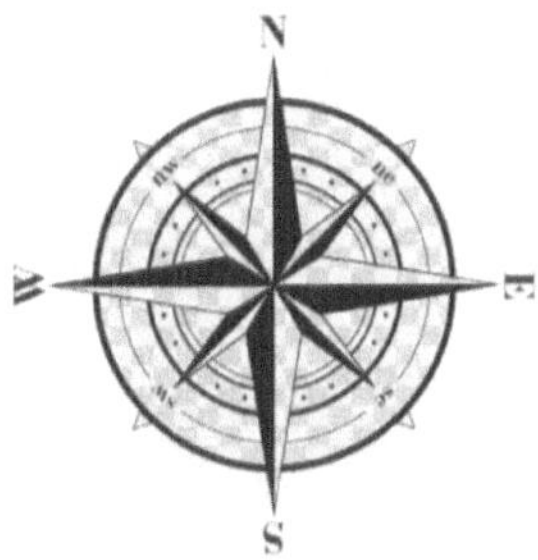

Approaching Target Vessel

The Adriatic Sea, off the coast of Croatia

Dawson gunned the engine of the inflatable zodiac, and raced toward the black silhouette on the horizon. As soon as they had a visual on the ship, they had deployed the boat, and he had jumped with four of his men. Wings had backed off the chopper to allow them to board the vessel, hopefully without the hostiles becoming aware, but time was ticking.

The Russians were closing in fast, and the latest update from Control was that there was no stopping them. They wanted their Amber Room, and would stop at nothing to get it. Half a billion dollars of Russian pride was stored in crates aboard the vessel, thought lost to history.

He just hoped that whatever happened over the next few minutes, left it intact and undamaged, along with Laura Palmer.

They pulled up to the stern, no indication so far they had been observed, their approach covered by the noise of the massive screws. They were now only feet from the port side of the ship, and he activated his comms. "Zero-Two, Zero-One. Status?"

His second in command and best friend, Red, responded with an update from a drone overhead, monitoring the deck and its hostiles. "You're clear, over."

"Copy that. Proceeding." Dawson launched a pneumatically fired grappling hook, and watched as it sailed through the air, dragging a rope behind it. It reached the deck, its rubberized membrane deadening the thud. He yanked it back, tightening up the slack before it caught. He gave it a few good tugs then rushed up the side of the ship, a mid-sized cargo vessel with no lights on from bow to stern.

He reached the railing and lowered his night vision goggles, spotting no one in the immediate vicinity, though there were half a dozen armed men about halfway down the deck, and more could appear at any moment. He swung over the railing, signaling the all-clear with a tug of the rope, then readied his suppressed MP5 as he slowly advanced toward the blind spot at the stern.

Two men rounded the corner as he feared, and he pumped two rounds into each of their chests before they could get a warning out. He rounded the corner, finding it all clear, as Niner swung over the rail. Dawson grabbed the first body and tossed it over the side as Niner advanced to cover him. He passed Dawson as the second body was flipped over the rail.

"Zero-One, Zero-Two. You've got two more coming around the starboard side, over."

"Copy that."

Dawson and Niner advanced, weapons raised, hidden in the dark of an overcast sky. The two men were talking loudly in Arabic, a bit of a surprise, their intel indicating that the thieves spoke English with a Russian accent. He allowed them to round the corner so they wouldn't be seen by anyone farther down the deck when they dropped, then fired two more rounds, Niner immediately following.

Four down.

"On your six," rumbled Atlas from behind him. Dawson didn't bother checking as he continued forward with Niner, Atlas and Jimmy now dealing with the bodies behind them, Spock leaving with the boat to get the rest of the team.

The plan was simple. Thin out the enemy as much as possible before they even knew they were there, then take the rest of the ship by force if necessary, securing Professor Palmer, then the cargo.

A machine gun opened up above them, changing the plan.

Spock ducked as the rear of the boat was shredded. He dove over the side and hit the water as what sounded like an AK47 continued to fire.

Any time now, guys.

The firing stopped as if in answer to his prayers, and he resurfaced, cursing at the sinking boat.

"Zero-Five, Zero-One. Status, over?"

Spock stared at the last vestiges of their boat sinking below the surface. "I'm peachy, but the boat is gone. I'm going to need retrieval, and you're going to need to secure a landing zone, over."

"Understood," replied Dawson. "Hang tight, and we'll try to get to you before the sharks do. Zero-One, out."

Spock's eyes widened as his head swiveled.

Sharks?

Niner and Jimmy quickly climbed the ladder to the next level, Jimmy in the lead, Niner slowed by his M24A2 SWS Sniper Weapon System. The body of the shooter lay in a heap, a pool of blood rapidly expanding, his shooting spree lasting only seconds, but long enough to eliminate their ride, and their element of surprise.

Gunfire pinged off metal everywhere, the hostiles firing in the blind as he knew Dawson and Atlas continued to sweep forward, taking out targets of opportunity. Unfortunately, they had no clue where Professor Palmer was being held, though it was a good chance it was the crew quarters.

And with their boat gone, the plan had changed, and Plan Bs were always more difficult.

He reached the bridge deck and quickly set up his weapon as Jimmy eliminated the one hostile manning the helm, before turning spotter and mapping targets. He activated his comms. "Overseer in position, over."

Dawson replied. "Copy that, Overseer. Get to work, out."

Jimmy fed him the first target, and Niner got him in his sights, taking him out and moving on to the next, the herd thinning quickly, when suddenly all the lights on the boat blazed. He jerked back from his night vision scope, momentarily blinded, and cursed at how exposed they now were.

Gunfire from two positions poured lead at their nest, the metal deck protecting them for the moment, though judging by the amount of rust now visible, he wasn't sure for how long.

Red leaned out the side of the Black Hawk as Wings raced toward the target, now a bright beacon on the sea ahead. He spotted Niner and Jimmy trapped on an upper deck, several hostiles firing on their position, and he leaned out, Mickey holding him by his vest as he took aim. He pumped several controlled bursts at those firing, taking two down, leaving the rest to scatter.

Niner and Jimmy repositioned as he continued to provide cover fire. Wings banked the massive chopper toward the ship, and Red gripped the rappelling rope, sliding down as soon as he had deck below him, his MP5 belching death in a sweeping motion, keeping the heads of the hostiles down.

He hit the deck and rushed for cover as the rest of the team quickly followed, all on board within seconds, Wings banking away to let them get to work. Red pointed at his team, signaling for a perimeter to be established, then pushed forward as he heard the belch of Niner's SWS once again enter the fray.

A hatch flung open ahead of him, muzzle flashes erupting from the darkness. He dove to his right, wincing as he got bit on the shoulder by a ricochet. Prone, he fired half a dozen rounds into the darkness, silencing the hostile. He checked his left shoulder, the cloth of his uniform torn, a hint of blood seeping through.

I'll live.

Dawson yanked open a hatch and tossed in a flashbang before he and Atlas entered, Dawson breaking right, Atlas covering his six. From the layout of the ship provided to them by Control, he knew crew quarters were two decks down, the stairwell twenty feet from their current position.

He listened for footfalls, but heard none, the action still unfolding outside, and hopefully distracting anyone who might be guarding Professor Palmer. He moved forward carefully though with purpose, reaching the stairwell and peering inside.

Clear.

They rapidly descended the two decks, encountering no one, then Dawson inched the hatch on the crew quarters level open. The hallway was clear.

This is too easy.

And that usually meant something was wrong.

Niner took out another hostile, now almost too easy with them engaged by the rest of the team. The enemy was too busy worrying about what was in front of them rather than what was above and behind. His count was nine down by his weapon, and at least another half-dozen by Red's team. The gunfire was dwindling, so the excitement, at least topside, would soon be over.

Wings' voice came in over the comms. "Control says four Russian choppers are inbound, ETA eight minutes, over."

Niner cursed, glancing at Jimmy. "Nothing like Russians to ruin a perfectly good day."

Dawson cursed as the last of the crew quarters turned out to be empty. There was no sign anybody had been held prisoner here, and more concerning, was that every hostile they had encountered so far appeared North African.

Not a Caucasian among them.

"Control, Zero-One. Can you confirm we're on the right ship, over?"

Colonel Clancy's voice replied. "Zero-One, Control Actual. Confirmed, you are definitely on the right ship, over."

Dawson shook his head at Atlas. "Control, are we sure that the correct ship was identified? We have no hostiles here matching the descriptions provided by Interpol, and have found no evidence of the target, over."

"Stand by, Zero-One."

Colonel Clancy was a man he trusted implicitly, and if something had been messed up on this mission, Clancy would get to the bottom of it. He had no doubt it wouldn't have been anyone at Delta HQ that had screwed up—if there were something wrong, it would be Washington or the Europeans.

But his money was on neither.

They had encountered at least a couple of dozen well-armed hostiles. They just weren't the hostiles they were expecting. The ship had been running dark, and he didn't believe in coincidences.

There was no way they just happened to be sent to attack a ship that was also a den of illicit activity.

No, he expected Clancy would confirm they were on the right ship, but for the wrong reasons.

This was feeling more like a Charlie-Foxtrot if there ever was one.

He looked at Atlas. "Do you get the feeling that whoever provided the intel on this one had the wool pulled over their eyes?"

Atlas grunted. "Yup. I've got a feeling somebody has been watching the magician's wrong hand."

"We need to find out what the hell is going on."

They proceeded up one deck and Dawson threw open the door to the galley, a burst of gunfire greeting him, hammering harmlessly into the opposite wall. "Lower your weapon, or die."

No reply, except another spray of gunfire.

He tossed a flashbang into the room, at least half a dozen screams responding. They rushed inside, weapons raised, finding only one armed hostile, half a dozen others crying, their senses still overwhelmed by the grenade. He put two in the armed one, deciding the planet could use one less bad guy, then grabbed the best dressed of the group, hauling him to his feet.

"Who's in charge?"

The man stared at him, confused. He asked again in Arabic. A shaky finger pointed to another, cowering under a table. Atlas reached under with a massive paw and yanked the man into view, his white captain's shirt covered in grime, the epaulets tarnished.

"Where's the hostage?"

The man shook his head, waving his hands in front of him, terror in his eyes. "No hostage! Just cargo!"

Dawson grabbed him by the throat. "Where are the other men? The *white* men?"

The man's eyes were wide with fear, and his entire body trembled. "Never here! They were never here! They delivered the cargo, then left."

An all-clear from Red came in over his comms as the dull thuds of the guns went silent. He tossed the man against the wall, processing this new information as he decided whether the man was telling him the truth. While he was reluctant to accept what was said at face value, it certainly fit the facts.

His comms beeped. "Zero-One, Control Actual. I've reviewed the footage personally. You are *definitely* on the right ship, but none of the hostiles appear to have boarded after the cargo was loaded, over."

Dawson shook his head. "Copy that, stand by. Zero-Two, send two men to cover the galley, over."

"Copy that, Zero-One."

Dawson pointed his MP5 at the captain. "Show me the cargo."

The man shook out a nod, his hands up as he hugged the wall toward the door, stepping out as Niner and Jimmy arrived.

The captain yelped.

Niner eyed the man. "Is that any way to welcome your guests?"

Jimmy shook his head. "I'm definitely making a note of the name of this vessel and instructing my travel agent to never book travel aboard her."

Niner agreed. "And I think we're in a bad neighborhood. I'm sure I heard gunshots!"

Dawson jerked a thumb over his shoulder at the room filled with their prisoners. "If you two are done your routine, watch them."

Niner grinned. "Ooh, a *captive* audience."

Jimmy gave him a thumbs-up. "Niiice, I see what you did there!"

Atlas shook his head. "Those two deserve each other."

Dawson chuckled, pushing the captain toward the stairwell. They followed him down a series of stairs and through several corridors, before they finally reached the hold, a hold containing two dozen crates stacked in the center, and no other cargo visible.

And the stench of human waste was almost overwhelming.

Atlas pointed to a far corner, a stack of soiled mattresses evident. "Looks like they're human traffickers."

Dawson frowned. "Remind me to sink this ship when we're done." He activated his comms as he eyed the crates. "One-Two, Zero-One. Get Professor Acton in here, now."

"Roger that."

Acton gulped, staring down at the heaving deck below, the waves picking up. He had done this a few times before, but never in these conditions, and always hooked to a harness. In this case, he had been told there was no need and no time, Wings the only one on board to hook him up, and he was too busy piloting the chopper.

"Just hug it, Doc, and you'll be fine."

Acton frowned. "You can't land, can you?"

"Not in these seas."

Acton sighed. "Fine." He wrapped his arms and legs around the rope and hopped out, sliding down the thick and surprisingly steady bundle of material, thankful Wings had handed him a spare set of gloves. He controlled his descent as best he could, and was surprised when he felt hands on him so quickly.

Maybe if you hadn't closed your eyes the entire time.

"Good job, Doc. We'll make an operator out of you yet!"

Acton laughed at Red as he let go of the rope. "I think I'll leave it to the pros."

Red pointed at one of his men. "Go with him. He'll take you to the cargo."

"Any sign of my wife?"

Red shook his head, frowning. "Negative. We're searching stem to stern right now."

"Okay, thanks." Acton wasn't surprised. From the chatter he had picked up from Wings, it looked like the men who had kidnapped him and Laura weren't on board, which probably meant Laura was still with them. The only explanation he had been able to come up with, was that they didn't want to be trapped on a ship in case the authorities, or Delta Force operators, dropped by. They had likely intended to pick up the cargo when it reached its destination, then give it to their buyer, using Laura to authenticate it.

Or she's already dead.

He chastised himself, refusing to go where his mind so desperately wanted to.

She's still alive. Never doubt that.

Reading dropped beside him, cursing the entire way down about getting too old for this shit, and needing to hit the gym.

Acton grinned at him. "You keep saying that, but you never seem to get around to it."

Reading gave him a look. "I get enough exercise chasing after you two."

Acton laughed, then they followed the Bravo Team member to the hold as the chopper banked away. Their escort seemed confident their route was secure, but he wasn't so sure, still holding out hope that Laura might be on board, and if she were, she was likely guarded by somebody yet to be found.

And that meant there could be others still lurking in the darkness.

They entered the hold to find a couple of dozen crates piled in the center, Dawson, Atlas, and another man Acton presumed was the captain of the vessel by the way he was dressed, stood next to them. His eyes narrowed as he approached the crates, all painted jet black.

Dawson motioned toward the cargo. "I didn't want to touch anything in case I damaged it."

Atlas held up his massive hands. "I offered, but he said my paws weren't made for delicate things."

Acton chuckled as the man pouted. "He might be right." He pointed at the paint job. "These weren't black when we found them."

Dawson stepped closer. "Looks fresh. Maybe they painted them to try and disguise them."

Acton nodded. "That's a possibility. They did have Nazi markings on them, so painting them black would cover pretty much anything in case they had been pulled over for some cursory inspection." He spotted a crowbar and grabbed it off the floor, quickly opening the lid to the closest crate. He carefully lifted it then tossed it aside.

"What the hell is this?"

Wings took the opportunity to return to where Spock had taken his spill, quickly spotting him waving up from the water below.

"Hang on buddy, just give me a second, over."

There was no response, Spock's comms apparently offline. With the rope Acton and Reading had just used still in play, he positioned himself overhead as best he could, then waited a ten-count. Leaning over and shifting his craft slightly to the right, he spotted Spock waving the go-ahead. Wings gave a thumbs-up then pulled up on the collective, gaining some altitude, before heading back to the ship, making sure he was high enough that he didn't slam his friend against the hull.

He decided he better seek a second opinion. "Somebody want to make sure I don't pop him like a zit, over."

Red's voice responded. "You're good. Your about fifty feet off the deck. Bring him down gently."

Wings expertly guided the Black Hawk lower, his concern not his skills, but the heaving deck.

"We've got him! You're clear."

Wings breathed a sigh of relief. "Copy that." He banked away then yanked back on his cyclic as four sets of powerful lights filled his field of vision.

He cursed.

"Zero-One, One-Two. The Russians have arrived."

Dawson cursed at the report from Wings, then at another crate filled with nothing but stacks of newspapers. "So what are we saying, Doc? Was there ever an Amber Room?"

Acton threw up his hands in frustration. "Yes, there definitely was. I opened the crates myself. It was definitely there. They must have switched them at some point. But when?" He cursed, kicking the crate.

"I have to go topside and deal with the Rooskies." Dawson turned to Atlas then pointed at the captain. "See if you can get something useful out of him."

Atlas slapped his paws together. "Want me to tenderize him?"

Dawson suppressed a smile. "Do whatever it takes to make him talk." He sprinted out of the hold then up the winding stairs and onto the deck. Wings was facing down the four Russian Mil Mi-24 Hind helicopters by himself, but the Black Hawk was no match for them. If this turned into a firefight, Wings would be blasted out of the sky, and his men would be shredded within seconds. He had to defuse the situation.

"One-Two, Zero-One. Fall back and hold position two hundred meters off the port side."

"Roger that, Zero-One." The Black Hawk banked away, repositioning as instructed, and Dawson ordered his men to lower their weapons.

"Let's look friendly, boys." Dawson waved at the choppers, then pointed at the clear deck. One of the choppers dipped forward, positioning overhead, half a dozen troops rappelling down, their weapons raised as they hit the deck. Dawson left his resting by the strap, the others doing the same. He strode toward the man who appeared in charge. "Sir, welcome aboard. I'm Sergeant Major White."

"Major Vasiliev. We are here for our property."

Dawson frowned. "I'm afraid we've both been misinformed, Major. Your property is not aboard."

The major cursed colorfully in Russian. "Forgive me if I don't believe you, Sergeant Major."

Dawson held out a hand, pointing toward the stairwell. "Please come with me, and I'll prove it to you. I'll just ask that your men lower their weapons, so there are no unfortunate accidents."

The order was given and the weapons lowered. Dawson led the major and two of his men to the cargo hold, where Acton had finished opening all the crates. Dawson pointed at the worthless cargo. "As you can see, Major, we've been had. They made a switch somewhere, and we don't know where."

The man frowned. "Perhaps it was never found. Perhaps this was all a hoax from the beginning."

Dawson held out a finger behind his back, a finger he hoped Acton would notice. "Perhaps." The professor remained silent.

"We will conduct a search, of course, to confirm it isn't held elsewhere."

Dawson bowed slightly. "Of course. We should coordinate, as my men are also searching, and we wouldn't want any misunderstanding. I suggest teams of four. Two from your team, two from mine?"

The major smiled, returning the bow. "Good thinking, Sergeant Major. Let's be efficient about this, so no more time is wasted on this endeavor."

"Agreed."

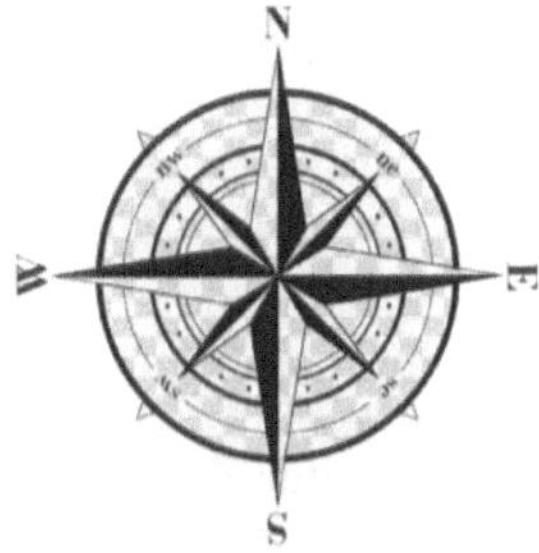

Portoroz Airport

Secovlje, Slovenia

Tankov watched as the last of the crates were loaded onto the C-130H Hercules. The two trucks that had served them so faithfully, their high-tech equipment removed, were driven away by two local hires who knew nothing, the vehicles to be stripped for parts and spread across Europe before dawn.

He boarded the plane with his men, the diplomatic status of the transport aircraft allowing them to escape the hassles normally associated with an international flight, and minutes later, they were in the air, the men with smiles on their faces, the payday huge.

Utkin lit a cigar, sending rings into the cabin. "I'd say that went off about as perfectly as could have been expected."

Tankov agreed. The fact they had taken off, meant their pursuers had fallen for the decoy. The trucks they had were capable of being loaded from the sides, one advantage of fabric siding. Both trucks had already been loaded with black decoy crates matching the shape and size of those in the photograph from the idiot who had leaked the find on social media, and while all witnesses were inside the mine, his men had loaded the Amber Room in the front half of their transports, painting them to match. At the dock in Slovenia, they had unloaded from the rear, so any footage captured would look as if the trucks had been emptied, the cargo loaded on the ship. The genuine cargo, still aboard the transports, was then brought here to the waiting Hercules sent by their employer, whose diplomatic ties assured a clean departure.

Tankov lit his own cigar. "One hundred million Euros for two days work including planning. Not bad, boys! Split eight ways, well, who the hell knows what that is? I'll hire a human calculator to figure it out!"

His men roared with laughter and he checked his watch. "Okay, let's get some rack time. We'll be there in two hours, then I want to be back in civilization as soon as possible."

The job wasn't over yet. A healthy down payment had already been made to the tune of fifty million, but the remainder wouldn't be transferred until they delivered the goods, and convinced their buyer that the item was genuine.

He just hoped that part went as smoothly as the rest of the plan.

He glanced over at the female professor whose husband had proven such a challenge. Unfortunately for her, he had planned on the possibility of an escape, and Team Three had been in position, just in case. She had been recovered quickly before she could make her phone call, sedated, and hadn't been a problem since.

But he needed her awake to confirm to the buyer that their cargo was genuine, then he had to decide what to do with her. Killing her would be the simplest thing, though she had done nothing wrong, and he wasn't a fan of killing women. If it were Acton he still had, he wouldn't hesitate to kill him, but not a woman.

He'd still do it, though he would have reservations.

Yet this was no ordinary woman. They had pulled her files using some deep contacts from his former Spetsnaz days, and it turned out not only was she extremely wealthy, she was very well connected.

Which meant if they killed her, those contacts might never stop hunting them.

He sighed as he stared at her.

What to do with you, Professor Palmer?

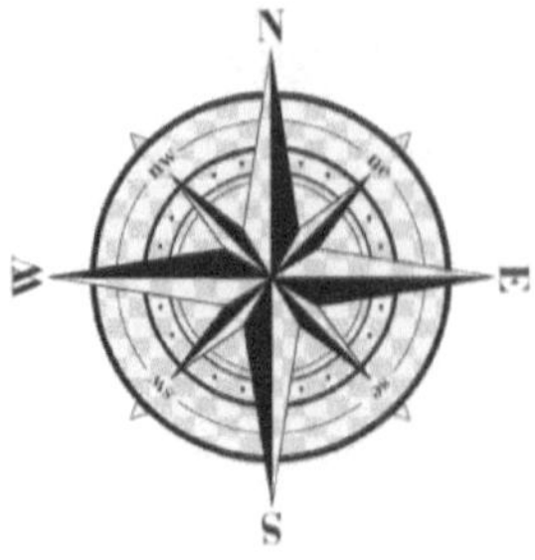

The Adriatic Sea

Acton watched as boats from the USS Philippine Sea approached, Wings already having landed the Black Hawk on her deck. The vessel they were on had been searched from bow to stern with no sign of the genuine cargo, or more importantly, Laura, the failed search sending the Russians on their way.

It had all been a misdirect, the past several hours a complete waste of time, though a couple of dozen bad guys were dead, and another vessel in the tragedy that was human smuggling would be out of the picture.

Only to be replaced in short order, he was certain.

Acton turned to Dawson. "Is there anything you guys can do to help?"

Dawson frowned. "Only if she's outside the European Union, or in international waters like this. Apparently, the State Department has said we're not to mess with internal European affairs. Frankly, Doc, the only reason we're here is because the Russians were on their way, and the Polish government didn't want to lose. We were the only ones with assets in the area that could react quickly enough."

Acton sighed. "So we're back to square one. My wife is nowhere to be found, and the Amber Room is once again lost."

"I wish I could help you, Doc, but you guys got pretty far on your own. I'm sure you'll pick up the trail. If it turns out she's somewhere we can operate, you know how to reach us."

Acton extended a hand. "Thanks for everything you did tonight. It's appreciated."

Dawson shook Acton's hand. "Always a pleasure, Doc."

Niner and Atlas strolled over, Niner with a massive rifle over his shoulder. Acton gestured at it. "Compensating?"

Atlas roared with laughter, his deep voice causing everyone to turn toward them. "Nice one, Doc!" He extended a fist for a bump.

Niner patted the weapon. "I'll have you know, I'm perfectly proportioned."

"So your mamma says."

"Don't be bringing mammas into this."

Atlas jabbed a meaty finger at Niner's chest. "Don't *you* be bringing mammas into this."

"Hey, you brought it up."

"Only because I knew you would. You always defend your inadequacies with references to your mamma."

"My mamma loves me. She told me so." He lowered the barrel of the SWS, aiming it at Atlas' chest. "Does your mamma love you?"

Atlas raised his hands slightly. "Not as much as yours does, apparently."

"That's what I thought." Niner slung the weapon. "Now that that's settled, your mamma's so fat, when someone asks 'where's the beef?' she smacks her ass and says, 'right here.'"

Atlas stared at him. "Your mamma is so fat—"

Niner raised a hand, cutting him off. "Have you seen my mamma? She's a tiny little Korean woman without an ounce of fat on her."

Atlas frowned. "Yeah, what's the point?"

Niner grinned. "So, do I win, or do you want to hear another one?"

Dawson shook his head then looked at Acton. "Be thankful you don't have to put up with these two day in and day out, Doc." He turned his back on the comedians. "Why do you think they still have your wife? They seem to have given everyone the slip."

"They wanted us to authenticate the Amber Room to their buyer. My guess is they'll keep her until they've completed the sale."

Reading frowned. "And when that's done…"

Acton's chest tightened as the jocularity of the men surrounding him was shoved aside, everyone growing quiet. "When that's done, I—" His voice cracked, and he took a moment to regain control, Reading's hand on his shoulder providing him with some strength. "I think they'll kill her."

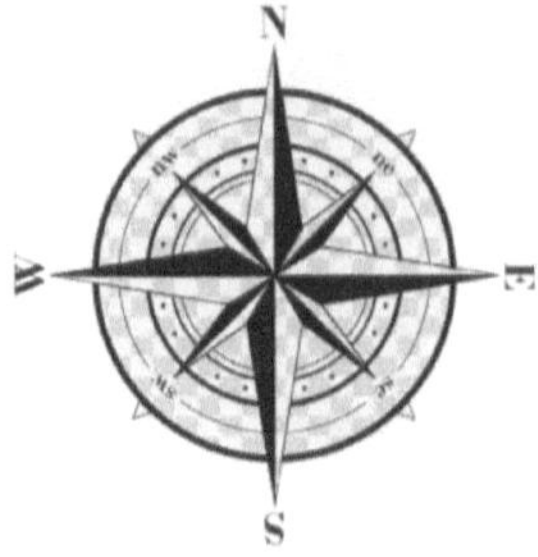

Unknown Location

Laura woke to find her face covered with something made of cloth, her face damp and hot from her breath. Her head was pounding as if it were New Year's Day and she was in her twenties again, and her entire body was vibrating. It took her a moment to realize she must be on an airplane, a propeller-driven one that had just taken off and was still gaining altitude. And it sent her heart racing, which didn't help her headache.

How long was I out?

She desperately had to pee, suggesting it must have been quite a few hours since her last relief. As she listened to the sounds surrounding her, she tried to piece together what had happened. She had escaped, found the phone, then heard something behind her. Before she could react, something sprayed in her face, and she had passed out almost instantly.

Then woke here.

I wonder what happened to James.

"Ahh, you're finally awake."

She frowned. Someone must have noticed a change in her demeanor—perhaps she had been breathing heavily in her sleep. Whatever had given it away, it didn't matter now. Simply listening wouldn't tell her anything anymore. "Yes."

"I apologize, but I'll be leaving the hood on. I can't risk you seeing anything that might give away our destination. I've read your file, and you're a very resourceful woman."

Laura rolled her eyes. "Thanks, I'm sure."

"Do not worry, Professor. I have no intention of hurting you, as long as you cooperate. You and your husband are far too well connected for me to risk the wrath of your friends. You will authenticate the find to my buyer, then you will be free to go."

"Bollocks."

The man chuckled. "I guess you'll have to trust me." His voice got closer. "But hear this, Professor. If you do anything to screw up this deal, I won't hesitate to kill you."

And his tone had her believing every word.

USS Philippine Sea

Acton lay on the narrow bed in the guest quarters arranged for him and Reading. His friend was snoring below him, but sleep continued to elude Acton. There was no way he could sleep until Laura was found.

They had said their goodbyes to the Delta team a short while ago, their helicopter taking them to parts unknown, though he hoped somewhere safe. Yet that wasn't their lot in life, and he had known some who had been killed, even killing one himself when they had been first sent to eliminate him, believing he was the leader of a domestic terrorist cell.

I can't believe how far we've come.

He had forgiven them long ago. They had been used, just like he had, and those guilty were now dead.

He just wished they could have stuck around to help retrieve Laura, but their job was done as soon as the crew, all known human smugglers, was taken into custody and their ship impounded.

Though he couldn't care less about that.

In fact, he couldn't care less about the Amber Room.

He only wanted Laura, and the worry was consuming him.

There was a knock at the door.

"Come!"

A sailor entered. "Sorry to disturb you, sir, but you have a call. A Mr. Tommy Granger? He says it's urgent."

A shot of adrenaline surged through his system as he rolled out of the bed and gave Reading a shake. "Wake up!"

Reading grumbled then rolled over. "What is it?"

"A call from Tommy. He says it's urgent."

Reading's eyes shot wide. "Give me a second." He sucked in a few deep breaths then looked up at him. "Give an old man a hand."

Acton yanked him to his feet, then they both followed the sailor through the bowels of the ship, finally arriving at a room with a phone. He pressed a couple of buttons then handed Acton the receiver. "I'll be outside if you need me, sir."

"Thank you." Acton pressed the receiver to his ear. "Hello, Tommy?"

"Oh thank God, when your cellphone stopped working, I didn't know what to think, so I called Dean Milton, and he called—"

"Yes, yes, I'm fine. What is it? You said it was urgent?"

"It is. I think I might have found Professor Palmer. At least where she was a couple of hours ago."

A wave of goosebumps swept over his body as hope returned. "Where?"

"I tracked the trucks to an airport in Slovenia. They were loaded on a plane, a cargo plane, that according to what I can find out, had Saudi diplomatic status. You need to find out where that plane went. It could be still in the air."

Acton's heart was pounding, and he wasn't thinking straight. He finally spoke. "I'm going to put Agent Reading on. Tell him what you told me."

He shoved the phone at Reading who took it and immediately began questioning Tommy, his notepad out, then collapsed in a chair as he processed what had just been said, and the inevitable conclusion it demanded.

Once that plane landed, Laura was likely dead, and that was at most only a few hours away.

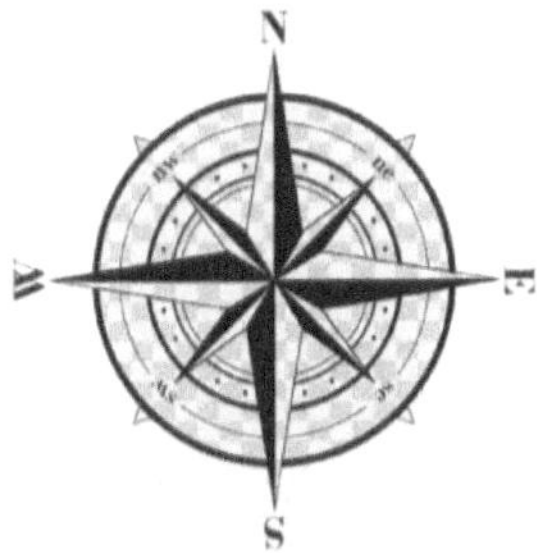

Unknown Location

Laura was led to the rear of the plane, squinting at the bright sunlight flooding in the rear as the ramp lowered. From the dry, hot air that swept in, and the barely two hours of flying time from Europe, she knew they had to be in a country rimming the Mediterranean. She had been recaptured in Poland, and the light through her hood and her previously unrelieved bladder, suggested it was the next day. They had obviously traveled a good distance by land, since two hours in the air from Poland would at best put them in Spain or Italy, neither countries she could see these men taking their cargo to.

And politics also reduced the possibilities. Turkey was likely out of the question, Syria and Israel definitely were, which left North Africa. She could see Egypt, Libya, or Tunisia, perhaps even Algeria, but that would be about it.

Yet knowing that didn't help her while still a captive.

A man in flowing white robes typical of a Saudi sheik, climbed the ramp, his head covering and sunglasses concealing his identity fairly well. Laura made it a point not to look at him, just in case he got nervous she might identify him.

"Show me."

Two of her captors opened several of the crates, revealing parts of the Amber Room dismantled by the Nazis over 70 years ago. A finger was run gently along the revealed panels, a finger that seemed to be trembling with excitement.

"How do I know it's real?"

Her captor stepped forward, holding a hand out toward Laura. "I've brought an expert."

A tablet was handed to the sheik, and she caught a glimpse of her photo. "Professor Laura Palmer. Currently with the Smithsonian." The sheik turned toward her. "Tell me, Professor, is this the genuine article?"

She hesitated, and her captor's eyes flared, reminding her of his threat. As desperately as she didn't want to cooperate, she could see no point in lying or delaying the inevitable. It would merely ensure her death. Her shoulders slumped, and her eyes drifted to her feet. "Yes."

"You're certain."

"Yes. I'm convinced it's genuine, as was my husband."

He looked at the tablet. "Professor James Acton."

Her heart ached at the mention of him. "Yes."

"Very well." He handed the tablet back then flicked a wrist at one of the men who had accompanied him. "Transfer the money."

A laptop was produced, keys pressed, and moments later, one of her captors was smiling at the man in charge.

"Our business is concluded?" asked her captor.

The sheik nodded. "Yes. I insist you visit me when it has been reassembled. You should see what you and your men have accomplished."

Laura couldn't resist. "Why are you doing this?"

The sheik appeared surprised, his eyebrows rising past his sunglasses as he turned to her. "Excuse me?"

"Why are you taking this? This is a part of history. The public should be able to see it."

"And they will, in time. But for now, it is mine, and I, along with *my* public, will be able to enjoy it in peace."

She glared at him, reaching out for the crates protectively. "This is wrong."

Her captor stepped closer. "Professor Palmer, I highly recommend you shut your mouth now, or you just might find our agreement terminated, and you along with it."

She bit her tongue, and the sheik smiled. "Professor, do not worry. Your discovery will be perfectly safe, but at least now, some will get to enjoy what was presumed lost forever. In time, I will tire of it, and it will be sold to someone else. Eventually, somehow, somewhere, it will be once again shown to the masses, though as we both know, it never really was, now was it?"

Laura frowned, the man right. It had been created for royalty, and in fact, had spent most of its existence hidden away. She decided holding her tongue was for the best, and she merely nodded, turning to her captor. "Now what?"

"Now we say goodbye."

She frowned, her heart hammering. "Why do I doubt that?"

Her captor smiled. "I don't know, why would you?"

"I've seen your faces."

The man laughed, waving his hand in front of his face. "Professor, you've seen *this* face. I've had many, and I'll have many more."

Her eyes narrowed. "So you're just going to let me go."

"Nothing is ever quite that simple."

He stepped forward and sprayed something in her face.

Laura woke to yet another headache, her mouth dry, her bladder protesting even more than before. She sat up, discovering she was in the back seat of a car, a rather cheap one at that.

And she was alone.

Somebody tapped on the window and she flinched, scurrying to the other side of the car as a uniformed man peered inside, asking something in Arabic. She opened the opposite door and climbed out.

"Where am I?"

He gave her a look, surprised at the ridiculousness of the question. "Tunis. Are you okay?"

She nodded, debating whether she should confide in the man. She surveyed the area quickly, then gasped at the most beautiful sight she could imagine.

A Union Jack, fluttering in the wind.

She smiled at what she assumed was a police officer. "I'm fine, thank you." She pointed at the flag. "I'm just going over there."

She quickly headed toward what she prayed was the embassy, and as she rounded the corner, she nearly cried in relief, breaking out into a run as she neared the gates. She grabbed the bars, and a soldier approached. "Yes, ma'am?"

"Please, I'm a British citizen. I was kidnapped and don't have my passport. My name is Laura Palmer, please let me in!"

His eyes widened. "Did you say your name is Laura Palmer? Professor Laura Palmer?"

She nodded, then paused.

How does he know I'm a professor?

The man stepped back, waving to someone. "Open the gates!"

The gates parted and she stepped inside, relief washing over her as she was now on British soil, safe from whatever might harm her only paces away. The guard disappeared into a gatehouse, and she could see him on the phone.

Somebody shouted from the entrance of the embassy, and she turned toward the sound, shielding her eyes from the blinding sun, then her shoulders heaved as she recognized her beloved James.

"Laura!"

She couldn't move, her legs frozen in place, her shoulders slumping as the tears rolled, her body finally giving in to all the tension and pressure of the past day, finally knowing it was all over, that James was safe, and they would soon be home.

He grabbed her and lifted her into the air, hugging her hard as they both cried. "Thank God you're okay!"

She held his face in her hands as she stared into his eyes, still not believing it was him. "What are you doing here?"

"We received a call. We were told that you would be showing up here at some point today, and that you were okay."

She sighed, then hugged him again.

"Glad to see you're okay."

She smiled at the sound of her friend, and let go of James, grabbing Reading, giving him a kiss on both cheeks, and she knew he was relieved to see her by his lack of protests. He returned the hug then gently pushed her away. "Let's get inside. They'll want to debrief you, then fly us back to Europe."

Acton put his arm around her shoulders, leading her to the embassy. "We lost the Amber Room. We thought we had tracked it to a ship, but it was a decoy. We eventually figured—"

"I saw it."

"What?"

"They made me authenticate it to the buyer."

Reading stopped, turning toward her. "Who was it?"

She shook her head. "I have no idea. Looked like a Saudi sheik, but could have been anyone from that part of the world."

"The transport you were on had Saudi diplomatic status," said Reading, resuming walking.

Laura sighed. "I'm afraid we're never going to see it again."

"Why did he take it?"

She laid her head on her husband's shoulder. "For his private collection."

He cursed. "We need to find it."

"I don't see how, unless you can track the airplane."

Reading shook his head. "It won't matter. Not with diplomatic status. We can't touch it."

She frowned. "Which means we can't touch him."

James growled. "We should at least be able to catch the thieves. We got a good look at them, and they were on enough cameras."

Laura shook her head. "No. They apparently change their faces all the time. I got the impression they do this for a living."

Reading grunted. "I think you're right. Unfortunately, the only lead we had on them, their contact with the Dark Web troll, turned up nothing. Everything was handled through encrypted messengers, and paid with Bitcoins. It's a dead end."

Acton sighed. "I can't believe that the Amber Room is once again lost to the world."

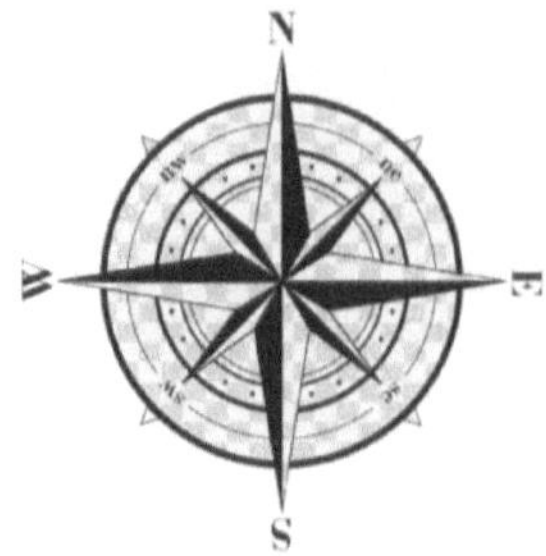

Outside Riyadh, Kingdom of Saudi Arabia

Sheikh Khalid bin Al Jabar sat in his chair, one that sat on a pedestal with a hand control allowing him to spin gently so he could take in the entire breathtaking display. To say he was once again excited with life, would be an understatement.

He was ecstatic.

And it was all because of the man who now stood beside him.

"What do you think?"

Tankov shrugged. "Not my style. Too garish."

Khalid chuckled. "I think you are missing the point. Whether or not you think it is aesthetically pleasing, you are looking at something that is priceless, and one of a kind. Never before, and never again, shall there be a room such as this. This is worth half a billion dollars by some estimates. Nobody today would ever build such a thing. You are in the presence of something that most can't even conceive of, and you shrug your shoulders."

Tankov smiled. "I'm not in it for the art, I'm in it for the money and the thrill."

Khalid sighed. "It's really too bad. Some of the pieces you have retrieved for me and my fellow collectors, are truly quite remarkable, yet you cannot appreciate what they mean."

Tankov stared at the walls surrounding them. "I appreciate the money they represent."

Khalid shook his head, giving up. "Now that you have one hundred million Euros, what will you do?"

Tankov turned toward him. "I think I'll relax on a beach for a while until the next job comes along."

Khalid nodded. "How much more do you need?"

Tankov wagged a finger at him. "Now it's *you* who don't understand. "It's not all about the money, it's all about the mission. We get to do what we want, when we want, with no consequences except success or death. There's no in between."

Khalid's head bobbed slowly as he thought about what was just said. "I understand completely." He extended a hand, Tankov shaking it. "Call me the next time you have something of interest come across your radar."

Tankov bowed slightly. "Rest assured, sir, you *will* hear from us again." He pointed at his face. "Though you might not recognize me."

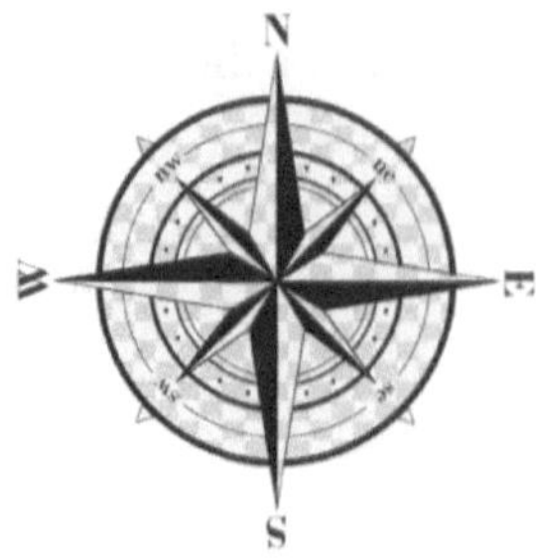

Mai Trinh Residence

St. Paul, Maryland

Tommy grabbed Mai, pulling her in tight for yet another kiss, giggles erupting from both of them as Acton stood with a heavy box in his arms, waiting for them to get out of the way.

"If you're going to play grab ass, then move it before this old man gets a hernia."

Tommy's eyes widened and Mai blushed. "Sorry, sir!" cried Tommy as the two of them pressed against the wall, letting him get by.

Acton stepped inside Mai's apartment, placing the box of what must be lead bricks, on the kitchen counter. "What the hell is in that?"

Tommy shrugged. "Weights, I think."

Acton growled at him, baring his teeth in mock anger as Laura passed him carrying a pillow in each hand. She grinned at him.

It was a pleasant end to what had been a frustrating couple of weeks. The plane with the Amber Room had left Tunisia, flying directly for Riyadh, Saudi Arabia, and as Reading had predicted, they weren't cooperating. From that point on, nobody knew what had happened to the cargo, and the world was poorer for it, though he took some small comfort in knowing that at least it was out there, somewhere, not destroyed during the war.

Reading had stayed behind to tie up some loose ends with the authorities in Poland, the Czech Republic, and Slovenia, and they had asked him to visit when he was done, but he hadn't been able to, apparently his boss ready to fire him if he didn't return.

Professor Lisowski was expected to fully recover, and the rest of the find, still an incredible one, would keep her and her team busy for years to come. Though the Amber Room might have been recovered only briefly, thousands of pieces of artwork would hopefully be reunited with their rightful owners over the coming months and years.

It would be a slow but worthwhile effort.

He watched Tommy and Mai, giddy with excitement at this new stage of their relationship and lives, and was very proud of the two of them. He almost thought of Mai as a daughter, and Tommy was rapidly becoming like a son. If it weren't for them, they might never have been found, though that wasn't the real reason he was proud.

They had finished their job after Laura's release, visiting the second family of the murdered engineer, bringing them a copy of his great-grandfather's records, and telling them of what had happened.

The body of Hermann Lang had been confirmed to be among the bodies found in the mine, and his remains had already been reunited with his family. It had been a moving, solemn occasion, one that he and Laura had decided was necessary to attend along with Tommy and Mai.

For this man was no one's enemy. He was simply an engineer, doing his job, and murdered for it. And one day, Acton hoped that the cargo he had transported on that fateful night would be found and shared with the world, and his important role could be celebrated.

And his soul could finally rest in peace.

As he was sure Tommy's great-grandfather's now did.

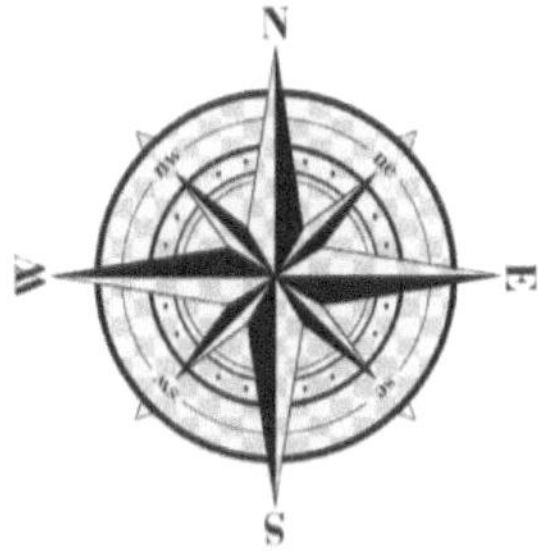

Outside Karlsruhe, Allied Occupied Germany

May 10, 1945

Wolfgang Vogel stood at the end of the long driveway leading to the family farm, his arm around his wife, his two children in front of them, waving at the column of American troops passing by. Some waved back, others tossed supplies to them, and as he had suspected he would all along, he felt liberated, as opposed to conquered.

The war was over.

Germany had lost.

And he didn't care.

These were the Americans he was expecting, not the evil army that would slaughter children and rape women, as the propaganda machines had warned. No, these were men who held no animosity toward the civilian population, and he was thankful he had been able to get his family out of Berlin where the Russians now held control.

He didn't trust them at all, and the rumors were horrifying if true.

A GI walked up to his son, handing him a chocolate bar. "Share that with your sister, okay."

Vogel smiled. "Thank you."

"Don't mention it, buddy."

The kids were thrilled, and so was he. If these men represented their enemy, then they truly did have no reason to fear them. He stared down the road at the city, heavy damage evident from the bombing, much of Germany destroyed. It would take years to rebuild, and the struggle would be hard. He could never return to Berlin, not with the Russians in control.

He had nothing but the clothes on his back.

He closed his eyes and wondered about Frau Lang and Frau Maier. Had they survived the war? Were they now under Soviet control? Was Frau Maier holding out hope that it wasn't her husband beaten to death like he had told her in his note to her? Was Frau Lang still waiting for her Hermann to come home?

He wished he had something more to tell them, to give them a reason as to why their husbands had paid such a high price, but unfortunately, he was as much in the dark as they were.

And with the mine now in Russian territory, he doubted the world would ever know what the SS had hidden there one cold night in January.

Though perhaps with time, and a little luck, the secret too many had died to protect would be revealed.

He turned to his wife and smiled at her, then the children, so thankful they had all made it through the war.

And a thought occurred to him.

"How would you feel about going to America?"

THE END

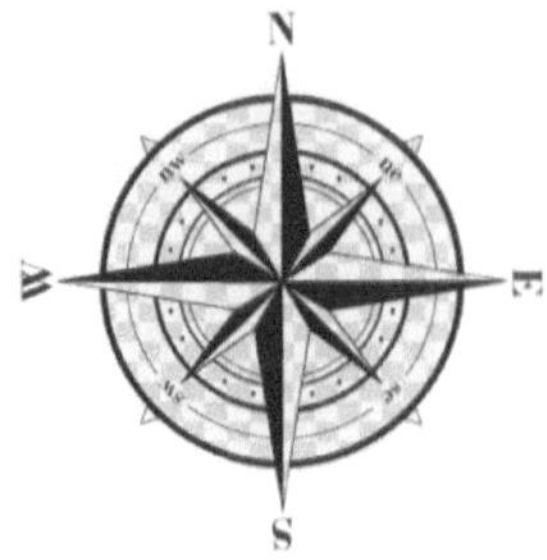

ACKNOWLEDGMENTS

First, a quick note on the title. Some might be thinking that the proper title would be The Nazis' Engineer (and still some The Nazis's Engineer), but both would be incorrect. The title refers to a singular Nazi, not the Nazis as a group, making the title grammatically correct. And that singular Nazi, of course, was Konrad, the museum administrator's go-to guy for whenever he needed someone.

This book was a lot of fun to write, especially the historical elements. I've always been a history buff, particularly when it comes to World War II and the European campaign. Having lived in Germany in my youth for seven years, and my father a history major, we traveled throughout the continent, visiting places such as Normandy, the Maginot Line, and other famous battle sites.

The history was unavoidable, and I loved it.

As usual, there are people to thank. My dad for all the research, Michael Heintz and those who participated on Facebook in choosing a video game for our bad guys to be playing (follow me on Facebook to participate in these things), William Viktora for some Czech help, Brent Richards for some weapons info, "Captain" Fred Newton for some nautical terms, and Greg "Chief" Michael for some metal detector info. And, as usual, my wife, daughter, and mother, as well as the proofreading and launch teams.

To those who have not already done so, please visit my website at www.jrobertkennedy.com then sign up for the Insider's Club to be notified of new book releases. Your email address will never be shared or sold, and you'll only receive the occasional email from me, as I don't have time to spam you!

Thank you once again for reading.